"Clay." She pre
looking flustered. "I don't know
what that was, but it was no big
deal. You didn't expect me to be
in your bedroom. I startled you."

"You startled something, all right."

She bit her lip, hiding a smile. "I'm just saying it didn't mean anything."

"C'mon, Shelby. I wasn't the only one affected in there." His gaze dropped to her breasts and he could see the faint impression of tight nipples beneath her sweater. He forced his gaze to her face. "I saw you," he rasped.

Shelby squirmed. "What are you talking about? It was no big deal."

"So that's why your body responded to mine, why your—"

"All right!" She blushed furiously. "Okay, so I... noticed you noticing. Just because I responded doesn't mean I should have. Or that I will again."

"Maybe you're right, but I don't think so." He stretched his arm along the top of the seat, hit with a purely macho urge to prove she would respond to him again. "I don't know why something's started between us, but it has."

Dear Reader,

The idea of best friends falling in love has always fascinated me. Perhaps it's the excitement of two people who think they know each other so well, only to be surprised and amazed by romantic feelings they never expected. I wanted to do a story of a man and woman who have only ever felt strictly friendship for each other, who fell in love with other people first. And then one day, bam! Hormones and emotions go wild. Where did *that* come from?

Firefighter Shelby Fox and Detective Clay Jessup have been there for each other through thick and thin, through death and divorce. Their bond is unbreakable and reassuringly familiar. So what are they supposed to do when their friendship suddenly feels anything but platonic? When they are both hit with the temptation to give in to their closest friend...who now doesn't seem close enough?

Happy reading!

Debra Cowan

DEBRA COWAN
Wild Fire

Silhouette®

INTIMATE MOMENTS™

Published by Silhouette Books

America's Publisher of Contemporary Romance

SILHOUETTE BOOKS

ISBN 0-373-27474-2

WILD FIRE

Books by Debra Cowan

Silhouette Intimate Moments

Dare To Remember #774
The Rescue of Jenna West #858
One Silent Night #899
Special Report #1045
"Cover Me!"
Still the One #1127
*Burning Love #1236
*Melting Point #1370
*Wild Fire #1404

*The Hot Zone

DEBRA COWAN

Like many writers, Debra made up stories in her head as a child. Her B.A. in English was obtained with the intention of following family tradition and becoming a schoolteacher, but after she wrote her first novel, there was no looking back. After years of working another job in addition to writing, she now devotes herself full-time to penning both historical and contemporary romances. An avid history buff, Debra enjoys traveling. She has visited places as diverse as Europe and Honduras, where she and her husband served as part of a medical mission team. Born in the foothills of the Kiamichi Mountains, Debra still lives in her native Oklahoma with her husband and their two beagles, Maggie and Domino.

Debra invites her readers to contact her at P.O. Box 30123, Coffee Creek Station, Edmond, OK 73003-0003 or via e-mail at her Web site at: www.debracowan.net.

In memory of my grandfather, R. E. Warren. The kindest man I've ever known and also a master storyteller who passed that love on to me.

Acknowledgments

Many thanks to David Wiist, retired Chief of Fire Prevention, Edmond, OK, and to Jack Goldhorn, PIO, Norfolk Fire Rescue, Norfolk, VA. You've both been unfailingly gracious and patient. I lucked out when I met you guys and I have the greatest respect for you both.
To Linda Goodnight, nurse, writer and friend.
To Patti Hager, for her help with all things Spanish, and to my nephew, Mason Banta, for answering my questions on bows and arrows.

Chapter 1

Typical male, thought Presley firefighter Shelby Fox. Wouldn't cooperate even with a willing female.

The May night was unseasonably warm for Oklahoma. She stood completely still outside Station House Three, pressed against the brick wall as she watched the stray tom-cat slink warily through the shadows and approach the food she had left out for him.

The other firefighters fed the animal but didn't care if he was social. For the last month, Shelby had been trying to coax the gray furball into sight. Three-quarters of the way through her twenty-four-hour shift, she should probably be trying to catch some sleep before the next call, like every-one else inside, but—

Someone screamed, the sound startling in the midnight quiet. She snapped to attention, her gaze going across the usually busy two-lane street to the nearest residence in the subdivision.

The sound had come from M. B. Perry's house. Unsure if

there was an emergency, Shelby decided to check it out herself. She dashed across the street, wondering if what she had heard had been a sound from one of those horror movies the petite schoolteacher loved so much. But it wouldn't have been that loud, would it?

All was quiet except for the chirp of insects as Shelby reached the neatly tended lawn. Her gaze skimmed the short, trimmed hedge along the front porch. No sign of an intruder. No sign of anything unusual. Shelby had seen M.B. park her car in the garage a couple of hours ago and she didn't think the woman had left. There were no cars in the driveway, so it appeared M.B. didn't have visitors.

Welcoming light shone from the porch, behind the large, curtained front window and from M.B.'s bedroom upstairs. It wasn't unusual for the woman to stay up so late on a Sunday night, but something was wrong. Shelby knew it by the sharp tingle in her fingertips, the same buzzed nerves she got every time she faced a fire.

The house was quiet, too quiet. She hurried up the few steps to the front door. Just as she knocked, she heard another scream, this one abruptly cut off. She tried the door, found it unlocked and opened it. "M.B.! Are you all right?"

Soon after moving into the older neighborhood, Mary Beth Perry had quickly endeared herself to the firefighters of Station House Three by bringing over all manner of fattening goodies twice a week. Shelby wasn't the only firefighter who loved M.B.'s pecan brownies or had given fire station tours to dozens of M.B.'s high school students.

"M.B.?" Eerie silence greeted her. Alarmed now, Shelby's stomach took a dive. She stepped inside, hit with an arid sticky odor as her gaze tracked up the stairway to her left, across the tall ceiling. Hair spray?

Hair spray? Could that be what she smelled?

A wrought iron banister and railing led up to the landing

that looked over the formal living area where Shelby stood, giving the house an airy inviting openness.

Quickly she scanned the formal living area in front of her. A squatty brass lamp spilled soft light into the room, over the Queen Anne sofa with its curved lines and glossy wooden back that M.B. had refinished. Warm beige-and-green rugs pooled on the dark hardwood floor.

As Shelby started to cross the living room to check the kitchen, she heard a hollow popping noise upstairs and smelled smoke. Moving toward the staircase, she glanced up and saw a thin gray wisp coming from what she thought was M.B.'s bedroom.

Grabbing the black iron banister, she took the stairs two at a time. The smell of hair spray—it was definitely hair spray—grew stronger. "M.B., are you up here? Answer me!"

It was unlike the teacher not to respond. Shelby headed for the bedroom, the first one to the left of the stairs. Light and smoke rippled from the open doorway, weaving around the stair rail spindles to sweep across the living room floor.

On the second floor landing, the sharp chemical odor of hair spray made Shelby's eyes water, as did thickening smoke. Rancid, bitter smoke that wafted out of M.B.'s bedroom. Shelby noted the new odor in the split second before she stepped into the doorway, blinking against the sting of smoke.

No! At first her mind couldn't process the horrible sight. Then it clicked into place—M.B. lay on the bed in flames! A man stood over her. A man Shelby knew! She froze in shock, then automatically recoiled from the gruesome scene. She was remotely aware of what was happening and how quickly.

Even as she recognized the man standing over M.B.'s body, caught the sour stench of burning hair and flesh, she backed up reflexively to run. The man charged across the room, putting his head down and ramming it into her stomach. His momentum, combined with her own, lifted her off the floor.

She grunted, her breath whooshing out as he plowed her backward, hard hands closing over her lower thighs and lifting her.

Off balance, she threw an elbow. The blow caught him on the side of the head, but it didn't slow him down. She pushed at him, trying to gouge his eyes. Something hard slammed into the small of her back. The railing. Her feet left the floor and she plummeted backward. Air rushed past. She screamed. Her hip hit the sharp edge of the couch. Her head cracked against the hardwood floor. Pain exploded, then nothing.

Clay Jessup hit the door of Presley Medical Center at a dead run. Jack's call that Shelby had been hurt and was being taken to the hospital had jerked him clean awake. Clay had pulled on jeans and a T-shirt, jammed his gun into the notch at the small of his back, put on tennis shoes and driven about eighty miles an hour to get to the center.

He didn't have all the details yet, but Jack Spencer, his friend and fellow cop who had caught this case, told him Shelby had been found unconscious in a house across the street from her fire station. The firefighters on Shelby's shift had also found a dead woman—a dead *burned* woman—in an upstairs bedroom.

Even at this late hour, the emergency room was half-full. Clay's nostrils twitched at the mix of ammonia, antiseptic and sweat. Nurses barked orders. Doctors conferred down the hall. The admitting nurse, sitting behind a sleek curved counter, calmly directed people to take a seat or to the patient they sought.

Clay flashed his badge, even though it wasn't necessary. He just wanted to get to Shelby. Fast. A short, trim nurse snagged his elbow to point him down the hall to the last trauma cubicle where his friend was being assessed. Three men in bunker pants, grimy boots and white, soot-streaked fire department T-shirts stood in a circle outside the curtain.

Clay recognized Jay Monroe, but not the others. His breath jammed in his lungs. He didn't want to think about the last time he and Shelby had been in a hospital together, but the memory was all over him.

Shelby wasn't hurt like her brother, his best friend, had been, Clay told himself. She wasn't going to die—

He cut off the thought, reaching her room and nodding to the waiting firefighters. The curtain to her room, one of three used to evaluate emergency room admissions, was slightly open and Clay took a deep breath, schooled his features into what he hoped was a calm mask.

He stepped inside and saw she was alone. His heartbeat jackhammered in his chest.

"Clay?" Her voice was weak, her eyes unfocused and dark blue with pain under the grainy fluorescent lights. The bed had been raised to a half-sitting position, and Shelby reached out to him with her right hand.

"Hey, blue eyes." He managed to keep his voice steady as he moved around the bed and squeezed her hand. Shelby wasn't big on hugging or touching, but he could tell how rattled she was when she didn't immediately release him. She was trembling.

His strong, athletic friend, who had competed in two triathlons, looked frail in her grimy white T-shirt and dark blue pants. Her black shoes smeared dirt over the snowy sheets beneath her. She was pale, the white bandage at her hairline and left temple glaring against her brown hair. Her soft features were pinched with pain.

His chest tightened. "This isn't your way of getting out of that dinner for the mayor, is it?" he teased.

Instead of shooting back with some cute retort, she said, "I…don't know." Tears filled her eyes, rocking him. "Clay, I can't remember anything."

"You mean about how you got hurt?" he asked.

Her fingers tightened on his. "Yes." She started to shake her head, then winced, releasing his hand to press hers to her temple.

"There's something wrong with my wrist—" She lifted her right one. "And my head. Why can't I remember?"

"What did the doctor say?"

"I…don't know." She frowned, panic edging into her voice. "She told me, but I couldn't follow."

Her words were slightly slurred. He wanted to calm her, wanted to calm himself. "I'll find out. It'll be all right."

"The doctor said she would be right back." Her eyes fluttered shut for a second. "How did you know?"

"Jack called me." Clay wondered what Shelby had been doing *alone* at the scene of a fire.

"Jack knows?" Opening her eyes seemed to be a struggle. "Why?"

So she didn't remember about the dead woman upstairs. Or maybe she hadn't even known.

"Clay?"

"They found you on the lower floor of a house across from the station. You'd…fallen over the stair railing."

She shook her head, confusion in her eyes. "Who found me?"

"The guys on your shift."

"There was a fire? Why would I be there by myself?"

"Yeah, there was a fire. I don't know much else."

"But…why would Jack be called to a fire scene?"

Clay hesitated. Procedure between Presley's police and fire departments stated that when PFD found a dead body in a fire, they worked to contain the blaze, then stopped and called Homicide. Shelby knew this, but that hit to the head had obviously jarred some things loose. "There was a woman in an upstairs bedroom," he said as gently as he could. "She was dead."

She touched a hand to her temple, her brow furrowing. "But I was at M.B.'s. I do remember going inside her house—" She gasped. "M.B.? Clay, is it M.B.? Is she dead?"

He hesitated. "I'm sorry."

"No!" she choked out. "How? What happened?"

He really didn't want to lay this on her right now. "I don't have all the details yet."

Other questions pressed harder at him. What had happened to Shelby? How had M. B. Perry died? As a result of that fire? All things Clay would have to find out.

A tear slipped down Shelby's lightly tanned cheek. "M.B. is dead? I can't believe it."

Clay could hardly breathe past the relief that Shelby hadn't met the same fate. He could have lost his best friend tonight. After what he'd been through with Megan and then losing Shelby's brother Jason, standing in a hospital room with an injured Shelby had Clay almost panic-stricken. That had to explain this urge he felt to touch her again, hold her for just a minute. He rubbed a hand across his sweat-dampened nape. "There are some guys waiting outside to see you."

"The doctor asked them not to come in yet."

"Should I have waited?"

"No. I need you in here."

"I called your mom. She's on her way."

An attractive blonde with a stethoscope hanging out of the pocket of a white lab coat breezed into the room. "Sorry I took so long, Shelby. I wanted to set up a CAT scan and wait for the X rays. Got 'em."

She lifted a large manila file jacket. The woman's hair was a mass of wild blond curls pulled into a ponytail. Despite the dark circles under her eyes, she was pretty and she gave Clay a faint smile.

Shelby raised a visibly shaking hand to the side of her

head. "Clay, this is Doctor...I'm sorry." Frustration tightened her voice. "What was your name?"

"Meredith Boren."

"Dr. Boren," Shelby repeated. "You've told me that before, haven't you?"

"It's all right. The confusion will pass and so will the difficulty you're having concentrating," the woman soothed, glancing at Clay. "Are you family?"

"Yes," Shelby said before he could answer. He knew her mother would agree.

"You'll probably ask the same questions for a bit," the doctor said. "That's due to the concussion. I expect that fogginess to dissipate in the next twenty-four hours or so."

"Concussion?" A new worry snaked through Clay. He'd gotten one years ago in a high school football game. But his had been mild; he'd suffered with only a headache, some nausea. His mind had never been this fuzzy, and he'd never forgotten anything. His voice was sharp with concern. "How long was she out?"

"We're not sure." The doctor's sober gaze told him she was concerned, too. "The EMTs who brought her in said she was unconscious when they found her. She woke up a couple of times en route, but I'd estimate she was out at least five minutes."

"That's a long time." Clay's stomach knotted as he scanned Shelby's heart-shaped face. She had an injured wrist, a cut and some bruises on her golden-ivory skin, but what was going on internally?

"I've looked at your X rays," Dr. Boren said to Shelby. "Your wrist is sprained. We'll need to wrap it and stitch up that gash at your hairline. That's not what worries me, though."

Clay stiffened. "What does?"

The woman's warm gaze took in both of them. "Shelby, you have a grade three concussion. That's pretty severe. The hit you took to the head had some momentum behind it."

That put a hard knot in Clay's chest. "Meaning she was pushed?"

"Or fell from some height."

"I wish I could remember what happened," Shelby said impatiently. "How long will this last?"

"I can't say. With a grade three concussion, it's possible the post-traumatic amnesia will last longer than twenty-four hours. I want to keep you overnight to monitor you and to see if your memory improves at all. At this juncture, I don't think your skull is fractured, but I want to watch for a change in symptoms in case there's a small hematoma I haven't detected."

Blood clot. Clay knew that much. His mind reeled with all the information, the sight of his strong, irrepressible buddy lying feebly in a hospital bed.

"Besides the confusion," the doctor continued, "you'll have headaches, dizziness, possibly some disturbance in your vision. I want to run a CAT scan and check for visible contusions on the brain."

"What's that, Doc?" Clay dragged a hand down his face.

"Bruising on the brain. Sorry." The woman smiled.

"I can't remember anything except walking into M.B.'s house." Shelby frowned.

"Do you remember what time that was?" Clay asked. "Or why you went over in the first place? Did you see anyone else?"

"You have on your cop face," she muttered.

The vise around his chest finally eased its grip, and he grinned.

"I know it's hard, Shelby," Dr. Boren said. "But do *not* make yourself try to remember. What you need to do is rest, and I can give you some medication to help with that. We'll see how you do tomorrow. Try not to get ahead of yourself, all right?"

"Hello?"

Hearing the warm, familiar voice outside the door, Clay glanced up.

The doctor turned as Paula Fox moved into the room in a swirl of loose flowing skirts.

"Hi, Mom."

"Paula," Clay murmured.

The woman, who had been like a surrogate mother to him since his own had left, moved up the other side of her daughter's bed, her gaze searching Shelby's face.

"I came as soon as Clay called." Paula's brown kinky hair was pulled back with a headband, her pretty features wan with worry.

He knew all three of them were thinking about the last time they'd been in a hospital together. The night Jason had died. The older woman looked terrified and Clay certainly understood why.

"I'm okay, Mom." Shelby squeezed her mom's hand. "This is Dr. Boren."

The blonde smiled. "Mrs. Fox, I was just explaining to Shelby and Clay that I want to keep her overnight."

"It's standard procedure," Shelby explained.

When Clay nodded in agreement, some of the rigidness left Paula's shoulders.

Dr. Boren scribbled something on a chart. "I'll send in a nurse to wrap your wrist and stitch you up, then we'll get you into a room. I want you to get some rest, even though we'll bug you every two hours to check your vital signs."

"All right."

"Thanks, Doc," Clay said.

The doctor left, closing the door on her way out. Paula frowned at the bandage on her daughter's temple. "Shelby Marie, what happened?"

"All I remember is I went across the street to check on a

friend. There wasn't a fire when I got there. At least I don't think so. Somehow I fell."

Clay decided not to mention the possibility that she could also have been pushed.

Paula frowned. "You don't remember anything else?"

"No."

"Do you have a concussion? Is that why the doctor wants to admit you?"

"It's nothing to be overly concerned about. You know how hard my head is."

"What about your memory? What does she say about that?"

Shelby glanced at Clay and he saw the strain of worry in her eyes. "Dr. Boren thinks the memory loss may last only twenty-four hours."

Clay hoped that by tomorrow Shelby would be able to recall those lost minutes.

"I'll stay with you tonight." Paula smoothed a wing of Shelby's short brown hair away from her face.

"You don't have to."

"You need someone."

"She's right, Shelby," Clay put in.

Shelby nodded. "Okay."

Clay didn't want to leave her. Telling himself she'd be fine with Paula did nothing to unlock the muscles that had gone rigid when he had heard about Shelby. He needed to do something. "I'm going to call Jack. Be right back."

He slipped out and leaned a shoulder against the wall. The three firefighters who'd been there had moved down the hall. Upon seeing Clay, they walked toward him.

Jay Monroe, wiry and ruddy-skinned, shook his hand, introducing the other two men. "The doc already told us we can't see her tonight. How's she doing? How bad is she hurt?"

"She's hanging in there." He recounted her injuries.

"Could've been worse," one of the others murmured.

Which was why Clay couldn't get his heart to stop hammering.

Jay nodded. "I left a message for Captain Oliver so he'd know what was going on. Tell her to keep her chin up and we'll check back."

Clay nodded, walking with them to the exit doors before calling Jack. He wanted to know if his buddy of ten years had a problem with Clay requesting to be assigned to the fire death case. Jack didn't, even offering to speak to Lieutenant Hager when Clay did. He also told the other man about Shelby's amnesia. Jack agreed Clay would have a better chance of getting answers from her by waiting until tomorrow to question her.

Clay hung up his cell and jammed it back in his jeans pocket. He went back inside, still rattled over what might have happened to Shelby tonight.

Just as he reached her room, he saw Vince Tyner stalking toward him. At the sight of the paramedic whom Shelby had dumped a month ago, Clay planted himself in front of her cubicle. Shelby had told him Vince still called her, even though she ignored him. The muscle-bound guy had dated Shelby only for a couple of months.

"I heard from dispatch that she's hurt." The other man halted, concern darkening his brown eyes. "How bad is it?"

Clay told him, thinking that Tyner looked genuinely alarmed.

"I want to see her."

"That's not a good idea."

"Why not? I want her to know I'm here if she needs anything."

She doesn't need it from you. "The doctor doesn't want anyone else in there tonight. She still has to get her arm wrapped and her head stitched up."

"It can't hurt for me to go in for a few minutes." The man made to move past Clay.

Clay blocked his way. "No, Tyner."

"She might say different."

"She won't."

Anger flared in Tyner's face and he visibly struggled to control it. "It can't hurt anything for me to just stick my head in there."

"Think about Shelby, why don't you?"

A dull flush crawled up Tyner's neck and his hands curled into fists. He took a step toward Clay. "Is there something going on with you two?"

If Shelby weren't lying hurt in the next room, Clay would've laughed. "No."

"Then who are you to tell me I can't see her? You have no claim on her."

"Neither do you."

"I have as much right to see her as you do."

"Not gonna happen."

Something cold and sharp flashed in Tyner's eyes, a volatility that had Clay's cop sense on alert.

He had always believed this guy's Prince Charming act was just that. "I know you've been calling her and she hasn't returned your calls. What does that tell you?"

Tyner's gaze went to Shelby's curtained doorway, then sliced back to Clay. He didn't budge. Silence stretched out, pulsing with tension. The other man looked ready to erupt.

"Fine. Have it your way," he snapped. "It won't be for long."

Clay watched the guy stomp down the corridor toward the exit. Did Tyner really think there was something sexual going on between Clay and Shelby? *Sex?* That was the one thing they had never shared. She and Jason had helped him through Megan's long fight with cancer and death. He and Shelby had been there for each other after Jason's death. And everything since.

He would tell her about Tyner's visit, but not tonight.

No way was Clay leaving now. He didn't trust the paramedic to stay away, and he wasn't letting anyone upset Shelby. That hard light of slyness in the other man's eyes was enough for Clay to make a mental note to keep an eye on him.

The door opened behind him and he turned as Shelby's mom stepped out.

"How is she?" he asked.

"She's resting." Paula slid an arm around his waist and hugged him tight. "I'm glad you're here."

He squeezed her in response. From the age of twelve, when his mom had left the family, Clay had spent as much time at Shelby and Jason's house as he had his own. His dad, working two jobs and raising three kids, had needed help. Curtis and Paula Fox had given it.

She stepped away. "I'm going home to get a few things. Do you mind staying until I get back?"

"I'm staying anyway."

"Good." The look in Paula's eyes said she believed he was staying out of a sense of responsibility. The responsibility he'd felt for her and Shelby after Jason's death, but also *because* of Jason's death. Maybe that was the reason. For the last four years, Clay had provided as much support as he could.

He walked Paula to her car then returned to Shelby's room. Her face was turned toward the opposite wall, her chest rising and falling evenly. Clay was glad she was finally getting some sleep. But as he moved around the bed and up to her shoulder, he saw she was awake. She smiled wanly at him, her blue eyes drowsy. "You leaving?"

"No way." She had sat with him for hours after his dad's stroke years ago, pulled him out of a bottle and literally saved his life after Jason had died.

"Even if the doctor makes you?" she asked faintly.

"She can try." He lightly squeezed Shelby's shoulder, her

warmth reassuring him that she was all right. He intended to see she stayed that way. "I'm bigger than she is."

Her eyes fluttered shut. "Good."

There was a nine-year difference in their ages, but she was the one person he could always depend on, and he was the same for her.

She was every bit as good a friend to him as Jason had been, and Clay would never take their friendship for granted. Or do anything to jeopardize it. He wouldn't let anyone else, either.

Chapter 2

"Except for the headache and the big black hole in my memory, I feel fine," Shelby told Clay the next evening in her hospital room.

Tall and lanky, he filled the small space done up in sterile white and soft pastels. Her mother stood at the foot of the bed.

Shelby had spent the day alternately sleeping and attempting to follow doctor's orders about not forcing her memory. Her friend's death was overwhelming enough, but not being able to remember what had happened at M.B.'s house intensified the ache in Shelby's bruised shoulder and back. Panic needled her and she felt as if she might crumble at any moment.

Frustration, combined with her efforts to let her mind work in its own time, tweaked the pain in her skull. She had thought she might remember something today, but she hadn't. Except for the last time she and Clay had been in a hospital together, and she couldn't handle thinking about her brother right now.

Clay moved up the right side of her bed, holding a large

brown paper bag. His deep green eyes twinkled. "If you're doing so well, maybe you don't need this."

Shelby peeked inside to find a six-pack of Diet Coke and several bags of microwaveable popcorn. "Oh, you're a lifesaver!"

He grinned. "I figured if you didn't get your daily fix, the doctor would have to restrain you."

"Thanks." She smiled, knowing his presence was responsible for easing the tension in her shoulders. She set the bag beside her. She had been trembling off and on all day, her nerves raw as her mind tortured her with what might have happened to M.B.

Shelby couldn't catch any of the elusive shadows hovering on the edge of her mind. All she had were fragments, none of which made sense or seemed connected.

Clay had left about mid-morning, saying he was going to grab a shower, change clothes and meet with his lieutenant. He had called throughout the day to check on her, not able to get back to the hospital until after six o'clock.

His sandy brown hair, streaked gold by the sun, was disheveled where he had run his fingers through it. His eyes were bloodshot and he looked tired. He stood over her, his hands in the pockets of his khaki slacks. The short sleeves of his red-and-tan plaid shirt revealed strong forearms dusted with hair the same dark brown as his eyebrows. "What did the doctor say today?"

"Dr. Boren said my CAT scan showed no blood clots or fractures, which is good, but she now suspects my memory loss might be due to something besides the concussion."

"Like what?"

"Like maybe I saw something horrible at M.B.'s and I just don't want to remember."

He frowned. "How's your head?"

"It still hurts, but not as badly as yesterday." She choked back the frustration screaming through her. "The doctor said I could go home in the morning if nothing changes."

"But you have to rest," her mother reminded her.

Clay nodded, studying her intently. She knew that look. If she didn't rest as ordered, he would tie her to the bed. "I got your car home so you don't need to worry about that," he said.

Her mom moved up the other side of the bed, her blue eyes warm as she took out a bag of the popcorn Clay had brought. "Would you like some of this?"

"Yes."

"I'll find a microwave. And some ice for your Coke."

"Thanks." As Paula left the room, Shelby glanced at Clay. "Sit down. You look beat."

He eased down into the hard, vinyl-covered chair next to the bed, scooting over to give himself a little room from the table at her shoulder that held a phone and a brown plastic pitcher.

"Did Lieutenant Hager agree to assign you to the case?"

"Yeah."

"Was Jack all right with that?"

He nodded, scrubbing a hand over his face. The fluorescent light running in a track overhead shone harshly on the tiny lines fanning out from his eyes.

"So what did you find out about M.B. today?"

"I've been talking to Collier. He's working the case for the Fire Investigator's Office."

Collier McClain was the newest of Presley's two fire investigators. He had been a former station mate of Shelby's when she worked out of Station House Two a couple of years ago. Only a fire cop since January, McClain's first solo case had been a doozy. A prominent female defense attorney had turned out to be a serial sniper who had been killing Presley firefighters.

"Right now, he's trying to determine if the fire at M.B.'s was arson or an accident."

Shelby knew the two men would work together until one of them proved M.B.'s death was an accident, suicide or murder. It must have been an accident. M.B. was a delightful person. Who could possibly want to kill the school teacher?

Clay leaned forward, propping his elbows on his knees. "Earlier today, Collier and I went to the high school where M.B. taught and talked to the other teachers, a few kids. She was well liked, very involved."

"Yes. She was the science club sponsor. I guess you found that out?"

"Yes." His gaze searched her face. "I need to ask you some questions. You up for it?"

She nodded. "I want to help."

"Do you recall seeing her that night?"

"Yeah, when she got home, which was about ten or ten-fifteen. She parked in the garage and waved to me before she shut the door."

"Do you remember what you were doing before you went over to her house?"

The headache Shelby couldn't shake throbbed at the base of her skull. "I was outside feeding the cat. A stray that started coming around the station house about a month ago. We call him Smoke. I heard a scream…"

She gnawed on the pad of her thumb, surprised at how clearly she could recall that, but when she probed for more, her mind became a mass of fractured light. "That's why I went over to her house. At first I thought it might have been the television—M.B. loved horror movies—but it was too loud."

"And you didn't see anyone at her house after she went inside?"

"No. I did try to notice if anything was unusual when I got to her front yard, but I didn't see anything or anyone."

A knock at the door had Shelby turning her head, wincing at the sharp jab of pain up the back of her skull. Her captain, Rick Oliver, and another shift mate, Dylan Shepherd, walked in. Dylan carried a bouquet of colorful balloons with bags of microwave popcorn tied to the end of each ribbon.

"We come bearing gifts, little invalid." Dylan's eyes sparkled. "This is from everyone at Station House Three."

Shelby laughed, exchanging a look with Clay. "I should have enough popcorn to tide me over for a while."

She introduced Clay to the black-haired, black-eyed firefighter who was a couple of years younger than she was. Clay shook hands with both men, having previously met Shelby's congenial captain at a city function.

Captain Oliver's sharp gray gaze scoured her face. "How are you, Fox?"

"I'm all right, Cap."

"You sure? Monroe said you couldn't remember anything."

"Not yet, anyway." She smiled at the fighting-trim man with close-cut gray hair. "Other than that, I'm okay."

"How long before you can come back to work?" he asked.

"Since my job is considered high-risk, I have to go at least seven days without concussion symptoms. The doctor has to examine me again then and if she likes what she sees, I can return."

"We can keep you on light duty around the station house until your wrist heals."

"All right." At one time Shelby would've protested, but having come so close to *never* returning, she was content to be off full duty for now.

Dylan's free hand closed over the rail at the foot of the bed, his dark eyes hot with interest. "That gives you a week to think of where you want to go on our date."

He had been asking her out for two months. Broad-shouldered and lean-hipped, the former school teacher was gorgeous. And a genuinely nice guy. "Now, Shep, if I went out with you, I'd have to go out with all the guys at the station house."

"Hey, I'm the one who carried you out." He flashed her a quick grin. "Don't you think you owe me?"

"I like you too much to date you," she said wryly. After being blindsided five years ago by her bigamist husband, Shelby's motto was leave and leave first. Her other hard-and-fast rule was don't get involved with anyone at work.

Her relationship with Clay was the longest one she'd had with a man and that was because they were only buddies.

Dylan let it go, but she saw the determined glint in his eye. It was a shame she wasn't interested.

"You really had me worried, Fox," her captain said. "I better tell Aubrey she can't have any more asthma attacks during my shift. You obviously need me around to supervise."

Shelby grinned at his teasing, but her thoughts went to Rick's daughter, who had severe asthma. The two-year-old had ended up in the emergency room several times. "How is she?"

"She's okay." Rick's face softened. "As hardheaded as you."

Dylan placed the balloon-and-popcorn bouquet on the window sill. "The nurse told us we could only stay five minutes so we'll get out of here."

"Thanks for coming."

"We'll be checking on you," Rick said.

After the two men left, Clay grinned at her. "How long has Shepherd been chasing you?"

"A couple of months. He only likes me because I say no."

His gaze softened as it skimmed over her face. "Maybe he thinks you're pretty."

She shrugged. "Maybe."

"He's definitely interested, but you're not, huh?"

"You know I don't date guys from my station house. After a few dates, I'm finished. If they aren't, things get messy."

"Like with Vince?"

"Yeah."

Clay folded his arms. "He came by last night. I told him about your injuries, but I wouldn't let him see you."

"Thanks. Was he a jerk about it?"

"Not too much." Clay eased down on the edge of the window sill, crossing his long legs at the ankle. "Tell me whatever you remember about last night."

She rubbed two fingers in a circle against her throbbing temple. "Well, like I said, I heard a scream. When I got to M.B.'s front porch, I knocked. I heard another scream, but it was cut off. So I opened the door and called out. When she didn't answer, I went inside."

She paused, forcing her mind to play through what she had just told Clay, but when she tried to remember beyond stepping inside the house, she came up with snatches of darkness and light, garbled unidentifiable sounds. In other words, nothing.

The dull ache at the base of her skull sharpened into a stunning pain that radiated up the back of her head, stabbing behind her eyes. She clasped her head in her hands, massaging her temple. "That's all I remember."

Clay straightened, moving toward her. "You okay?"

"Yes, it's just this headache. It comes and goes."

"Do you need something for the pain?"

"I took a couple of ibuprofen about an hour ago. Maybe I'll take some more."

His eyes dark with concern, he rang for the nurse.

"Oh!" she said. "M.B. told me she was seeing someone."

"Yeah?" Clay's gaze held hers expectantly.

"She never told me who. I think he was married."

"Did you ever see a man at her house?"

"About a week ago, I saw a red Corvette at her house, an older model, but I didn't see who was driving it. I saw a man about a month ago in a different car, but only once."

"Remember what either of them looked like?"

"I never saw who was driving the 'Vette. The other man

was Hispanic, but I couldn't describe him. That's not much help, is it?"

"It's a lead and we have too darn few so far." He smiled.

The nurse delivered more pain medication and left. Shelby searched her mind, trying to recall anything else. All she had were shadows, elusive bits and pieces of…something. She couldn't even determine if they were thoughts or pictures. "I want to know what happened."

She sensed Clay tense subtly, the strain not visible in his face. Only in the barely perceptible shift along his lean muscles. Shelby knew he was keeping something from her. "What are you not telling me?"

Mouth grim, his steady gaze met hers. "Ken Mason, the medical examiner, had to go in for an emergency heart bypass a couple of days ago so it's going to be a while before we find out M.B.'s exact cause of death."

"Doesn't he have an assistant?"

"Yes, but she isn't certified to sign off on CODs. We've been able to piece some things together from what Collier learned at the scene."

"Enough to rule out an accident?"

Clay nodded. "He checked for cigarettes and frayed wiring. Everything he's found so far indicates the fire was arson. Most likely to hide another crime."

Shelby's fingertips tingled from that mix of adrenaline and apprehension she always got heading into a blaze. She didn't want to ask the question that had dread fisting in her gut. "You mean—"

"Murder," Clay said quietly, his large hands wrapping around the bed rail.

The shock of the words had her going still; then her entire body quivered. "Do you think I saw something? *Someone?*"

"I don't know."

"Do you think Dr. Boren's right? That I can't remember

because I did see something horrible? But if I saw who murdered M.B., wouldn't they have made sure I was dead, too?"

"They tried," he said tightly. "Your station is right across the street from her. A fire had started, so I don't imagine the killer felt he had time to make sure you were dead before your crew arrived."

Sickened at the thought, she laid back on the pillow.

Clay squeezed her shoulder, his eyes hard. "I'm not taking any chances. Until we know you're not in danger, I'm sticking to you like white on rice."

Clay was as good as his word. He stayed again Monday night with her and her mom at the hospital, and the next morning helped Paula load Shelby into the car to take her home. She finally got settled to her mother's satisfaction and convinced Paula she'd be fine. Shelby wanted to be in the comfort of her own home, not that huge empty house her mom had bought with the ample insurance settlement from Dad's death.

Stepping inside her kitchen eased some of the tension in her shoulders. The white of the cabinets, countertops and island top was broken by splashes of red on the wallpaper, in the curtain across the single, floor-to-ceiling window. Deep black-cherry candles and a floral arrangement spread color across the dining table. The familiarity soothed her.

Paula fixed lunch for all three of them, some bean sprout-tofu thing that wouldn't satisfy a bird. Shelby was hungry, but more than that, she was jumpy. Her entire body ached. She was frustrated at the missing minutes in her memory and edgy over what had happened during those minutes.

Paula rose to get more tea. "Vince has called me several times to see how you're doing. He wants you to call him back."

Shelby shook her head.

"Are you sure?" Her mom refilled her glass. "He seems genuinely concerned."

"It's one thing to check on me. It's another to keep coming around. Clay said he was at the hospital last night, too."

Shelby glanced over, noting how his jaw had tightened. He had on his blank cop face. The phone rang and Paula answered. Shelby tensed, hoping it wasn't Vince.

Her mom brought the phone over. "It's your captain."

Relieved, Shelby spoke to her boss, assuring him that she didn't need anything and promising to let him know her progress as she recovered.

Clay cleaned up the dishes while Paula made a list of things to buy at the grocery store. Shelby wandered into the living room, sank down on her oversize saddle-brown couch.

Her mom left for the store and Clay put in a call to his lieutenant. Shelby couldn't sit still. Pain jabbed at her temple. Her nerves were raw, urging her off the couch and to the large plate glass window that looked into her backyard.

M.B. had been murdered. Clay's words kept circling in Shelby's head. Did she know anything about it? Were the answers buried somewhere in the writhing shadows of her mind? Had she lost her way in the smoke and fallen? Or had she been thrown over that railing?

Panic swelled inside her and she fought it, afraid if she gave in that she would fall apart. But it was hard to dismiss the fact that her friend was dead. And that at least ten minutes of her life were missing. Gone. As if they had never existed, hadn't been even a hiccup in time.

She wrapped her arms tightly around herself, cradling her injured wrist. What if she never remembered? Besides feeling that she would be letting M.B. down, Shelby didn't know how she would accept such a blank space in her life. In the scheme of things, maybe five or ten minutes wasn't much, but a murder had been committed in front of her. Maybe she hadn't seen anything, but if she had, she wanted to know what.

Shelby had tried not to think about the danger Clay felt she might be in, but for the first time since being rescued, a frozen, slow-moving fear climbed over her, suffocating her. What if she had died, too?

Clay stood in the wide archway that led from Shelby's kitchen into her living room, frowning as he saw her looking out into the backyard. He said her name, but got no response.

Surrounded by the warm light of the midday sun, she stood motionless in front of the large picture window. She wore a baggy red T-shirt, with Presley Fire Department written in thick white letters across the back, and khaki shorts that drew attention to her sleekly muscled legs. She was barefoot.

She didn't move. Didn't appear to know he was there at all.

He walked around the edge of her sofa and stopped behind her. "Shelby?"

Still she didn't move, didn't speak.

Clay stepped up so he could see her face. And was startled at the tears streaming down her cheeks. She stared outside, unblinking, her breathing shallow.

His heart lurched. He had only seen her cry like this at the hospital when the doctors had given them the devastating news that Jason was gone.

Clay pushed away a zing of guilt as something close to panic unfurled inside his chest. He teasingly bumped her shoulder with his. "This means you wanted popcorn instead of that grass stuff your mom made, right?"

Her face crumpled and she looked away.

"Hey." He slid an arm around her shoulders.

His touch seemed to break the lock on her emotions. She turned into his chest, choking out a sob, her good arm going around his waist and holding tight. Her palm rested on the small of his back.

Careful of the bruises on her back and shoulder, he curled his left arm loosely around her waist. His right hand went to the back of her neck, slipping under the short ends of her hair. He brushed his thumb soothingly back and forth across her nape.

They stood like that for a long moment, her sobs quiet but deep enough to rattle her body. Nearly thirty-six hours after the incident that had caused her injuries, Clay figured everything was hitting her at once. Grief over her friend. Frustration and uncertainty over the loss of her memory. The realization that she could've been killed.

That one certainly scared the hell out of him. He snuggled her face into his neck and rested his cheek against her hair. He stroked her nape, murmuring to her over and over until finally she stood quietly against him, drawing in ragged breaths.

Her vise-like grip on him eased, but she stayed where she was, her breath fluttering against his skin. He rubbed her back. He realized then that she wasn't wearing a bra and the feel of her breasts flattened against his chest had his body going tight. Jolted by his reaction, Clay's mind froze for an instant.

He inhaled the light floral scent of her shampoo. "It scared me when I heard you were hurt."

She looked up at him with glistening blue eyes, her dark lashes wet and spiked. A wobbly smile lifted the corner of her lips. "You? A big bad cop scared?"

"Yeah." He suddenly wanted to hug her close again, calm the brutal fear that reared up inside him just as it had at the hospital. "You're my best pal. It would be hard to replace you."

Tears welled in her eyes and she smoothed his navy tie, rubbed at the spot on his light blue shirt that she had wet with her tears. "You could go on one of those reality shows. Surely they have one about finding friends."

"Think I'd be able to find somebody who would drag me out of a bar and keep me captive until I swore on my badge that I was sober and never going back?"

"That *was* special, wasn't it?" she said wryly, wiping the tears from her face.

"You saved my life," he said quietly. He'd told her before. With everything they'd shared through the years, they had both agreed not to keep count anymore, but he knew he wouldn't be standing here if it weren't for Shelby.

"You've done the same for me. I wouldn't want another best friend. It would be hard to find someone who knows everything about me and would still put up with me."

He grinned. "I don't know everything. I don't know where that tattoo is."

She smiled, which was what he wanted. The small fox tattoo on his left shoulder matched the one she'd gotten at the same time. It had been Shelby's idea to get a physical symbol of Jason, and she had wanted Clay to take her to the tattoo parlor on the first anniversary of her brother's death. To this day, she'd refused to tell him *where* she'd gotten tattooed.

"I have to say, Jessup, you're good with hysterical females." She dabbed at her eyes again. "Must come from having two sisters."

"You were hardly hysterical." Unsettled at how the feel of her lean curves had affected him, Clay released her as she stepped away. "Wanna talk about it?"

"I guess I had a meltdown." She held her injured arm against her stomach, folding the other one underneath it.

"You're entitled. You've been dealing with a lot."

"I can't stop thinking that I might know what happened to M.B. And that it could've been me instead of her."

"I know," he said fiercely, clenching his fists tight. He had been responsible for Jason's walking into danger, but he wouldn't make that mistake with Shelby.

Her gaze, knowing and sad, searched his. "The hospital made me think about him."

"Me, too." Most of the time he lived with the memory just fine, but sometimes pain raked through him and nearly ripped a fresh wound. Like when he'd seen Shelby in that hospital bed.

"Why couldn't I have lost *those* memories?"

The agony in her voice clutched at his chest. Their gazes met and he knew the memories in her eyes were the ones that hit him now. Jason hadn't wanted to go climbing that day, but Clay had pushed until his friend gave in. They had scaled the ragged mountain face just fine, but coming down, Jason's harness had broken and he had lost both his handholds and footholds.

Clay, secure in his harness, had scrabbled and grabbed, but Jason had fallen. Sometimes even now, four years later, Clay would dream about it, hearing over and over the sickening thud of his friend hitting the ground. Reliving the horror, the guilt.

Pain flashed across Shelby's features, then was gone. "If only I could remember something. Anything. There are only…shadows in my mind. No definition."

"Shelby." Clay didn't like the guilt that flashed across her face. "Don't torture yourself. You know it doesn't help. And the doctor said not to force anything."

"I know." She shoved an unsteady hand through her short brown hair.

"You hungry for some real food?"

"Yes." She fell into step with him as they walked around the edge of her sofa. She squeezed his arm and gave him a small smile, telling him she was all right.

A pair of ceramic dalmatians flanked either side of the wide entry that led from the living area into the kitchen. She fixed drinks while he made turkey sandwiches. He glanced at her as she slid into the seat next to him, putting diet colas on the table at both their places.

"I went back to M.B.'s school today to follow up on what you told me about her being involved with someone. No one I spoke to knew anything about the affair, but I left my card for a woman named Gail Cosgrove, M.B.'s closest friend there. She's the school secretary. Right now she's in Arizona moving her elderly mother back here. I couldn't reach her by phone, so I left a message at the school for her to call me when she returns."

"Hopefully M.B.'s friend will know something." Shelby stole a pickle from his plate. "It's only been about two weeks since she told me about him. Maybe she broke things off."

"Do you think it was the Hispanic man you saw once?"

"I don't know."

"Did she tell you what her new guy looked like? Age?" Clay pushed the jar of pickles toward her. "What kind of car he drove?"

"No. I assumed she wouldn't tell me his name or anything because he was married, but maybe that wasn't why."

"Maybe she kept it a secret because he's someone prominent," he suggested.

"Maybe it was another teacher or someone else at school."

"Like the principal? A custodian?"

"Or the school cop?" Three years ago, the city had instituted a program that assigned an officer full-time to the two high schools. The presence of law enforcement had cut down drastically on everything from fights to drugs.

He nodded. "One or both of them could've feared losing their jobs. I'll go back this afternoon and see if I get anywhere with that."

The door that led to the garage opened and Paula walked in carrying two grocery sacks. "There's a police car parked out front."

"I called for one." Clay rose and took the bags from her, setting them on the counter.

"Even though Mom's here?" Shelby asked.

"Even though." He wasn't taking any chances with her safety. Or her mom's, either. He made a mental note to keep a close eye on Vince Tyner.

Paula glanced over as she began unloading items. "You're still planning to stay, aren't you?"

"Yes. Until Shelby remembers whether or not she saw anything. Until we know what happened to her *and* the victim."

"Thank you, Clay." Tears shone in Paula's eyes. "I feel better knowing you're here."

"You should go back to the store whenever you need to, Mom." Her mother's bead and jewelry store, To Bead Or Not To Bead, did a thriving business, enticing customers from Presley as well as Oklahoma City and other nearby towns. "I'll be fine."

"Tracy can handle things there for a couple of days."

Clay wrapped up the rest of his sandwich to take with him, then said goodbye to her mom. Shelby walked with him to the front door.

"Thanks for a while ago," she said, not quite meeting his eyes.

That was a first, too. As long as he'd known her, even as a teenager, Shelby looked directly at someone, whatever the situation. Was she avoiding his gaze because she'd felt his body's insane, mystifying reaction to her? "I've got a ways to go before I make up for the solid week you stayed with me after Jason died."

"Yeah, that was a hardship."

"You're trouble in your own way." He grinned, opening the door. Still off balance at the unexpected pull of want he'd felt, he searched her face. "I can have the department assign a female cop to stay with you at night, if you'd prefer." He didn't even consider a male officer. "I've already requested one for during the day when your mom has to get back to the bead store."

"No."

"Shelby," he said firmly. "Until we know what happened in that house, I'm not leaving you alone without protection."

"I meant no to somebody else. I want you."

At her words, heat inched under his skin. What was going on with him? "You sure?"

"Yes."

"Okay, you've got me. Call me if you need something or want me to bring you anything."

"All right."

"Lock up after me."

She gave him a lazy two-finger salute. "Yes, Mr. Po-lice Man."

"Smart aleck." He stepped outside and waited until he heard the turn of the dead bolt, the click of the knob lock. Walking to his truck, his head felt fuzzy, as if he'd been out in the sun too long. He rubbed a hand across his chest, the spot Shelby had dampened with her tears.

He should be thinking about the case, about putting in a call to Collier McClain to tell him they needed to make a repeat visit to the high school, but instead his mind was stubbornly, startlingly fixed on Shelby not wearing a bra. The incredible softness of her skin, the feel of her breasts against him. Something hot and reckless and totally unexpected had charged through him. His body had gone hard; it still was.

He rolled his shoulders, uncomfortable with what could only be called desire. For *Shelby,* for whom he'd only ever had platonic feelings. He had to be wrong. There was something else going on, probably a combination of his reaction to her close call, fatigue, his self-imposed celibacy.

After Megan's death, he hadn't been interested in dating at all. About the time he'd become interested, they'd lost Jason. Since then, he hadn't had the time or enough interest for a relationship.

Lusting after Shelby? His best friend? No way.

Chapter 3

Something strange had happened with Clay. Something physical. He had wanted her.

That couldn't be right, Shelby decided. Things had never been that way between them. They weren't now, either. The stupid concussion was to blame. Just because she didn't need to have things repeated so often didn't mean her brain was back to operating the way it should.

That...incident had happened on Tuesday. Today was Friday and she hadn't stopped thinking about it, even though nothing like that happened again. Everything between them had been perfectly normal, just as it was right now.

She slid a look at him as they walked into the largest chapel at Presley Memorial Gardens. Clay had insisted on bringing her to M.B.'s memorial service. The funeral would be a family-only affair after M.B.'s body was released by the medical examiner. In the days since M.B.'s murder, he and

Collier McClain had been conducting interviews at her school, with the firefighters on the scene and with neighbors.

Shelby's mother had left this morning on a buying trip to New York City and wouldn't return until Monday. If things went well and Dr. Boren agreed, Shelby would be back at work by then. She hadn't recalled anything about M.B.'s murder yet, but surely she would. How long could amnesia really last?

She and Clay took a seat next to Collier just before the service began. Well over a hundred people listened in the flower-packed room as M.B.'s oldest brother, Glen, walked to the podium to give a eulogy. Almost half the crowd consisted of the students M.B. had taught and their parents. The others were teachers, administrators, friends and almost every fire-fighter from Station House Three. Shelby's captain sat with several of her station mates in the row of dark blue dress coats across the aisle to her right.

The scents of roses and lilies mixed, the amount of flowers nearly overwhelming. She wanted to follow the funny story Glen Perry told about his sister, but the headache returned, the pain stabbing brutally from her temple to the back of her skull. She shut her eyes for a second and it seemed to ease. Looking again at M.B.'s brother, Shelby tried to pay attention.

The agonizing throb behind her eyes persisted, shooting flashes of light and shadow through her brain, but nothing else. No memories, no nothing.

As the somber, sturdily built man spoke, she closed her eyes. Shelby remembered M.B.'s contagious laugh, her ready smile, her sunglasses in every color. The void Shelby had felt since the murder grew deeper inside her, colder.

Her hands shook and she became aware that her entire body trembled. Maybe it was delayed reaction? Maybe just the realization that a service like this could also have been held for her? She might have the information to help find M.B.'s killer, but it was lost somewhere in her mind.

Glen Perry's voice cracked and Shelby's heart ached for him, ached for M.B.'s parents who were burying a child. She thought about her own mother having to bury Jason and couldn't imagine how Paula would cope if something were to happen to her, too. That put a painful lump in her throat.

Stop! she told herself. Clay leaned forward with his wrists resting on his knees and she focused on the sight of his strong, gentle hands.

Finally the service was over. She fought a rising sense of suffocation as she waited with Clay and Collier to walk out. Once they stepped into the warm May sunshine, Shelby let out a sigh of relief. After telling Clay where she was going, she moved over to join the people in line to pay their respects to the Perry family. Returning to her friends, she tried to keep from bursting into tears. If she knew who'd killed M.B., why couldn't she remember?

Feeling helpless and frustrated, she turned her attention to the tall man beside Clay. "Collier, how much longer before yours and Kiley's wedding?"

"One week, one day and—" He glanced at his watch. "Seven hours. Y'all are coming, aren't you?"

Clay and Shelby both nodded.

She was amazed at how perfect he and Detective Russell were for each other. "I never thought I'd see you walk down the aisle."

"My momma didn't raise no dummy. I'm not letting that woman get away."

Shelby grinned, trying to keep her thoughts from sliding back into fear.

Clay nudged her shoulder, saying in a low voice, "See that guy over there in the white shirt and jeans? He's a custodian from M.B.'s school named Antonio Sandoval. Everyone Collier and I spoke to said he spent a lot of time with M.B."

"Why?" She turned, following Clay's gaze to a lean, darkly

handsome man with raven hair, a deep tan and striking bone structure. Double-take gorgeous.

"She was teaching him to read and write English."

"He speaks the language well," Collier added. "But he says he's never learned to read or write it."

"What reason could he have for wanting to kill M.B.?"

"We have to find out if he did have one." Collier studied the Hispanic man. "Some of the other janitorial staff think there was more going on than reading lessons."

"They think he was M.B.'s lover?"

Clay nodded. "Could Sandoval have been the guy you saw at her house that time?"

She frowned. "I don't know."

"He denies things went that far with M.B."

Shelby's throat knotted. She watched the other attendees move slowly among M.B.'s family members, heard a sob coming from someone. She looked away, filled with anger over her friend's death, the chilling realization that she could easily have met the same fate, frustration over her memory loss.

Why couldn't she remember? She wanted to help M.B., wanted whoever had killed the teacher to be brought to justice. All Shelby had was a yawning black hole in her mind, a fluid blurry memory that floated out of reach any time she tried to latch onto it. And a rage that flared occasionally. Dr. Boren had said the head injury would cause intense, often unfamiliar emotions.

The younger of M.B.'s two brothers leaned down to their mother and Shelby heard choked sobs coming from them both. Tears burned her eyes and she turned away.

Clay squeezed her shoulder. "You okay?"

"I'm ready to go," she said unsteadily.

"You got it."

They said goodbye to Collier and walked quietly to Clay's black pickup truck. As they pulled onto the main road, she felt his concerned gaze on her. Fighting to keep from crying, she didn't speak for several long minutes. "I keep thinking that service could've been for me."

Clay's free hand, resting on his thigh, curled into a fist. He didn't prod her to continue; he just waited.

"I feel...terrified and I don't even know why." Her voice thickened. "Why can't I remember? Why can't I help her?"

"It'll come, Shelby."

"What if it doesn't? What if a killer gets away with murder because of me?"

"First of all, it won't be because of *you*. And secondly, I'm going to find this killer." He looked at her somberly for a long moment. "But if you never remember anything, we'll figure out a way to handle it."

She felt so strange, confused and wobbly, as if she'd lost her footing. Reaching over, she slipped her hand into Clay's. He linked their fingers and a sense of relief moved through her.

"I couldn't do this without you," she said quietly. "I'm so glad you're my best buddy."

"Back at ya." He squeezed her hand.

She marveled at how the least word from him could reassure her. Looking into those familiar green eyes, she saw steadiness, concern, the always-present acceptance. Nothing heated or sexual or unexpected. Nothing like what she thought she'd seen the day she had come home from the hospital. She'd only imagined the hunger there, the reaction of his body to hers.

There was relief at the realization, but it was joined by an emotion she couldn't identify. What mattered was that she had misread the situation with Clay that day. Completely misread it.

When Shelby returned to work on Monday, things were still normal between her and Clay. The odd physical awareness that had sprung up between them wasn't what had her feeling backed into a corner. It was Vince Tyner, who stood in front of her at the firehouse.

She'd been carrying in groceries and found her ex-boyfriend in the kitchen. Her spine stiffened. Had he simply walked in? Where was everyone else?

"I wanted to come by and see you." His smile seemed forced. "I've called several times, but I guess your buddy, Clay, didn't tell you."

"He told me. I appreciate you checking on me, Vince. As you can see, I'm fine."

He moved around the long, scratched dining table, the muscles in his massive arms straining at the fabric of his paramedic's uniform shirt. His gaze slid over her as his voice lowered suggestively to say, "You look good."

"I'm well enough to come back to work," she said brightly, although her guard was now raised. "Which is what I should be doing."

"I want to talk to you, Shelby." He eased closer, brown eyes glittering sharply. "I need to."

"About what?" She stayed where she was, making sure to keep the open doorway at her back.

"About us."

"This is where I work. You shouldn't be here."

"I'm not leaving until you talk to me. You won't return my calls. Jessup won't let me anywhere near you. This is the only way I figure I can talk to you about us."

"I'm not interested in an *us*."

"Is this what you told all those other guys, too?" he demanded hotly. "I know you feel differently about me than you do all of them."

No, I don't. She didn't want to be so blunt, but maybe she should. "I don't want to get serious with anyone, Vince."

"Are you seeing someone else?"

"Not that it's any of your business, but no."

"Then why did you just up and tell me you didn't want to go out with me anymore?"

"Because I don't," she said firmly. "I didn't like what happened that night, Vince."

"I know I got carried away, but I apologized."

"And I accepted. Doesn't mean I want to reconsider." They had been to a movie and when he'd brought her home, he had wanted to come in. She had said no. He had stopped just short of forcing himself on her. That had been enough for her. "I don't want to hurt your feelings, but I'm not interested. Why can't you accept it's over?"

"You can't dump me like you did all those other guys. I'm better than that."

Her temper stirred. "You need to leave. The firehouse is no place for this conversation."

"I'll pick you up after your shift ends tomorrow and we can have coffee. Talk."

"No, Vince."

Something cold and sharp flared in his eyes; a dull flush colored his handsome face. "I'll let you think it over."

"I don't need to think it over. Please don't come back here. And don't call me anymore."

"Don't jerk me around," he snarled.

"I'm not. I don't like it when you act this way." In fact, she was growing alarmed. She started out the door, intending to go get the last bag of groceries.

A hard, hot hand clamped on her shoulder and spun her roughly. "Don't walk away from me!"

Startled at the forcefulness of his grip, she tried to shake him off. His fingers bit into her flesh. "Get your hands off me, Vince."

"That's not what you said the other night," he sneered.

"Let go right now," she said through clenched teeth.

He yanked her toward him. She raised her uninjured arm and drilled an elbow into his chest. "Back off."

"You listen to me, you little—"

"Get away from her, Tyner."

Captain Oliver appeared and grabbed the other man's arm. Vince shook free, releasing Shelby. "This isn't over," he hissed.

"Yes, it is," she said more steadily than she felt. "Don't come back here."

Savage fury twisted his features and he took a step toward her. Oliver pushed between them. Dylan Shepherd appeared, and so did Jay Monroe.

Vince's gaze locked on each of them and lingered, challenging. Shelby knew he was sizing up his chances in a fight. She didn't think he could take Shep's powerful build or Monroe's wiry strength.

The glare Vince gave her was so full of venom that her skin prickled. She'd never seen him this upset.

He pivoted and stalked out. Her captain turned, eyeing her intently. "You okay?"

"Yes." Her muscles, gone rigid as Vince talked, finally relaxed. The headache returned. "Thanks for stepping in, y'all. I guess he just didn't want to take no for an answer."

"We'll keep an eye out for him." Shep's dark eyes reflected concern.

Captain Oliver's gaze narrowed as he watched Tyner pull away from the curb in his ambulance. "I don't like him coming around my firehouse."

"I'm sorry, Cap. I had no idea he'd come here." Shelby tried to calm the boiling mix of fear and anger inside her. "I've told him more than once that things are over."

"It's not your fault, Fox."

The phone in his office rang and the captain jogged past Shelby to answer it. Shep and Monroe moved up beside her.

"You sure you're okay?" Jay's ruddy face was as serious as she'd ever seen it.

"Yeah, thanks. I don't know why the guy won't leave me alone."

"He might be a jerk," Dylan said, "but he knows a good woman when he sees one."

She cut him a look. "Don't start with me, Shepherd."

He grinned, opening his mouth to say something only to be interrupted by the shriek of the fire alarm. He and Monroe bolted for their gear; Captain Oliver rushed out of his office, stepped into his own bunker pants and steel-soled boots, and climbed into the driver's seat.

Shelby wished she were going. She stayed out of the way and in two minutes flat, the truck roared out of the garage. She waited until they disappeared and then went into the kitchen, shaken up more than she liked by Vince's visit. She finished putting away the groceries, giving in to a little self-pity that she couldn't go on the call with the others.

Glancing at the clock, she saw it was nearly three. Her usual time for a snack. She took a bag of popcorn from the cabinet and stuck it into the microwave.

As it cooked, she fixed a bowl of cat food for the firehouse cat and carried it outside. Just as she started back in, an explosion ripped through the air. Training had her ducking as metal clanged against metal, thudded into the wall. Debris shot through the kitchen's open doorway and across the bay's cement floor. Smoke rolled out. She jumped to her feet, awkwardly grabbed the nearest fire extinguisher with her uninjured hand and then raced into the kitchen, killing the small blaze in short order.

She stared in disbelief at the powder-covered mess. The microwave's door was across the room, its glass shattered. What if she'd been standing in here, watching the corn pop as she usually did? She might've been killed.

Fear formed a knot in her belly. Making sure all the embers were dead, she left things as they were and called Clay.

He arrived in less than ten minutes, his jaw stiffening when he saw the microwave. Despite having left for work early this morning when she had, his navy slacks and green-and-blue striped polo shirt looked fresh.

He took her chin in his hand and looked her over from head to toe. "Are you okay?

"I'm not hurt. I was just coming back into the firehouse when it happened."

"Blue eyes, you're gonna give me a heart attack."

"Tell me about it," she muttered. She wrapped her arms around herself. "This is too strange, Clay."

He brushed her hair away from her forehead and eyed her healing cut, then propped his hands on his hips. "Show me where you were and what you did."

Shelby walked him over to the cabinet where she kept her popcorn. "After Vince was here, the guys got a call—"

"Tyner was here?" he asked sharply.

She nodded.

"When? How long? What did he want?"

"It was less than half an hour ago. He was here maybe five minutes. He wanted to talk about getting back together. At first, I told him here wasn't the place to talk, but he wouldn't leave so I told him—again—that I wasn't interested in seeing him anymore."

"How did he take it?"

"Not any better than last time. He kept after me until Cap and Monroe and Shepherd came out, and told him to back off."

"Did Tyner threaten you? Try to push you around like he did the night you broke up with him?"

"No, he just grabbed me."

A savage light flared in Clay's eyes. "I really want to hurt that guy."

A police cruiser pulled up. Two uniformed officers stepped out of the black-and-white, met at the end of the sloping firehouse drive by the crime scene technician who was removing his work kit from a white van.

"Are you bruised?" Clay asked.

"No. He scared me more than he hurt me."

Clay's eyes turned cold and hard. Shelby knew that look. He waved the crime scene tech into the kitchen then turned back to her. "Where did you first see Tyner?"

"In here. I came in with a bag of groceries and he was waiting."

"Was he alone?"

"Yes."

His gaze shifted to the destroyed microwave. "How long after he left did the microwave blow up?"

"Maybe five minutes."

"Did you know he was coming?"

"No."

"He was in here alone for a bit before you knew he was here. Maybe no one else knew he was here, either."

Her eyes widened. "Do you think he did this? But why?" She felt sick. "Just because I broke up with him?"

"People do take revenge for those kinds of things, Shelby. But it might not have been that at all."

"What else?"

He searched her face, then said quietly, "It could be related to M.B.'s murder."

"Clay!" Her surprise left in a rush as realization sank in. "You mean, Vince might've killed M.B., then come after me?"

"I have to look at all the angles."

"But he hardly knew her."

"Are you sure?"

She froze. "No."

"I want to find out what connections he had to Ms. Perry."

"She met Vince a couple of times here when she brought over goodies. He took his ambulance to her school and showed the kids around." Could there have been more between the paramedic and the teacher? Something that might make Vince want to hurt M.B.? Shelby suddenly couldn't breathe.

"Did you notice if any of the firefighters were in here alone at any other time?"

"You're scaring me."

"Did you?"

"Alone?" She thought hard. "Maybe Shepherd."

Clay nodded. "I'll check him out, too."

"We already know he was friends with M.B. We all were."

"How did he act around her?"

"Flirty, like he does with every woman."

"We've been assuming M.B.'s lover was married, but maybe not."

"That's true," she said slowly, her stomach still in knots. "You really think Shep could've had something going with M.B.?"

"We'll have to find out."

"You're making me paranoid, as if Vince weren't enough," she muttered.

"Sorry." His gaze searched her face. "You sure you're okay?"

She nodded. "Thanks for getting here so fast."

"I need to talk to your captain, as well as Monroe and Shepherd."

"Just to see if they saw or heard anything, right?"

There was something in his face.

"You don't suspect either of them?"

"I suspect everyone until I have a reason not to. I want you to wait for me, then you're moving to my house."

"Do you think that's necessary?"

"I think Tyner would've hurt you if your captain hadn't stepped in. And I'm real suspicious about the timing of Tyner being in the kitchen just before the microwave blew."

"What do you think caused the explosion?"

"We'll have to wait for the lab guys to give us a solid answer. Was popcorn the only thing in there?"

"Yes, but that by itself couldn't cause an explosion."

"Even if the bag overheated and caught fire?"

"Even then. There has to be a lot of heat and pressure behind an explosion like that. If the bag caught fire, it would burn, but probably not even crack the glass. There had to be some power to make the glass shatter and for the door to blow off," Shelby explained.

"Power caused by what? An accelerant?"

"Yes. Or maybe a malfunction of some kind."

"You mean electrical?" Clay looked pensive.

"It's possible."

"What about accelerants? What could be used?"

"A piece of metal, maybe?" The growing realization that the incident could've been deliberate made her shudder.

"Something big? Small?" he asked.

"Could've been as small as a paper clip or a coin."

"Or flammable liquid inside the bag?"

"Yes, any of those." Had someone really tried to kill her? Or was the microwave faulty and she had just happened to be using it when it malfunctioned?

"I'll have the lab guys look at it. From your time together, Tyner knows you eat popcorn every afternoon. He could've planted something in the microwave before you tossed in your bag. So could Shepherd."

"I can't believe Shep would do something like this." It was frightening to realize she wasn't sure about Vince.

"I'm checking them both out anyway. I want you to take a leave of absence until we figure out what's going on."

"But I just came back to work today."

"I know, but if this was an attempt on your life…. Until the lab guys tell me this explosion *wasn't* deliberate, I don't want you here. I want you to be somewhere I can control the security."

His words chilled her. She knew he wouldn't suggest a move and a leave from work if he didn't believe it was necessary.

"I want to talk to the crime scene tech. Then I'll drive you home to get your things."

She nodded. "I'll talk to Captain Oliver when he returns."

"I won't let anything happen to you, Shelby."

She met his serious green eyes. She knew he was thinking about Jason, about the accident that he still blamed himself for. Why couldn't he accept that what had happened to her brother hadn't been his fault? "I know," she said quietly.

She didn't like taking a leave from work. She felt as if she were running away, giving in to a scare tactic; it chafed, but she trusted Clay. If he said he feared for her, then he had a reason. There was probably no place safer for her than his house.

Just before eleven-thirty the next morning, Clay walked into his kitchen from the garage, returning from a domestic dispute call he'd received at 5 a.m. He and Detective Kiley Russell had finally convinced a man holding his estranged wife and two-year-old daughter hostage to let them go. There had been no bloodshed, a major victory in itself.

Erin, the older of his two younger cop sisters, stood at the sink rinsing dishes. She turned when she heard him, her straight, dark hair sliding over one shoulder. Concern shadowed her green eyes, a shade lighter than his. "How'd it go?"

As he moved around the oak dining table, he told her about the outcome and then excused himself to go shower.

"Want me to fix you a sandwich or something? Shelby and I have already eaten."

"A sandwich would be great. Thanks."

She nodded, walking over to the refrigerator and opening the door.

"How were things here?" He stopped in the wide, arched doorway leading into the hall.

His sister straightened, bracing a hand on the top of the fridge door. "Fine. She talked a little bit about the explosion yesterday. Tyner didn't call, but her mom and Dylan Shepherd did."

The information about Shepherd annoyed Clay for some reason, despite his having learned that Shep hadn't been in the kitchen before the explosion as Shelby had thought. Shepherd wasn't a suspect at all right now. Neither were any of the other firefighters who'd been in the firehouse. They all had solid alibis, since they were off on a call. Clay dragged a hand across his tired eyes. "Did she say anything about Vince?"

"No. She only mentioned him when she talked about the microwave. Do you think she's afraid of him?"

"A little. After what she told me about their last date, I don't want him coming anywhere near her."

"Since you've got me and Brooke for backup during the day, he won't. Not on our watch anyway."

"Thanks." Clay did feel better knowing both his sisters would be with Shelby. "Where is she?"

"Putting on her clothes."

He started down the long hallway, passing the guest room on his left. The door leading into the light, airy space done in red, blue and yellow plaid was closed.

He figured Shelby was in there getting dressed, just as his sister had said. Before he could stop himself, he recalled holding her. Felt the press of her breasts against him, the soft skin of her neck beneath his hand.

He shook his head. Whatever had happened with Shelby last week hadn't occurred again. And wouldn't, Clay told himself. That unexpected, unfamiliar awareness he'd had of her body must've been some weird fluke. Things were back to normal between them and he was glad. The uneasiness nagging him now was due to the microwave explosion yesterday and learning about Tyner's presence there just before it happened.

Clay felt much better knowing Shelby was at his house. They had spoken to Paula last night after she'd returned from her buying trip, and the older woman agreed that Shelby should stay with him. As did Clay's dad, a cop who'd retired and started a private security company in Presley.

Clay walked into his room and pushed the door shut. As he moved toward the heavy king-size bed and matching chest of drawers, he pulled his gray Presley PD T-shirt over his head and dropped it on the floor. He toed off his tennis shoes, turning with his hand on the top button of his jeans just as the door to his bathroom opened.

Shelby stepped out, her eyes rounding in surprise. "Oh."

Sweet son of a—

His breath backed up in a painful knot.

Her short hair was dry except for a few strands that curled onto her nape. Steam from the bathroom glossed her neck, the curve of her shoulder. She wore only a bra and panties, and she looked damn good. The sight of all that bare golden skin had Clay's entire body going rigid.

"Erin's using the other bathroom or I wouldn't have—"

"It's fine." His throat was so tight it hurt to talk. A subtle feminine scent drifted to him. Something light and frothy and Shelby. It made his mouth water. He told himself to move, to look away, but he couldn't. His pulse hammered hard.

Her underwear wasn't sheer. It wasn't even a sexy color. Just serviceable white. But the plunging lacy bra and high-cut panties were enough to make his chest ache.

Who the hell knew she wore underwear like that? His gaze moved over the swell of her breasts, the sleek line of her belly to her lean legs, then drifted back to her breasts. His gut clenched when her nipples tightened against the silk.

She gave a nervous laugh. "Why are you looking at me that way? I mean, you've seen me in a bikini that shows more than this."

Jerking his attention to her face, he struggled to keep his voice even. "What way?"

"Like…I don't know," she said slowly, her left foot rubbing the top of her right.

Tension swelled between them. Her smile faded, replaced by confusion.

Trying to ease the moment, Clay went with the first thing that came to mind. "Where is that darn tattoo?"

Uncertainty flashed across her gamine features, then she arched a brow. "Wouldn't you like to know."

Hell, yes. He'd like to find it with his hands, his mouth. It took everything he had to pretend that raw, primal need wasn't clawing through him. "You know I'm going to find it one of these days."

He saw her take a deep breath and struggled to keep his gaze on her face. Not that it mattered. The sight of her half-naked would be carved into his brain for the rest of his life.

Of course he'd noticed her before. She was right—he'd seen her plenty of times in a bathing suit. She was a good-looking woman with a great body. But he'd never felt like *this* when he'd noticed. Never been so aware of the powder-fine texture of her skin, the tempting fullness of her breasts, her taut waist. She wasn't as tall as either of his sisters, but her legs were leanly muscled and strong. The image of those legs wrapped around him exploded on his brain. Startled at his thoughts, he slammed on the mental brakes.

It was too late. The confusion he'd seen earlier in her blue eyes was now panic. She moved toward him, keeping a healthy distance. "I didn't know you were coming home."

"Finished my call and thought I'd come back to clean up." The heated rush of his blood took him off guard.

She stood nearly even with him now, close enough to touch. And he *wanted* to.

Slanting one arm across her middle, she curled her palm around the side of her neck in a self-conscious motion. "I'm going to go get dressed," she said huskily.

It was only then that Clay realized her gaze had dropped to his bare chest. Her lips parted slightly and she stared with a feminine appreciation he couldn't remember ever seeing. At least, not when she looked at him. His heart thudded hard.

She looked up suddenly, and her gaze crashed into his. Something flickered in her eyes. Was it just his imagination, or had the air in the room turned electric? A strange sensation traveled up his arms.

Whatever was going on had him off balance and from the look on her face, he wasn't alone. He thought about tossing her a robe, but he didn't have one. She looked dazed. And nervous. She moved toward the door.

He started for the bathroom, trying to sound normal, as if lust weren't boiling him from the inside out. "I'll be out in a minute," he said gruffly. "Meet me in the living room."

She nodded, turning quickly to leave. As he stepped into the bathroom, he heard her shut the door in the bedroom. Bracing an arm against the door frame over his head, he cursed. He was turned on as hell right now, but he'd seen her face. She hadn't been afraid; she'd been wary, guarded. *With him.* He didn't blame her. There had been nothing friend-like in the way he'd looked at her.

After telling himself for days that the previous instance had been a fluke, that his body's response to hers hadn't meant anything, Clay was forced to admit he'd been dead wrong.

Until now, no woman had affected him since Megan's death. Not physically, not emotionally. Why did Shelby have to be the one? She'd seen his reaction and hadn't bought his lame explanation about why he was practically drooling over her. For a split second, he'd seen an answering heat in her eyes. Before the nerves set in.

He knew how she was about romantic relationships. Still, he couldn't deny that he wanted her. Wanted her with more ache than he could ever remember feeling, even for his late wife.

He didn't know what these feelings were or what they meant. He had told himself that he could ignore what had happened before, that he could make the lust, this increasing physical awareness of Shelby, go away. The cold hard truth was he couldn't. What the hell was he going to do?

Chapter 4

Whoa, *whoa*, *whoa*. That was all Shelby could think as she and Clay drove to Presley's oldest high school. Her skin tingled as if he'd put his hands on her. He hadn't, but he'd looked as if he wanted to. And she had wanted him to. As hard as she tried, she couldn't deny it.

She was uneasily aware of her body. Of the two feet that separated them. Of the current of sensation humming between them. She stared out the window; she didn't trust herself to look at Clay. Not yet, anyway.

She plucked at her pink, lightweight sweater, ran damp palms down the legs of her khaki pants. Was her response due to the concussion? Another of the erratic, uncontrollable emotions Dr. Boren had warned her about?

Coming out of the bathroom to find him had been a surprise, but what had jolted her senses like a live wire was the way Clay's gaze had done a slow, appreciative glide down her body.

He wasn't the only one who'd looked. He'd been wearing only jeans and as she followed the lines of his powerful body, she'd become suddenly and profoundly aware of his smooth, supple skin, the tan that faded into paler skin at his hips, the thin bands of muscle across his abdomen. She'd seen his chest before—they'd spent countless summer days at the lake—but *yowza*. It was all hard angles and planes and sleekly defined sinew, just like his shoulders and his arms. Dark hair coiled on his chest and formed into a thin line down the center of his ridged abdomen. He'd caught her looking. She couldn't help it; he was something else.

The moment had grown between them, clutching deep inside her and igniting a tiny flame of temptation. She could still smell his flesh-warmed woodsy scent, see the hard throb of his pulse in the hollow of his throat. She'd tried to dismiss her body's response, but she couldn't halt the heating of her blood, the heavy ache in her breasts, the tightening in her belly.

At first, he'd looked as startled as she'd felt, and then he'd looked…hungry. A shiver rippled through her. No man had ever looked at her that way, not even her ex, Ronnie, when they'd begun dating and things had been hot and heavy between them.

What was going on with Clay? And her? He was nine years older than she was. She had never felt toward him exactly as she had toward her brother, but she'd never wanted to jump his bones, either. Certainly never considered that he might want to jump hers.

Jeez, Louise! This was Clay! Restlessness moved through her. Her skin felt tight. She ordered herself to stop thinking about his chest, his body, his *everything*.

It wasn't until they were walking through the school's front door that Shelby had the presence of mind to speak. "You never said exactly why you wanted me to come to M.B.'s school with you."

"Oh," he said gruffly, pausing at the corner of a long corridor before starting across the vinyl-floored hallway for the school office. Fronted by glass walls, a long counter stretched along the width of the rectangular room. Several women and students worked behind it. "I thought you might get a glimpse of someone here that would help you remember something."

"Good idea. I hope it works." It was on the tip of her tongue to say something about that bizarre exchange in his bedroom, but for the first time in their long friendship, she didn't feel she could talk to him. Not now, anyway. Not when she could still feel this tight pull in her belly.

As she and Clay made their way to the office, the low roar of children's voices came from the opposite end of the building. The cafeteria, she realized. The silence between her and Clay was different than usual, heavier, but she noted that he didn't try to break it, either. If he was reeling over it as much as she was, she understood.

Once in the office, Clay asked to see Gail Cosgrove, M.B.'s friend who had called this morning to tell Clay she was back at work and eager to help any way she could. As the school secretary, Gail was responsible for making any travel arrangements for school-sponsored trips, local or out-of-town.

"M.B. and I were friends for ten years," the trim blonde told Clay and Shelby as she motioned them into her small office.

Clay shot Shelby a questioning look and she shook her head. She didn't recognize Gail Cosgrove, and the woman hadn't sparked any memories. Neither had anyone else in the outer office.

"So you knew about the man she was seeing?" Clay asked.

He always gave people his full attention. Shelby tried to keep hers on the secretary, but her mind was occupied with the man who was her best friend. She could smell the deep musk of his aftershave, a faint whiff of fabric softener. He'd shaved; the smooth line of his jaw was every bit as compelling as it was with stubble.

Gail nodded. "I knew about him, but I didn't know who he was. She wouldn't tell me."

"Why not?"

"She said it could cause trouble for both of them. I have no idea what she meant. It was the first time in our friendship she'd kept anything like that from me. M.B. wasn't a secretive person by nature. She was outgoing and straightforward. What you saw with her is what you got. I never understood why she wouldn't tell me. She knew I wouldn't have said a word to anyone."

Clay glanced at Shelby. "Could it have been because her telling you might have threatened you in some way?"

"In what way?"

Shelby knew what he meant and watched the other woman's face carefully.

"Are you married, Ms. Cosgrove?"

She gave a small laugh. "Oh, I see where you're going, but M.B. wouldn't have had an affair with my husband. And even if she'd wanted to, Wes would never have cheated on me."

"You sound pretty sure."

"I am." Her gaze went from Clay to Shelby and back. "Aren't there some things *you* know in your gut and your heart?"

Shelby's gaze met Clay's. They both had an unshakable confidence that they knew the other person inside out. At least, she had felt that way up until an hour ago.

Breathing in his flesh-warmed scent gave her the same reassurance it always did. Yet the familiar, comforting feeling now had an edge of awareness. A sharp edge that had wariness stealing through her.

She didn't want to be affected that way by him. Clay and her mom were the only people with whom her relationships had never changed. She knew what to expect with him. Or she had until everything had turned topsy-turvy.

Shelby had thought she'd known her husband, too. But during the last three years of their five-year marriage, he'd split his time between her and another wife in another city. Learning about Ronnie's bigamy, and the fact that he had a child with that other woman, had shattered Shelby's confidence in everything except her job and her relationships with Mom and Clay.

Gail leaned down to jot something on a piece of paper, then handed it to Clay. "This is my husband's work number and address. You can talk to him if you want."

"Thank you. We appreciate that."

"I want to help you any way I can. Wes will, too."

"Can you tell me if there was anyone you suspected of being M.B.'s lover? Someone she spent a lot of time with or showed an interest in?"

Gail shook her head. "Whoever the mystery man was, she dated him for quite a while. I always wondered if he was married. Sometimes I thought yes, sometimes no."

Shelby had entertained the same thoughts.

Clay took a newspaper clipping from his wallet and unfolded it, showing a picture of Vince Tyner to the other woman. "Have you ever seen this man?"

She studied it carefully. "Yes, he's been to the school before. M.B. asked him to come talk to the kids about being a paramedic."

Shelby recognized the photo as having come out of the weekend edition of *The Presley Reporter*. Vince and two of his co-workers had been interviewed as part of an ongoing series about local EMTs and other rescue workers.

"Did you see him around at any other times? Here or away from school with M.B.?"

"No. And the only other visitors she had here were parents." The secretary returned the paper to Clay. "M.B. entered those kids in science competitions all over the country. This spring alone, they competed twelve times. Five of those were out of the state."

"The other times were here?"

"Or nearby. Oklahoma City, Norman, Tulsa, Stillwater."

Clay slid his wallet into the back pocket of his navy slacks. "How many children are in the club?"

"Ten."

"That's a lot of children for one woman to handle."

"Oh, she didn't do it alone. The parents always helped her. Typically, at least two would go with her, sometimes three if they were traveling out of state."

"Moms and dads?"

"Yes. They had a rotating schedule. Well, except for Mac. He went on all of the trips until last month. Then he just stopped cold."

"Mac who?" Clay's voice sharpened.

"Mac Hayward."

Shelby didn't recognize the name, but Clay seemed to.

"He has twin daughters in M.B.'s—" Gail broke off, biting her lip. Tears sheened her eyes as she continued, "I mean, in the science club."

Clay gave her a minute before asking, "Why did he suddenly stop going on the trips?"

"I don't know. She never said."

"Why do you think she wouldn't tell you the reason?"

The secretary's frown deepened. "I don't know. Would you like Mac's phone number?"

"I have it, thank you. I spoke to him a few days ago."

"I assume you've already spoken to the teachers?"

"Most of them."

"As of this morning, Karen Lemley is the new sponsor of the science club. If you haven't already talked to her, she'd be a good place to start."

"Thanks for your help, Ms. Cosgrove."

Her voice thickened. "You're welcome. I hope you're able to find out who did this to M.B."

Shelby swallowed past a lump in her throat. "We will."

She and Clay walked out of the office and down the hall toward the teachers' lounge. "What do you think?" she asked.

"At least we have a name."

"Hayward?"

Clay nodded. "Collier and I did a dump on Ms. Perry's phone records. There were several long calls between her and Hayward. When I interviewed him last week, he said the calls were about the science club trips, planning and whatnot. Until now, I didn't have any reason to think he might be hiding something."

"I wish I could help more. I didn't recognize Ms. Cosgrove from anywhere."

As they made their way down the hall, Shelby was aware that several women looked on from their classrooms. Watching Clay. The two of them spoke to Karen Lemley, who also mentioned Mac Hayward. They had planned to talk to the man anyway, but his name coming up twice made it a slam dunk.

Shelby studied Clay surreptitiously. He was the same rangy, sometimes shy guy she'd known her whole life. So why couldn't she stop looking at him? She had never noticed that darker rim of green around his irises. Or just how hard his body was, especially his arms. She kept seeing his bare chest, the small fox tattooed on his left shoulder.

She tried to steer her thoughts to the present and deal with only one thing at a time, which meant each interview Clay conducted. As they spoke to several teachers outside the lounge, then others in their classrooms, Shelby noticed the admiring looks he was getting. The more-than-friendly offers to do *whatever* they could to help. The emphasis that he could call them day or night.

She tried to focus. A couple of times, she added what she hoped had been semi-intelligent questions to Clay's. The whole time, like a hard-to-reach itch, she was aware of the women's attention on Clay.

Women's gazes trailed from his slightly ruffled sandy hair down the lean strength of his body, as if they were picturing him naked. That struck an uneasy chord in her. Why hadn't she ever noticed how really wide his shoulders were? Why hadn't that tiny dimple at the corner of his mouth caused a little hitch in her pulse before now? Those women saw the same long-lined athletic build, the broad chest covered by dark green knit, the crook in his nose that made him rugged instead of pretty. And the look in their eyes was the same lust she'd felt in his bedroom. Still felt.

Lust. She couldn't call it anything else. And no matter how often she dodged the thought of what had happened between them earlier or how much time had passed, she couldn't seem to steady her pulse. Knowing things about Clay that those women didn't only made him more appealing. Such as his always calm demeanor, the gentleness in those big hands, the losses he'd suffered.

She wanted them to stay away from him. Especially the woman who gave Clay her phone number on the torn-off corner of a test paper. Surely *that* had to be against some school policy.

As they left the school and drove to the oil company where Mac Hayward worked as an engineer, Clay stuffed the paper into his empty ashtray. He glanced over, looking sheepish when he realized she'd seen him.

"Does that happen a lot?" she asked.

"What's a lot?"

"More than once." She really wanted to know.

He shrugged.

Which meant it had definitely happened more than once

Shelby realized there would've been a time she would have encouraged him to call the woman. This time, she kept her mouth shut. She didn't ask herself why; she didn't want to know. What she did know was that she had no intention of sacrificing their friendship for some fluke physical reaction that had nearly buckled her knees.

If either of them had intended to address it, she would've been the one. She wasn't going to and she knew Clay wouldn't, either. All she had to do was act normal and things between them would go back to normal.

Clay tried hard to sidestep the image of Shelby half-naked in his bedroom. Or at least keep it tucked away where it didn't totally distract him. Now that he'd seen her in next to nothing, he wanted to see more of her. And he kept imagining that tattoo in all kinds of places.

All during the interviews at M.B.'s school, Shelby had watched him. Sometimes with curiosity in her blue eyes, sometimes with bewilderment.

He felt the same confusion he saw in her face. If this had been about any other issue out of the ordinary, she would've been the first one to confront it, but this wasn't just about something out of the ordinary. It was about *them*.

He knew she wouldn't bring it up. He sure as hell wasn't going to.

At the Presley YMCA where Mac Hayward's secretary had told them Mac spent his lunch hours, Shelby kept studying Clay like a code she couldn't break. He tried to pretend she wasn't looking at him, because right now he didn't need to be distracted by her or the strange, unexpected thing that was happening between them.

Once inside the red brick building, they were taken upstairs to the free weight area. The long room was lined on three sides with mirrors. Weights, bars and benches were arranged along the far wall. The older woman who'd led them upstairs pointed out the man they'd come to interview.

Just under six feet and probably in his mid-forties, Hayward sat on a bench in the far corner doing bicep curls. With close-cropped blond hair, he was muscular without being bulky. Clay flashed his badge and introduced himself, then Shelby.

The man's gaze lingered on her, sending a flare of irritation through Clay. Shelby smiled pleasantly. Clay knew she was trying to recall if she had ever seen the other man with M.B.

She glanced at Clay and gave a small shake of her head. *No.*

He turned his attention back to the man in front of him.

"You want to talk to me again about M.B.?" Hayward asked before Clay could speak.

"Yes." The man hadn't appeared upset about M.B.'s death the first time Clay had spoken to him and he still didn't. Clay decided to rephrase some of the questions he'd asked last week and see if he could lead Hayward into telling him that he'd abruptly stopped going on the science club trips. "How did you and Ms. Perry get along?"

"Great. She was my girls' favorite teacher."

Clay glanced at his notebook, although he didn't need to. "You have twin daughters?"

"Yeah."

"How long did you know her?"

"Um, my girls have been in the science club for two years now." He dragged an arm across his perspiring forehead.

"How *well* did you know her?"

"As well as anybody, I guess."

This Hayward jerk had known her for two years and didn't act at all bothered by her murder. "Did anything go on between the two of you?"

"I already said we got along just fine," he said with a conspiratorial wink at Shelby.

Clay wanted to thump the guy. "I meant when you were out of town together."

The man tensed, his full attention now on Clay. "No, absolutely not."

"You two ever date?"

The man looked decidedly uneasy. "I don't know where you heard that."

"Did you?"

"No."

Clay found it interesting that Hayward hadn't issued a flat denial. Or still didn't seem upset over the victim's death. People dealt with grief differently, but to show nothing?

Two women walked past, then stopped a few feet away in front of a water cooler. Hayward's gaze followed them. Clay glanced over at the pair, noting the thin, almost bony frames encased in skintight exercise pants and what looked like sports bras. Both women focused their attention on him with an avid interest that made him uncomfortable.

He turned back to Hayward. "You said you went to the science club competitions with Ms. Perry."

"Yes."

"Why did you suddenly stop going?"

"Who told you that?"

"More than one person." That was the second question the man hadn't answered directly. "*Did* you stop accompanying the club on their trips?"

"Yes. Things got too busy at work. I'm a drilling engineer and my company started several oil and gas wells about the same time, so I've had to be out in the field a lot. All the engineers have."

"You know we'll check this with your boss."

"Sure, yeah." He smiled at Shelby. "Are you a cop, too?"

"She's my partner," Clay said before she could answer. "Where were you the night of May 9th, between the hours of 10 p.m. and 2 a.m.?"

"When was that? Like…nine days ago?" Realization skipped across Hayward's features. "That was the night of M.B.'s murder."

"Right. Where were you?"

He thought for a minute. "I was out in western Oklahoma waiting for a well to T.D."

"To reach its total depth," Clay explained to Shelby before asking Hayward, "Did anyone see you out there?"

"Sure. Lots of people. The drilling crew, the foreman, a logging service guy. I can give you their names and the names of the companies they work for."

"Good." Clay passed the man his notebook and pen. "Where did you stay?"

Hayward named a national motel chain. Clay would call and check out the man's story. "When did you return to Presley?"

"Not until a couple of days after M.B.'s, uh, what happened to M.B."

Clay nodded, pulling out the newspaper photo of Vince Tyner. "Have you ever seen this man?"

Hayward stared at the picture. "I think so," he said slowly. "I'm trying to remember where."

"With M.B.?"

"Yes." Realization spread across his blunt features. "At a restaurant one evening."

"Which restaurant?"

"Little Italy."

The small eatery, located right off I-35, was renowned for its pasta dishes. "When did you see them?"

"Maybe six weeks ago."

When Shelby was still dating Vince. Clay could tell by the

stillness of her body that she hadn't known. What other things had M.B. and Vince done that Shelby hadn't known about?

"If I see him again, should I call you?"

"Call if you remember anything else." He handed Hayward a business card. The man was cooperative, almost too eager about it, yet showed not one whit of being upset over M.B.'s murder. Clay turned to leave and Shelby did, too. "Stay available. We may have more questions."

"Sure. Anything you need. Anytime."

Clay and Shelby walked down the stairs. He glanced at her. "I take it you didn't know about Vince and M.B. going to dinner."

She shook her head. "That must've been why she asked me how serious I was with him."

"Was this before you broke things off with him?"

"Yes. A couple of weeks, maybe."

So it was possible the paramedic had been having an affair with the victim. Clay didn't say it out loud. Shelby didn't need things spelled out for her. They reached the first floor and he looked over at her. "You okay?"

"Yes. I'm just wondering what was going on with the two of them. I'm glad I broke up with him."

"Me, too."

She smiled, both of them stepping aside as a young, muscular guy jogged past them and up the steps, focused intently on his destination.

She glanced over her shoulder at him. "Do you think people like that live at the gym? Those two women back there were as close to perfect as I've seen."

"You've got to be kidding." He opened the door and followed her out into the warm May sunshine. "They were nothing but bones."

"Jessup, I know you didn't miss those 36 double D's."

"They weren't real."

She laughed. "How do you know?"

"I've seen real." Before he could stop himself, his gaze dropped to her breasts. "And those weren't."

A blush spread up her neck and she looked away quickly. "How many guys really care if they are or not?"

"I do."

"Are you saying size doesn't matter?"

"I guess it depends on what you're talking about," he said with a grin. "But I go for the whole package."

"Too bad more men aren't like you. We women spend way too much time trying to look model-gorgeous for y'all. Trying to get bodies like those two back there."

"Even you?"

She shrugged.

She didn't really think she needed to look that way, did she? "There's nothing wrong with your body, Shelby."

"My arms are too muscular, my legs are too short."

"I've seen you," he reminded her pointedly, his gaze flicking over her. "And for the record, wow. Trust me, there's not one thing wrong with your body."

His own was drawing up tight.

She gaped, but recovered quickly. "So if one of those women asked you out, you wouldn't go?"

"I don't know for sure, but probably not. They didn't seem that interested anyway."

"Yeah, right." Her eyes sparkled. "I almost suggested that you come out here and let me interview Hayward. The way those women stared, I thought they were going to strip you down."

He didn't care about those women; he'd barely noticed them. But he wouldn't mind if Shelby stripped him down.

"The only one I noticed was you," he said gruffly. He wanted to back her into the wall and kiss her, find out how she tasted. And if he did, he could sign his own death warrant. "You've been looking at me funny all afternoon."

She blinked. "Huh?"

They climbed into his truck and he started the engine, flicking on the air conditioner. He rubbed the taut muscles in his neck. "Are we going to talk about it?"

Long seconds ticked by, but when she spoke, she didn't pretend not to know what he meant. "I don't want to."

Neither did he. "We need to, blue eyes."

She stared at him, looking so uncertain, so damn cute that he wanted to pull her into his lap.

"I can't believe *you're* bringing this up."

"I can't, either."

"You hate man-woman talks."

"Yeah." He dragged a hand down his face, ready to get it over with, not sure how to start. His nerves pinged.

"I think we were both surprised," she began.

"You can say that again," he muttered, relieved she'd said something.

"But we're making too much of it."

"We are?" He angled a shoulder into his door.

"Yeah. I mean, we're in a weird situation. Things probably feel different between us because we're living together. We've never done that before."

"True." He didn't buy that explanation. Surely she didn't, either.

"It's probably some bizarre combination of that and me being nearly killed. All kinds of weird feelings are hitting me. Anger, sadness. Dr. Boren said I would experience a lot of unfamiliar emotions. That could be one of them."

"You think that explains why *I* wanted to get my hands on you a while ago? Why *I* couldn't stop looking at you? *I* wasn't the one who got whacked on the head. The only thing wrong with me is, I'm wondering why I haven't noticed you before now. I mean, *really* noticed."

"Clay." She pressed into the door, looking flustered. "I

don't know what that was, but it was no big deal. You didn't expect me to be in your bedroom. I startled you."

"You startled something, all right."

She bit her lip, hiding a smile. "I'm just saying it didn't mean anything."

"C'mon, Shelby. I wasn't the only one affected in there." His gaze dropped to her breasts and he could see the faint impression of tight nipples beneath her sweater. He forced his gaze to her face. "I saw you," he rasped.

She squirmed. "Oh, what are you talking about? It was no big deal."

"So that's why your body responded to mine, why your—"

"All right!" She blushed furiously. "Okay, so I...noticed you noticing. Just because I responded doesn't mean I should have. Or that I will again."

"Maybe you're right, but I don't think so." He stretched his arm along the top of the seat, hit with a purely macho urge to prove she would respond to him again. "I don't know why something's started between us, but it has."

"I don't know that I would call it *something*."

"Blue eyes, we've never tiptoed around things. We're not going to start now."

She huffed out a breath. "Well, what is it then?"

"Hell if I know, but it *is* something. Things are changing."

Her gaze jerked to his. "I don't want them to."

He nodded. He knew how she felt about him, about their friendship. He didn't want to fiddle around with it, either.

"We've never...been that way with each other," she said slowly, softly.

His blood stirred at the way her voice slid over him.

"So whatever is happening is probably temporary," she added. "Due to stress or tension or our living together."

Clay's gut told him that whatever was going on was too significant to be short-lived. His whole world was going into a tailspin. The thoughts, the emotions tumbling around inside him were uncontrollable and reckless. Arousing.

He knew any move on his part in that direction would send her running for cover. "You don't need to worry about anything happening, at least on my end." She looked so serious that he couldn't resist teasing her. "If it turns out *you* can't control yourself, just let me know."

She laughed then, the full-throated sound that he usually heard. "And you'll help me out?"

"Like I always do."

She shook her head, pulling her seat belt across her body and buckling it. "Okay, you were right to talk about it. I feel better."

"Good." Problem was, he didn't, but he didn't see any reason to talk it to death, either. Maybe she was right. Maybe this sudden awareness between them would wane.

As they pulled out onto Main Street, his cell phone rang. It was the lab tech and the information he gave Clay about the microwave explosion had him calling Collier McClain as soon as he hung up.

"Pete from the lab just called," he said when the fire investigator answered. "He said the microwave explosion at Shelby's firehouse yesterday had a high probability of being deliberate. When we finish at the high school, he wants us to come by the lab and he'll walk us through it."

After Collier agreed, Clay hung up, saying to Shelby, "I'll drop you off at the house, then meet McClain at the school."

"All right. What exactly did Pete say?"

"He said wires were tampered with and that's what caused the explosion."

"I was hoping it was a manufacturer malfunction," she said quietly. "Someone really did try to kill me yesterday."

"Yes," he said through gritted teeth. "It's too convenient that the explosion happened at a time when you're known to usually be using the microwave and that it happened on your first day back."

"I guess I won't complain about taking a leave from work. It's a good thing you moved me to your house."

Thinking about how close she'd come to being hurt a second time put a sick feeling in his stomach.

"So why are you and Collier returning to the high school?"

"To interview Antonio Sandoval again."

"Is he the guy M.B. was teaching to read?"

"Yeah, and he's an electrician. Pete said since that explosion was powerful enough to blow out the glass, it was probably caused by a combination of tampered wires and adding something else to the mix."

"Like an accelerant? Or a piece of metal?"

"Right."

"But I didn't recognize Sandoval from anywhere. And I've never seen him at the firehouse."

"Doesn't matter. He has a connection to M.B. and he has the knowledge to blow up a microwave."

She nodded. "I hope you and Collier can get a lead."

"Me, too."

She was subdued for the remainder of the ride. He didn't push. Her silence could've been due to learning the explosion most likely had been deliberate. Or it could've been about this new awareness charging the air between them.

Her scent drifted to him and his gut knotted. He studied her profile, the clean, classic lines of her heart-shaped face. His gaze moved over the curve of her breasts, her hip. The urge to touch her had his whole body going rigid. How could something this strong, this unmistakable be temporary?

He'd hoped getting the issue out in the open would have cooled his blood. It hadn't.

Chapter 5

That conversation with Clay made Shelby's nerves tingle. It also made her jumpy. Half an hour after he dropped her off, she sat on the edge of the bathtub in his guest bathroom, watching Erin slather on makeup.

"You're working a john trap tonight?"

Clay's sister would work the street undercover and whenever she was solicited for sex, the john would be arrested. "Yeah. Gotta look the part."

"You're getting there." Shelby eyed the denim miniskirt and tight lace-up top the other woman had poured herself into for her role as a hooker. She pointed to a pair of three-inch black stiletto heels in the doorway. "Can you really walk in those? I'd fall and break my neck."

"They kill my feet, but yeah, I can walk in them."

"Exactly where are y'all running this john trap? Presley doesn't have a hooker row."

"We'll be on Lincoln in Oklahoma City. I'm part of a multiagency task force working with the OCPD to bust a prostitution ring." The other woman flashed a smile as she lined her eyes with thick black color. "Since I'm not known to the johns or pimps down there, they won't automatically think cop."

"You've got a lot of guts, Erin. The whole operation sounds scary. It's got to be dangerous. I've done ride-alongs to that part of Oklahoma City. I know what it's like."

"Hey, I'm trained, just like you are. It takes guts to run into a burning building, too. Well, maybe *guts* isn't the right word so much as *nuts*." Erin shot her a wry look in the mirror.

Shelby grinned, wishing she could get that conversation with Clay out of her mind. Forget how the intensity in his green eyes had melted her, made her *want*. When had that ever happened? Never, that's when.

The whole thing was too bizarre. She couldn't believe he'd been the one to address what had happened in his bedroom. So much for her hope that things would get back to normal. He had no better idea than she did about what was happening, but she wanted to ignore it. Clay acted as if he wouldn't mind exploring it.

She couldn't believe the things he'd said to her, that he'd told her he liked her body. And that whole bit about breasts? A blush heated her face.

"Hey, what's going on?" Erin's light green gaze met Shelby's in the mirror. "You just turned about three shades of red."

Shelby thought about confiding in Clay's sister, but talking about it made it even more real, more confusing. "Nothing."

"Uh-huh. I grew up with you. Something's going on." Erin turned, brushing out her dark hair. "Spill it. There was some kind of tension between you and Clay when y'all left for those interviews at the school. Does it have to do with that?"

"What is it with you Jessups today?" she muttered. "Having to get everything out in the open?"

Because of their brothers, Shelby and Erin had been friends a long time. Maybe telling the other woman would help her put it in perspective. "Something did happen."

"Like what?"

When she didn't answer, Erin jerked around. "Something sexual?"

"No. Yes. I think."

"Whoa." The other woman's eyes turned serious. She began to tease her long dark hair with a comb. "Go on."

Shelby took a deep breath, feeling a little awkward. "When he came home earlier, I was in his bathroom."

"Yeah, because I wasn't finished in the other one when you needed it. So?"

"He walked in when I was coming out. All I had on was my underwear."

"I bet he liked that." Erin waggled her eyebrows.

Judging by that heat in his eyes, he had. Shelby's pulse hitched and she looked at the floor.

"Hey." Erin faced her, settling one hip against the vanity as she started on the back of her hair.

"He's never looked at me that way before," she said shakily.

"What way?"

"I don't know why it was such a big deal. I mean, he's seen me in a bathing suit before." She nervously fingered the collar of her sweater.

"He looked at you like *that*? Like he wanted you?"

"Yes."

"No way! And Clay talked to you about this? Clay Jessup?"

"He's the one who brought it up."

His sister's eyes went wide.

"I know. I couldn't believe it, either."

Erin hesitated for a second. "Did he do more than look? Did y'all kiss?"

"No! No, no, no." She pushed herself off the tub and moved to the door. "But I...responded. I wanted him, but I don't want to feel that way."

"Because y'all are best friends?"

"Exactly. If we acted on whatever this is and it turned out badly, I couldn't bear to lose him."

"You know he wouldn't hurt you?"

"Of course. It's not about him hurting me. If it didn't work out, there would be distance. Even if we stayed friends, things would never be the same."

Erin's eyes darkened with compassion.

"Anyway it was just a little thing," Shelby added quickly. "I surprised him. He surprised me. We dealt with it, so it's over. We can move on." She wanted that to be true. And yet she didn't.

Erin stared solemnly at her for a long moment, then picked up a can of hair spray and saturated her new hairdo. "You're right to be cautious."

"Really?" Shelby coughed and fanned herself as the cloud of spray floated around her.

Erin nodded, bending at the waist and giving her hair another dousing.

The dry, sticky odor was overwhelming, and Shelby sneezed.

"Remember Johnny Dollarhide?"

Erin was three years older than Shelby, but they'd all gone to the same school. "You guys were pals from fifth grade, right?"

"Yes. Our freshman year in college, we got together. It was the weirdest thing. One day we were only buddies, and the next day we were all over each other."

"It happened that fast?"

She nodded. "One night, we walked back to the dorm after studying and he kissed me. He did it on impulse." Her voice was distant with the memory, then strained. "It was great. For a while. But it didn't work out and when we broke up, our friendship suffered for it. It wasn't worth it. I still miss him."

"I don't want that to happen between me and Clay."

"You can't always help how you feel."

"That doesn't mean I have to do anything about it."

"True. And if you're smart, you won't."

Shelby nodded, but her heart squeezed hard. If she lost Clay as a friend, she wouldn't be able to bear it. His friendship was the one thing she could always count on. Boyfriends were a dime a dozen; best friends weren't. So why did she have the niggling sense that she stood to lose something anyway?

Erin gave her big hair one last coating of spray. Shelby sneezed again and eased back from the door, away from the thick, sticky mist. Something flashed through her memory, then was gone. She was right to keep things between her and Clay platonic. He'd said he wouldn't pursue it, and she knew he wouldn't. As long as she was clear that she didn't want their relationship to take a romantic turn, he wouldn't go there. That should've made her feel more confident about what she'd told him in the truck. Instead, she felt unsettled, full of doubt. She was doing the right thing, wasn't she?

Clay and Collier followed Gail Cosgrove out of the school office and down to the end of the long main hallway. As it was nearing two o'clock and all the kids were in class, the school was quiet except for the muffled thump of his and Collier's shoes and the sharp click of Mrs. Cosgrove's heels. She led them through an exit door, then down a flight of stairs. When she'd heard that they needed to talk to Antonio Sandoval, she offered to find the custodian and take them there.

Ever since dropping Shelby off at his house a while ago, Clay had been telling himself he could get past wanting her, get past this need that seemed to sharpen the more he tried to fight it. It wasn't as if he knew what was going on, either, or had his head screwed on straight. Or was even using his head, he thought wryly. He and Shelby had been forced to have that semisex talk because another part of his body was overruling his brain. That had to stop.

At the bottom of the stairs, he and Collier followed the school secretary through another door, met by the thick odors of ammonia and some generic cleaning fluid. The hallway, which appeared to stretch the length of the building, was brightly lit. A door marked Custodian's Office led into a square twelve-by-twelve sparsely furnished room. There was no one inside.

Down the hall, maybe two hundred feet from the office, was Antonio Sandoval. Surrounded by three girls who looked about sixteen, his attention was fixed on an object he held. He said something Clay couldn't hear and one of the girls tossed her long blond hair over her shoulder as she leaned forward to look at what was in the man's hand.

The door they'd come through creaked and groaned, but none of the four people down the hall seemed to have heard it.

"Sasha! Mandy! Gina!" Mrs. Cosgrove called loudly.

All three of the girls started, turning to stare solemnly at the older woman.

The blond girl grimaced, then pasted on a smile. "Yes, ma'am?"

"Sasha, aren't the three of you supposed to be in class?"

A long pause. "Yes. Antonio was just fixing my tape recorder so I could tape today's biology lecture."

"You know you're supposed to make that request through the office."

"Yes, ma'am."

"Go there and wait for me."

Clay asked in a low voice, "Does he get a lot of girls wanting him to repair things?"

"A lot of *people*. He can fix anything."

"Even electrical problems?"

"Yes." Mrs. Cosgrove made a shooing motion toward the girls. "Go on."

Sandoval returned the tape recorder. The blond girl, Sasha, glared at the older woman, but motioned to her friends and the three of them disappeared through another door a few yards away.

The custodian's eyes narrowed as he saw Clay and Collier. Did the guy have some reason to be concerned that they were back? Or did he just not like cops? They walked with Gail toward the man who pulled a rag from the back pocket of his coveralls and wiped his hands.

"Señora Cosgrove," he said politely. Despite a thick Spanish accent, his English was flawless.

"Antonio, haven't I told you that those girls can't be down here?"

"Yes, ma'am. That's what I told them. They were only here a moment before you arrived. I also told them to put in a request at the office."

She nodded, looking irritated. "Detective Jessup and Investigator McClain need to talk to you again."

The man's dark gaze shifted from Collier to Clay. "All right."

Gail glanced at Clay. "I'll leave you to it, then."

"Thanks, Mrs. Cosgrove."

"You're welcome." She left by the same door they'd entered through.

As soon as the door shut, Sandoval frowned. "Why are you back again?"

"We need to ask you some questions about your job," Collier answered.

"My job here?"

"Do you have another one?" Clay slid his notebook out of the back pocket of his navy slacks.

"No."

Collier gave the man a curious look. "You speak English very well."

"Thank you," Sandoval said stiffly.

Clay waited. He and Collier had decided that Collier, rather than Clay, should ask again about the man's lessons with M. B. Perry. Just to see if his story stayed the same.

"I'm wondering why you need to be tutored in English, since you do speak it so well."

Dull color spread up the man's burnished neck. "I can't read or write it. Speaking is easier to learn than those things."

Which was what he'd told them on their first visit. Clay nodded. "How long have you been in the United States?"

"Two years."

"Did you have a job similar to this one in Mexico?"

"Yes."

"Who did you work for?"

"Myself," he said grudgingly.

"How many years there?"

"Seven."

So he had plenty of experience. "Have you ever worked on microwaves?"

"What does this have to do with Señorita Perry's murder?"

"Microwaves," Clay repeated flatly. "Ever work on them?"

"Yes. We have some here."

"What kind of work do you do on them?"

"I fix them," he said impatiently, glancing around.

"Are we keeping you from something, Antonio?" Collier asked.

The man didn't answer.

Clay eyed Sandoval. "Ever had a problem with any microwaves?"

"A problem like what?"

"Like an explosion or a fire."

"No." He vehemently shook his head. "No."

"If a microwave or any other appliance had a wiring problem, could you fix it?"

"Probably."

Collier and Clay exchanged looks. From his back pocket, Clay pulled out the Polaroid photo of Shelby he'd taken earlier at his house. "Do you know this woman?"

Sandoval took the picture and studied it, interest plain in his eyes. "No. She's pretty."

"Have you ever seen her?" Clay asked sharply, not liking the heat that charged through his chest.

He returned the picture. "Yes, at M.B.'s funeral."

"And nowhere else? No other time?"

The olive-skinned man frowned. "Nowhere else." Sandoval met his gaze without hesitation. He appeared to be telling the truth.

Collier asked, "When does your workday begin?"

"Seven-thirty."

"And what time do you leave?"

"Usually between five-thirty and six."

Clay jotted a note in his pad. "So you were here yesterday between 8 a.m. and 3 p.m.?"

"Why?"

"Just answer the question."

Uncertainty flashed in the other man's dark eyes. "No. I had the day off."

Collier stroked his chin. "You don't have to be here every school day?"

"The head custodian and I switch off every other Monday."

"How did you spend your time yesterday?"

Sandoval stiffened. "I did chores at my apartment in the morning, and in the afternoon I went to a movie."

"Alone?" Collier fired the word at him.

There was the slightest bit of hesitation. "Yes."

Clay gave the man a flat stare. "Can anyone verify that you were at either of these places?"

"I did laundry. The apartment manager saw me there."

"Where do you live?"

Sandoval gave the name of a complex on the west edge of Presley, close to the city limits.

"What movie theater did you go to?"

"The theater at Quail Springs Mall."

The man lived only a couple of miles from the shopping center in Oklahoma City. "What movie?"

He hesitated. "*Diarios de Motocicleta*."

"Want to translate that?" Collier asked.

"*The Motorcycle Diaries*."

"Never heard of that one." Clay shared a look with McClain. "What time did it start?"

"About one-thirty."

"What time was it over?"

"Maybe…three-thirty?"

"What was the movie about?" Collier asked.

They would need to check movies and showtimes with someone who spoke Spanish. And knew something about Spanish films.

The custodian explained that it was a movie based on the journals of Che Guevara, a Cuban revolutionary.

Clay caught resentment beneath the man's words, on his sculpted features. "You have a problem talking to us, Sandoval?"

"I've already talked to you. I know nothing. Why do you continue to bother me?"

"Because you've got information we need."

"Why don't you go find who did this to M.B.? She was my friend. Go find who killed her and leave me alone."

"Did you ever go to the movies with her?"

Surprise flared in his eyes. "No."

Clay leveled a look on him; the man held his gaze. "We might want to talk to you again."

"I will be here," he said with a jerky nod.

As Clay and Collier entered the stairwell to return the way they'd come, Clay asked, "What do you think?"

"He's lying about something."

"I don't think it's about Shelby. Being alone at that movie?"

"Yeah."

"Since school hasn't let out yet, let's talk to the other students M.B. tutored. Maybe they can tell us if they ever saw Sandoval with anyone else or if he talked about anyone."

"We don't have much besides the fact that he can work on microwaves, maybe has the electrical knowledge to rig one to explode."

Clay slid a hand through his hair. "If he was the guy M.B. was having an affair with and word got out, there would be consequences."

"Like one or both of them getting fired?"

"Yeah."

"That might happen," Collier agreed. "At the very least they'd get a reprimand. He's here on a work visa. He couldn't get deported over something like that."

"No," Clay answered slowly. "But if he was discovered in an affair with a teacher and drew attention to himself, he might show up on someone else's radar."

"Immigration?"

"Maybe his work visa isn't in order. Maybe he was M.B.'s lover and she wanted to keep their affair a secret because his visa is expired, not because either of them was worried about a spouse finding out."

"Let's check out his work visa."

Clay dragged a hand down his face. "I can do that when I get back to the station. I'll let you know what I find out."

Collier nodded, pausing at the corner of a long hallway lined with lockers. "How's Shelby doing?"

"Okay." The question shot Clay's thoughts back to the discussion they'd had in his truck earlier.

"It's a good thing you moved her to your house. At least you know she's safe there."

"Yeah, this whole thing is making me hinky." And he was talking about what was happening between them as much as he was the attempt on her life.

She was safe from danger. And that was the main thing, Clay reminded himself. To keep her safe. To make her feel that way.

After what had happened earlier in his bedroom, he could see why she might be skittish around him. He didn't want that. Her safety was and should be his number one priority. The only thing he should be thinking about her body was how to guard it.

The memory of her in that lacy underwear would torture him the rest of his life, but he couldn't let her see how much he was starting to want their friendship to be more. She'd told him she didn't want a romance. It wasn't *her* problem that she didn't.

It was *his* problem and he wasn't going to make it hers. She had enough to deal with. He had to keep his brain engaged and his hands off.

No matter how tough it would be.

Several hours later, after Clay and Shelby had eaten, he was stretched out on the couch in his living room and she sat cross-legged on the floor at his feet, relaxing as the TV droned on in the background.

"Did you ask Vince about being at the restaurant with M.B.? The one where Mac Hayward saw them?"

He nodded. "I went by Tyner's paramedic station. He didn't deny being at Little Italy with her."

"Did you get the feeling they'd been seeing each other or was it just a casual dinner? Maybe a thank-you for Vince talking to her kids at school?"

"He didn't say specifically, but yeah, I think they had more than one dinner together."

"Loser." It was irritation, not hurt, that flashed across her features. "You didn't say much about your interview with the custodian while Mom was here."

After Erin had gone to work, Paula had stayed with Shelby until Clay had come home. She'd left a few minutes ago. "I wanted to wait until we were alone."

"Maybe what you learned will help me remember something," she said hopefully.

Clay sat up and swung his feet to the floor. He'd watched her carefully through supper, trying to appear that he wasn't watching her. She hadn't acted awkward around him after their talk in his truck; he didn't want her to start. "And you might be able to help me with further information. Plus I know if I didn't tell you, you'd be out there stirring up trouble."

She wrinkled her nose at him. Taken by the way the light glided across her velvet skin, shading one high cheekbone, his gaze lingered on her.

His body hummed. He wanted to move, to pace, but he forced himself to sit there. No sense winding up her nerves as tightly as his. "Sandoval gave us an alibi for the time of the microwave explosion, but not the night of M.B.'s murder. He said he spent yesterday doing laundry and going to a movie. Alone. Neither Collier nor I believe that part. We re-interviewed the other students in his tutoring group to see if they'd ever seen him with anyone or heard him mention anyone."

Shelby opened a bottle of hot pink nail polish, glancing up in a silent prod for him to continue.

"Two girls recalled seeing him with another student, a senior girl named Leticia Keane. They said Leticia has a big crush on Sandoval. We asked him about being seen with her and he said that it was one time, when he told her to leave him alone. I stopped by on the way home and talked to Leticia. She said basically the same thing. When she approached him, he told her he wasn't interested and she left it at that."

"So that's a dead end?" Shelby drew one knee to her chest and slicked bright polish across her first nail.

"No." His gaze slid up the length of her tanned legs. Her shorts gaped, right there where the crease of her thigh met her butt. "No, no. It's not a dead end yet."

He pinched the bridge of his nose, trying to ignore the glimpse of red satin panties he'd just had. And telling himself to stop wondering about that tattoo. "The two girls who told us about Leticia said there was an incident last year involving her and another teacher. A male teacher."

Shelby frowned. "What kind of incident?"

He was not going to stare at her. "Leticia claimed he tried to get her to do sexual favors for him in exchange for a better grade."

Shelby grimaced. "Gross. Was it true?"

"Who knows? We talked to Gail Cosgrove. She said a formal complaint was never filed and Leticia agreed not to bring it before the school board if the man was fired. Cosgrove said that did happen, and he moved to Tulsa. She pointed us to the guy's last known residence. There was a For Sale sign in the yard, and the house was empty. I called the real estate agent and got his name and phone numbers. I left a message for him to call me. I want to get his side of the story."

"Do you really think someone would lie about something like that?"

"It's happened before."

"So what are you thinking? That maybe Antonio and M.B. did have something going on? That Leticia found out about it and was jealous?"

"Maybe she thought if M.B. were out of the picture, Sandoval would pay attention to her."

"But kill M.B.?" Shelby shuddered, leaning down to blow on her wet toenails.

He dragged his gaze from her mouth. "It's an angle I have to check."

"So Leticia could be the one I saw at M.B.'s house, the one who pushed me or hit me with something?"

He nodded. "If she got a teacher fired, there's no telling what a girl like this might do."

"That is so twisted—" she stopped. "Do you smell hair spray?"

He laughed at her abrupt change of subject. "Where did that come from?"

"I've been smelling it since Erin left." Shelby smiled, pulling her other knee into her chest and dipping the brush into the nail polish. "She must've used a gallon of that stuff for her 'hooker' hair. Keep talking."

"Did M.B. ever mention this incident?" Clay smelled only Shelby's fresh softness. "The girl or the teacher?"

"No."

A lock of hair fell across Shelby's eye, and he stopped himself from reaching toward her to brush it away. "Ms. Cosgrove doesn't buy the rumor that Sandoval was the man M.B. was seeing. She said M.B. liked men closer to her own age, focused, with a sense of themselves."

"Well, I sure don't know." She again blew on her freshly painted toes. Why did that make his body tighten? "I'm starting to wonder if I knew as much about M.B. as I thought I did."

"Collier and I checked Sandoval's work visa, just to make sure it was in order, and it is. I also showed the guy your picture so I could get his reaction. He said he remembered seeing you at M.B.'s funeral, but not anywhere else."

She capped the polish and set it on the coffee table. "Do you believe him?"

"I don't know. He's hiding something, but I'm not sure if it's about you or himself. I don't think he's involved with the Keane girl. She acted embarrassed about chasing after him and being rejected. Still, I want to talk to the teacher she reported for putting the moves on her."

"What about the guy we talked to at the gym?"

He rubbed the taut muscles in his neck. "Hayward's story about being in a hotel and on that drilling rig the night of M.B.'s murder checked out. So I don't have anywhere to go on him right now."

Clay wouldn't have thought twice about touching Shelby before…the incident. Now he questioned every impulse. "The headache back today?"

"No, thank goodness. Except for the whole MIA memory thing, I feel normal."

His gaze traced her features, lingered on the circles under her eyes, the anxiety there. "You look tired."

"I am. You've got to be, too."

"Yeah, I'm ready to hit the sack."

"Will Erin be back tomorrow?"

"I think it's Brooke's turn."

"If there's anything you want me to do around here, just let me know. I don't like sitting around all day."

"Like ironing my shirts, cooking my meals, waiting on me hand and foot?"

"Don't push your luck, buddy."

He grinned as she walked past him on her way to the hall. Stopping in the archway, she smiled. "See you in the morning."

"See ya."

Nerves pinging, he waited until he heard her finish rustling around in the guest bath, until he heard the door to the extra bedroom close before he went to his own room across the hall. He stripped to his underwear, brushed his teeth and eased down onto his mattress.

For long minutes, he stared up at the moonlight spotting the ceiling. He'd said he wouldn't touch her, and he hadn't, but he wanted to. Not only in a sexual way, either. Earlier, he'd stopped himself from doing things he normally didn't give a second thought to. Like brushing her hair out of her face, squeezing her shoulder. Now he checked every impulse. Wondered if he should touch her at all.

He thought he was too frustrated to sleep, but he must've dozed off because something jerked him awake. Moving on automatic pilot, he rolled out of bed. Yanked on a pair of cotton knit shorts, grabbed his 9mm Glock and sprinted for the guest room.

As he reached Shelby's door, he realized what had woken him. A scream, then a thud. And now he heard sobbing.

Every muscle went rigid. His finger twitched on the trigger. He didn't see how anyone could've gotten in, but he was taking no chances. Easing up to the door, he turned the knob and silently pushed it open. Moonlight trickled around the edges of the blinds. He flipped on the light, cataloguing everything in two seconds. His gaze skimmed the dresser to his left, the window straight ahead. Around to the chest of drawers. The room was empty. So was her bed, just in front of him.

His heart crashed against his ribs. Where was she?

He was already moving into the room when a low, keening cry came from the other side of the mattress. He took two steps and found her huddled in a ball on the floor, shaking so hard he could see her muscles spasm.

He crouched at her feet, thumbing on the gun's safety and then laying his weapon on the bed. She wore plaid boxers and a skinny-strapped T-shirt. He touched her thigh. "Shelby?"

She cried out and scrambled to her knees, launching herself at him.

Catching her by sheer reflex, his arms went around her and he fell back against the bed with a grunt. "What happened? What's going on?"

She was crying, sobs so deep that she was gasping for breath. Her arms clamped around his neck; her short nails dug into his skin.

He braced his shoulders against the bed, trying to balance them both. Alarm streaked through him. What in the hell had frightened her so badly? He shifted her into the cradle of his arms, and she burrowed into him as if he were a blanket. "Blue eyes, what happened?"

"I...had...a nightmare," she choked out. "I was at M.B.'s and I was falling. Over and over and over."

And she'd tumbled out of bed because the dream felt so real? She shook so hard he felt her ribs knock against his. Holding her tight, he murmured to her, his mind racing. A nightmare about M.B.'s? Why tonight? "Is this the first one you've had?"

She nodded. Her sobs quieted and she shuddered, trying to drag in air. She moved on his lap, laying her head on his shoulder. Hot tears wet his skin, and her breath whispered against his neck. His right arm draped over her hips; his free hand slid up to stroke her nape.

"It was awful. Pitch-black. And hot. Burning up." She drew in a labored breath. "You know that feeling you get when you know you're dreaming, but you can't wake up? I was suffocating."

"You fell out of bed."

She blinked, looking dazed.

"Let me see you." She would barely release him enough for him to take a look. "Did you hurt your head? Your wrist?"

"I don't think so." She trembled violently as he ran his hands up and down her arms, checked her head carefully for a re-opened wound or a new one. He found none.

She gave a sobbing laugh. "I can't stop shaking."

"Want me to get you something? Popcorn? Hot chocolate?" She drank cocoa in cold weather and hot.

"No. I'll be good to go in just a minute." Her trembling arms tightened, clutching at him as if he were holding her together limb by limb.

The sight of her cringing on the floor looped repeatedly through his head, and his chest felt as if it might split open.

"What is going on? Everything is so weird." She shivered and buried her face in the crook of his neck, her breath tickling his skin. "What's happening?"

"I'm not sure. Do you remember anything else about the dream?"

"Just falling," she said raggedly.

Now that she was calming down and his pulse had slowed, Clay became aware of the silence of the house, their aloneness. Of her in his lap. She smelled like peachy soap. The press of her breasts against him had his blood heating.

Beneath his hands, she felt slight and fragile. Her skin was petal-soft, as delicate as down. Desire clawed through him, followed by a fierce urge to do something about it. He wanted to kiss her. Not just her mouth. Behind her ear, between her breasts, the crease where her hip met her thigh…

She gave a shaky laugh and wiped her eyes, keeping her head on his shoulder. "I don't think I've ever been so scared."

"Me, either," he said huskily.

"I haven't had a single nightmare about what happened at M.B.'s house. Why would I have one tonight?"

He shook his head, his throat tight as she shifted and her cheek brushed his. So close. Her mouth was right there. Clay squeezed his eyes shut, fighting the ache that pulled every muscle taut.

Don't do it. Don't do it.

He held her tight, trying not to move his hands, struggling to level out his breathing. He inhaled deeply, needing fresh air but getting her scent instead. She smelled sweet, sugary-warm, and he wanted a taste.

His muscles quivered with restraint. He didn't want her to look at him, didn't want her to see what was surely on his face.

She drew back slightly, her arms staying locked around his neck. His stubbled chin rested on her head. She felt the rising tension in his body, was suddenly, keenly aware of his clean male scent, his hard bare chest. His big hands no longer moved up and down her back; they remained still on her, as if to steady her. Or himself.

"I hate feeling so helpless, so terrified." She looked up. Clay's eyes were closed and his handsome features were taut.

With hunger.

Her stomach dipped. Before she could fully process the look on his face, he opened his eyes, staring at her mouth. She felt him then, hard beneath her bottom. Sensation fluttered in her belly as her gaze lowered to his lips. He had a beautiful mouth, his lower lip slightly fuller than his upper lip. Why hadn't she noticed that before? She wished he would kiss her.

The realization blanked her mind of everything she'd told him earlier. Caution and reason crumbled. Every tendon in her body strained toward him. *Her best friend.*

When her gaze dropped to his lips, Clay's heart nearly burst out of his chest. For the span of a heartbeat, he saw the same intense want on her face that seared his gut. She swallowed hard, her lips parting slightly. As if to invite him in.

His whole body went rigid. He didn't know he'd moved, but he must have because suddenly she levered herself off his lap and stood.

"I'm sorry I woke you. I'm sure you're ready to get back to bed."

Not really. Making some monosyllabic noise, he got to his feet because he knew she expected him to. His legs felt like sand.

"I'm fine now."

"You sure?"

Her gaze climbed over his lean legs, the low-riding shorts, the corded lines of his abdomen. Smooth skin stretched over lean muscle. Her voice, her body shook as if it were fifteen below zero. She cleared her throat. "Yes. I'm fine."

"You should call Dr. Boren, tell her what happened. See if she thinks you might have re-injured your head."

She nodded.

"Okay." He leaned down to get his gun, but not before she caught the longing in his face. Heat flushed her entire body.

"See you in the morning," he said gruffly.

She nodded, feeling disoriented. "Good night."

"'Night."

Shelby heard him pad across the hall, heard the faint click of his door closing. She sank down on the edge of her bed, staring blankly at the thick taupe carpet. He'd nearly kissed her and she'd been disappointed when he hadn't. Not glad, not relieved. Disappointed. To the point of aching.

She wanted him.

This was insane! Why now? They'd both been single for years. Why not after Megan's death? Or after Shelby's divorce? What was she going to do? What was *he* going to do?

She couldn't leave. Not only because of her safety, but because she needed Clay. He was her rock. She couldn't get through this without him. But how could she stay? She'd told him these strange feelings, their bodies' unexpected reactions didn't mean anything. She was so wrong.

Chapter 6

Three days after she and Clay had come so close to kissing, anticipation still drummed against Shelby's nerves. Restless during the day, fidgety at night, she kept waiting for something else to happen. For *it* to happen. But it didn't. She was ready to crawl out of her skin—her suddenly very sensitive skin—and so she had eagerly accepted Terra Spencer's invitation to lunch on Friday.

She and Terra had gone through the firefighter academy together. The other woman had moved into fire investigations a few years ago, the first female investigator in Presley's history. And she was Jack Spencer's wife.

Today Brooke Jessup, Clay's other sister who was also a cop, drove Shelby to the Fire Investigator's office. Brooke's sandy hair brushed her shoulders; like Clay's, it was streaked from the sun. Her eyes were a dark green like his, too. She was a year older than Shelby, quieter than Erin, but funny with a self-confidence that Shelby had envied growing up. Brooke left her with Terra, saying she'd pick her up whenever they finished their visit.

As she and Terra drove back to the other woman's office after lunch, her friend brought up the subject of her injuries.

"My wrist is still a little tender, but the cut on my head is healed." Shelby ran a hand through her hair. "I still haven't remembered anything and it's driving me nuts."

"Has Meredith said anything about the likelihood of that?"

Shelby's doctor, Meredith Boren, was a good friend of Terra's, as well. "She wants to give me a little more time to remember on my own. If things don't start coming, she said there are some different therapies I can try. So far, nothing's coming."

"I can only imagine how frustrating that is."

"She said for me not to try to recall things, but sometimes I can't help it. The other night, I had a nightmare about being at M.B.'s and I fell out of bed. Clay made me call Dr. Boren. He was afraid I had hurt my head again, but I'm fine. I really thought that might have jarred something loose, but it hasn't."

Nothing memorywise, anyway. Physically, yes. Ever since being in Clay's lap with his mouth so close to hers, Shelby's skin had tingled as if lit with tiny flames.

"All I can recall is walking into M.B.'s house, which I've remembered all along."

"I'm sorry. I'm sure you're ready to get back to normal."

"I am." While part of her might not want to move out of Clay's house, another part told her that the sooner she did, the better off they'd both be. "I imagine Clay's ready to have his house back."

"Collier said it sounded like he enjoyed having you there."

Had Clay told the other fire investigator anything else? Like what had nearly happened between them? She didn't think he would.

"Shelby?"

She blinked, realized Terra had asked her a question.

"Is everything going all right? You and Clay have been friends for a long time, but I guess it's a little different being roommates."

"He's great. We're great. I feel so much better at his house, knowing that whoever might be after me will have to deal with him. Plus, staying with him rather than my mom means she should be out of harm's way."

Shelby didn't doubt her safety. She didn't doubt for a minute that Clay would protect her. But after that near-kiss the other night, she was almost as anxious about what might happen between them as she was about the threats to her life.

For three days, her senses had been on heightened alert, her nerves knotted. Waiting, wondering, halfway expecting him to kiss her. He hadn't. Hadn't even come close.

And all right, it annoyed her. She didn't like admitting that. She should be relieved he hadn't kissed her, but she wasn't. Something had happened between them that night, stark and startling enough that Shelby couldn't deny it, and she had tried. Clay hadn't mentioned the incident and neither had she. All she had to do was think about the change their friendship would suffer and that put her back on an even keel. Or it should have.

She forced her thoughts to the murder case. "I know the medical examiner is still recovering from his heart bypass, but has Collier heard back on any of the evidence he gathered?"

Since Presley's fire investigations office had only a few pieces of equipment, they used the lab at the Oklahoma State Bureau of Investigation for more specialized tests.

"The tech at the OSBI told him that there was a small backlog." Terra turned onto the street leading to her office, an old red brick building visible just ahead. "Collier doesn't think it'll be more than another few days or so. He said they haven't been able to cross anybody off their suspect list yet."

"That's what Clay said, too." The custodian at M.B.'s school, Mac Hayward, who'd suddenly stopped going on trips with the science club, and Shelby's ex-boyfriend were all suspects at this point. "Getting those lab results will surely help get one more lead. I know Clay has a couple he's working on." Shelby stared out the window absently aware of passing the neatly trimmed grass and trees along the street leading to Terra's office. The May afternoon was mild and sunny, one of the few spring days without wind.

Terra parked the city's red Explorer in front of the old brick building that had once housed Presley's original fire house. A weathered metal sign over the door and black lettering on the glass itself identified the place as the Fire Investigator's Office.

As Terra turned off the ignition, the office door opened and a slender blonde, Darla Howell, stepped out. "Phone call, Terra! It's the mayor."

Terra slid out of the truck, glancing at Shelby. "Come on in. I need to run and get this call, but it shouldn't take long."

"All right."

"Hi, Shelby!" Darla called.

Shelby waved at the woman who had been Terra's secretary since she had been promoted to this office several years ago. Darla had also worked for the previous fire investigator, Harris Vaughn, who had died, the victim of a serial arsonist-murderer. Shelby had worked the fire at Harris's house and, sadly, Terra had been forced to work that case, too. Shelby knew the retired man had been close to her.

As her friend walked inside, Shelby unlatched her seat belt and opened her door. It felt so good to be out of the house, to go somewhere. Remembering she was supposed to call Brooke to pick her up, Shelby punched in the number on her cell phone. Clay's sister said she was less than ten minutes away, so Shelby said she'd wait inside with Terra.

She shut the door of the unmarked vehicle and started toward the door.

"Shelby?"

Recognizing Vince's voice, alarm shot through her. She turned, saw the muscular paramedic standing beside the back passenger side door. He was out of uniform, wearing jeans and one of those tight stretchy T-shirts that made her want to call him Dr. Spandex. Where had he come from?

"What are you doing?" she snapped. "You scared me to death."

"I wanted to talk to you. Without your watchdog."

Despite his dig at Clay, the other man's voice was mild and he didn't try to come closer. Still she wished Clay were here right now. "There's nothing to talk about, Vince. Please leave me alone." She turned to go, reached the hood of the Explorer.

"I have some information that might help find who murdered M.B."

She pivoted, stared hard at him. "What kind of information?"

"Come talk to me. For just a minute," he added when she shook her head. "Just one minute, and I'll tell you."

"Clay's the one you should tell. I'll call him and y'all can talk over the phone."

He shook his head. "You."

"Why can't you tell me right here?"

"Do you want to know or not?"

How did she even know he was telling the truth? She wouldn't put it past him to use that excuse just to try and strong-arm her again. "You're bluffing. You don't know anything."

Before she could take a step to leave, he said, "It's about the night Hayward saw M.B. and me at the restaurant."

Clay had said that he talked to Vince about being seen at that restaurant with M.B. But...Clay hadn't told Vince where he'd gotten the information about Little Italy. Hayward, Vince and M.B. hadn't been the only people in the restaurant that night. So why would Vince think it had come from Hayward? Unless he had a reason to think so.

She glanced at the glass door of the F.I.'s office. "You know Darla has a clear view out here."

He raised his hands, slid them into his pockets. "I'll keep my hands in here. I just want to talk."

"Leave your hands where I can see them. If you make one wrong move, I'll crush your grapes, Vince."

His brown eyes hardened, but he nodded as he did what she demanded. "I've seen you in action. I know you'd do it too."

"All right, talk."

A muscle corded along his jaw. "I figured out it was Hayward who must've sent Jessup my way. And I know why."

Shelby waited. When he didn't continue, she sighed. "Why?"

Vince took a couple of steps toward her, easing up next to the passenger door. "To get Jessup's attention off of him."

"Why would Hayward need to do that?"

"You know he used to go on all the school trips with M.B.?"

"Yes," she said impatiently.

"That night at the restaurant, he was talking to M.B. at our table when I came back from the restroom. She looked mad."

"Go on."

Vince shifted closer, his hands still in plain sight. "I could see the guy was upsetting her, so I told him to leave. After he did, she told me that the reason he stopped going on trips with the science club was because she'd caught him drunk one night on an out-of-town trip. He was responsible for getting five of the students back to their hotel by nine o'clock. When none of them showed, M.B. went looking for him."

Vince paused, studying her as if trying to read her reaction. "She found him in a bar, had an off-duty cop who worked there haul him back to the hotel and went out looking for those kids. It took her three hours to find them. They'd taken off when they saw Hayward wasn't paying attention and had gotten lost. They were terrified."

And lucky something hadn't happened to them. Clay would definitely want to know this.

"M.B. handled it herself. She didn't report it to the school, although she did talk to the parents. And she told Hayward he was finished. No more trips ever or she would see about filing charges against him. Child endangerment or whatever she could find."

"You'd think, after that, he'd steer clear of her. So why would he want to talk to her at the restaurant? Was he trying to change her mind about letting him go along?"

"Yes." Vince's eyes glittered. "And she didn't tell me this, but he threatened her. The waitress overheard him and thought I should know."

Shelby shook her head, astounded.

"You don't believe me?" he bristled.

"Actually, I do." She shot him an irritated look. "I was just thinking butter wouldn't melt in that guy's mouth. Man, I didn't pick up on him hiding anything like this. Anything, period." She eyed Vince thoughtfully, still wary. "Thanks."

"You're welcome."

That surely hadn't been the only reason he'd come, but when he didn't say anything more, she smiled and turned to go. "Well, okay. Thanks for the information."

"I wasn't seeing her, Shelby. While I was seeing you, it was only you."

She didn't care, but knowing whether that was the truth or a lie might help Clay. She turned and looked at the big man.

"I know you probably think I was, after what Hayward said about me and M.B."

"It doesn't matter now, Vince."

"Because that's not why you broke up with me."

"Right. You know why I did that."

"Okay, I was an ass. I get that's why you don't want to see me anymore." He extended a hand to her. "No hard feelings, okay?"

Her gaze went from his hand to his face. He hadn't yelled or tried to push her around. There was no anger or even irritation in his eyes. She tentatively reached out. The second her fingers brushed his, he clamped a hard hand on her wrist and yanked her into him, locking her there with one beefy arm across her back.

She stumbled, pushing at him as pain twinged in her injured wrist. "Let go, you jerk! You're hurting me."

"I want to hear you say you believe me."

You pig. Trying to remain calm, hoping Darla or Terra could see her, Shelby said, "I believe you. You weren't seeing M.B."

"Good." His gaze slid over her face, making her skin crawl. She tried to draw away from him, but he held her fast. "How about a goodbye kiss? For old times' sake."

"I don't think so," she snapped.

He dipped his head toward her and she ducked, hitting his chin.

He grunted, thrust one hand into her hair and jerked her head back. "Just one and I'll let you go. Jessup's nowhere around. He'll never have to know."

"You don't need to worry about Clay." She fought him, her hip banging into his as she tried to escape. "You need to worry about me."

"Lamb chop, I love the way you fight." He nudged his lower body into hers. "Feel that? I want some more."

A cold fury settled over her and she went completely still. He chuckled, his arms bone-crushingly tight around her.

She stood rigid, her mind racing for the best plan. Waiting for just one opening. "C'mon, Shelby. Give me something."

You can count on that. "And then you'll go?"

Satisfaction flared in his eyes. "Yeah."

She stared at him for a long minute, trying to control the greasy knot in her stomach. She forced herself to relax. "Okay."

The instant she felt his hold loosen on her scalp, she head-butted him in the face. The burst of pain in her forehead was worth it when he roared and took a faltering step back. Dropping one arm from her, he tried to tighten the other. Blood ran from his nose and he was so angry that veins bulged at his temples.

Her head was ringing, pain shooting down her neck, but when he raised his fist, she brought her knee up hard, dead center between his legs. Contact. He released her, groaning as he bent double. For one split second, Shelby thought about kneeing him again. She backed away, holding her head, fury rushing through her.

All of a sudden, Terra and Darla were there. And Brooke. Shelby hadn't even heard Clay's sister drive up.

Brooke rushed toward Vince. Terra took Shelby's shoulders and looked her over. "Are you all right?"

"Yes."

"When you still weren't inside after I finished my phone call, I came out to see what was going on."

"I called the police." Darla threw a disgusted look at Vince, who was being ordered by Clay's sister to put his hands behind his back.

Rattled, Shelby's gaze met Brooke's. Concern darkened the other woman's eyes. "Brooke's a cop," she said faintly.

Clay's sister grinned. "Y'all make sure Shelby doesn't fall down. It shouldn't be long before a cruiser gets here. You're planning to file a report, aren't you?"

"Absolutely." Adrenaline jagged through her, stinging her

skin as she paced in front of Vince. He was on his knees with his hands cuffed behind him. "Why couldn't you have left well enough alone, Vince?"

He glared at her. The idiot.

"Get up, Tyner. Here comes your ride." Brooke prodded his hunched-over frame.

Gingerly touching the bump on her forehead, Shelby followed the other woman's gaze over her shoulder to see a black-and-white police car pulling up.

Vince hesitated, muttering a string of vile curses.

"Stand up," Brooke snapped. "Or I'll let Shelby have another shot at you."

Shelby figured the other woman was kidding, but Vince stood as ordered. An officer named Lowell walked over and told Shelby he'd take her report. Shaking with fury, she told him what had happened while Brooke read Vince his rights and stuffed him into the backseat of the patrol car. She told the officer she'd meet him at the station to book the guy.

She walked over, waiting until Shelby had finished giving her report. Darla handed her a paper cup full of water.

"You all right?" Brooke peered closely at her.

"Yes. More mad than anything." Hands shaking, Shelby sipped the water.

"Nice shot," Terra said, watching Officer Lowell get into his car and drive away with the creep. "We may never have to deal with any little Vinces running around here. The whole world thanks you."

Shelby managed a shaky laugh.

Brooke gave her a quick hug. "I'm glad you're okay. If something had happened to you, Clay would have killed me. I'll take you home, then file a follow-up report when I go in later. I saw what happened. Would've been able to help if you weren't so quick."

Shelby smiled, trying to stop the trembling in her legs.

Vince had known Clay was nowhere around, had known Shelby was alone for that one moment. That meant he'd been watching her. For how long? And was it only to talk to her about Mac Hayward or to make sure she never remembered what she might've seen at M.B.'s that night?

Brooke unclipped her cell phone from the waistband of her slacks and punched in a number. "I'd better let Clay know."

"Wait." Shelby put a hand on her friend's arm. "Let me tell him. I want to do it in person."

After a pause, the other woman nodded. "Okay."

Shelby wished she didn't have to tell him about Vince at all, but what Tyner had said about Mac Hayward needed to be shared. Clay wasn't going to like how she'd gotten the information. Not one bit.

Forty-five minutes later, as they stood in the living room of his house, Clay's gaze scanned every inch of her. His jaw locked as he touched the spots of blood on the neckline of her coral top.

"It's not mine," she assured him.

He brushed her bangs up so he could see the quarter-sized knot on her forehead. "He hurt you."

"Not as badly as I hurt him. I think I broke his nose."

"You did." There was relief somewhere under his anger and fear, he knew. But he didn't like her joking about it. Too many things had gone on lately. Except for the bump on her head, he knew she was all right. He could see she was, but he wanted to feel it for himself. "I want to know exactly what happened," he demanded. "And I mean everything."

He paced from one end of the couch to the other. Word had gotten around the station that his sister had arrested Vince Tyner for assaulting Shelby. And as Clay had started out the door for home, Shelby had called.

Brooke had met him in the garage, telling him she and

Shelby had only been home for half an hour and warning him not to start with the caveman stuff. He knew Shelby hated that as much as his sisters. Right now, he didn't care.

As she told him how Vince had showed up at the Fire Investigator's Office, Clay cautioned himself to calm down. The information she passed on about Hayward was helpful, but didn't do one thing to cool his blood.

He took a deep breath, trying to get a hold of himself. She didn't need any more upset. She'd handled the jerk, but she had to be rattled.

"Is that it?" Clay planted his hands on his hips, staring out the patio door at the full, leafy trees, trying to leash the turmoil inside him. "You're leaving something out. There's no way Tyner told you about the incident with M.B. and Hayward out of the goodness of his heart."

She cleared her throat. "Well…I think we should focus on what he said about Hayward. Vince is in jail. I filed a report and I plan to press char—"

"He wanted something. Tell me." He looked over his shoulder, fixing her with a stare.

Her gaze skittered away and she shifted uncomfortably. "It's too stupid."

"Shelby."

"All right." She looked up at the ceiling. "He wanted me to kiss him."

Clay's jaw clamped tight enough to snap and he had to force the words out. "Did you do it?"

"Yeah."

His whole body shut down about the time she burst out, "Are you kidding me! No, I didn't do it! I can't *believe* you asked me that!" She glared at him. "I told him to get lost. He grabbed me. I hit him. End of story."

His pulse ragged, Clay fought to keep from crushing her to him. She was all right, but it was time for Clay to pay Tyner a visit. Clay had always felt protective of her, especially because of Jason's death, but that need to protect was starting to get tangled up with a growing physical need.

He had spent the last three days poring over every report from the case, revisiting the homicide scene, checking in at the OSBI lab as well as with Collier McClain to see if all the evidence had been analyzed, if the autopsy had been completed. He was glad for the new information, although it seemed damned little in comparison to Shelby getting threatened by Tyner. Again.

But it wasn't just the case spooling Clay's nerves tight. His desire for her was becoming harder to ignore. Harder to resist. Eroding his control, like water pounding on rock.

He was angry that Vince had waylaid her like that. Angry that he hadn't been there. Angry that he couldn't stop thinking about what would never be between them. Couldn't stop *wanting* it, even though he knew she didn't.

How long had Tyner been watching her, waiting for a chance to get her alone? Clay's gut knotted. What if Tyner didn't stop? What if he was the person trying to kill her? Or even worse, what if he wasn't? What if there was another person out there also trying to hurt her?

Clay had to keep her safe. He didn't trust anyone else to do it. "I don't want him anywhere around you."

"I don't, either. He won't be."

"What if you'd been alone? What if Brooke hadn't driven up?"

"I handled him."

"Shelby, if something had happened—" He wanted to hold her, so tight that dust couldn't squeeze between their bodies. His hands shook with the effort not to reach for her.

He had to get himself under control. She was fine. She had reassured him. Brooke had reassured him. Clay had seen for himself. It wasn't enough. He wanted to touch her, feel her breath on him, her warmth under his hands, the way he had when she'd had that nightmare.

He slammed a palm against the wall, shoved open the patio door and stalked outside. He felt her follow him out, heard the door slide shut. He stiffened. She shouldn't be out here, not when he was on the edge, his emotions churning. He leaned against the porch railing, curling his hands around the weathered wood as he stared blankly at the grass.

She came up beside him and flattened her palm in the middle of his back, saying softly, "I'm okay, really."

Bowing his head, he squeezed his eyes shut. She thought this was all about him being worried. There was that. But there was also a burning, wrenching need to have her, to claim her. He didn't understand. He'd never felt this with Megan.

Shelby rubbed his back. Her peachy scent drifted to him and he breathed her in. Muscles that were already tight turned rigid. Her touch wasn't even sexual and he was aroused. "He wants you."

"He can't have me. I've made that clear six ways from Sunday. I bet he'll stop coming around now."

"Just thinking about him touching you makes me want to put my fist through his face."

Her palm slowed, her fingers curled against his spine. "That's not like you."

"I don't feel much like myself these days." He turned his head and looked straight at her.

When her eyes went wide, he knew she understood what he meant.

"It's between us all the time now, Shelby. I know you feel it, too."

"It's tied to Jason," she said quickly, a flush tinting her cheeks. "I've been in danger and you don't want to let anything happen to me because you feel responsible for his dying, but it wasn't your fault. Neither Mom nor I have ever blamed you, and we wish you wouldn't blame yourself."

"I do feel responsibility for you, but this isn't about that and you know it. It's about you and me."

She went on as if she hadn't heard him. "You were afraid for me."

"Yes, but—"

"It's just because you weren't there when Vince showed up. You're feeling responsible for that, and—"

Something inside him snapped. Frustrated and on edge, he closed his hands over her shoulders and backed her into the wall.

"Hey!"

He kissed her. On the mouth, the way he wanted. He felt her surprise, the jolt that went through her body when his lips touched hers, the reflexive stiffening of her shoulders. And then she opened to him.

Sweet, deep heat. Her lips were soft, just like the rest of her. Clay wanted to drown in her. He slid his palms down her back and held her waist, then her hips. Her hands came up to his forearms, not to push him away, but to hold tight. She trembled against him, and he pressed into her. He could feel her breasts, her thighs. They'd never done this before. As he tasted her, he wondered why not.

He loved the wet heat of her mouth, the smooth velvet of her tongue, her honey-dark taste. He shifted his head a fraction and slowly seduced her mouth until a ragged moan worked its way up her throat. Every muscle in his body strained with the effort to keep his hands where they were.

When he lifted his head, he was breathing hard. He *was* hard. Her mouth was red from his, and savage, primal need clawed through him. After the other night in her room, he'd wondered how long he could last without putting his hands on her. Kissing her. Evidently, not long.

Her eyes opened, dazed and dreamy-blue, the desire there reaching right into his gut and grabbing tight. *"ClayJessup,"* she breathed. "Where did you learn to do that?"

The whispered way she ran his name together had need searing him in a molten rush. He kissed her again because he couldn't *not* kiss her. He didn't want to stop. She kissed him back, her mouth hot on his, her hands gripping his arms to pull him closer. He wanted to peel off her clothes and taste her all over. No way in hell could they ignore this. She would have to admit that.

He wanted her, wanted everything. But he knew Shelby. If he pushed her, she'd bolt. Although his brain had nearly locked down, he struggled to think past right now. Muscles quivering with restraint, Clay forced himself to pull away. To let her limp hands slide off his arms. Let her sag into the wall.

"Does that feel like responsibility to you?" he asked hoarsely.

Slack-jawed, she stared at him in stunned amazement. He was pretty amazed himself. From her sultry eyes to the lithe way she curved into the wall, her body plainly said, "Take me." And he wanted to. It cost everything he had to retreat a step. Then another.

If he looked at her mouth any longer, he would go back for more. He shoved an unsteady hand through his hair and turned for the door. She wasn't ready. Hell, he didn't know if he was, either.

Chapter 7

The man was a total stud, a total kissing stud. Clay. Her best friend. Breathing hard, Shelby braced herself against the wall.

How could she have known him all this time and not have heard about *that?* Her mind jumped back to the years when he and Jason were in college and she'd heard girls talking about them. If anyone had talked about Clay's kissing, she didn't remember. And if they hadn't talked about it, he must not have kissed them. Because who would keep that to themselves? *Un-be-lievable.*

She didn't know how long she stood there before she got her legs to move, her brain to reconnect. This was the second time he'd been the one to confront what was happening between them, which was enough on its own to throw her off balance. *Think!* This wasn't supposed to happen. *They* weren't supposed to happen.

"Oooh," she said through gritted teeth. Panic sent her marching into the house. She stalked across the nubby neutral-colored carpet, turned left at the arched doorway and continued down the hall to his bedroom.

The door was open. Battling a mix of excitement and wariness, she crossed his room to the bathroom. That door was partially ajar, and when she saw him in the mirror, she stopped short.

She wanted to groan. He was bare-chested, his hands at the zipper of his slacks. Her gaze slid over the triangle of hair between his pecs that narrowed to disappear below his sternum. The strong lines of his back made her want to drag her hands over his warm supple skin.

She must've made a noise because he looked up and saw her. His gaze flared hotly. "I'm changing clothes, Shelby."

"Well, don't." She shoved a shaking hand through her hair. "Come out here and talk to me."

He hesitated long enough that she thought he would refuse.

"Please?" She was surprised at the huskiness of her voice.

He was all hard muscle and sinew, the lines of his arms, chest and abs sketched in sharp definition. Just looking at him caused a flutter in her belly. What had she ever done to deserve this? He was delicious, a heck of a guy…and totally off-limits.

Leaving his shirt on the floor where he'd dropped it, Clay opened the door and leaned against the frame. His sandy hair was disheveled, his face carefully blank. His cop face. Her gaze went involuntarily to his lips.

"Shelby." The warning came through loud and clear.

A whiff of Clay's male scent drifted to her, tightening her throat. How could she concentrate with six foot two of gorgeous solid man in front of her? Especially now that he'd kissed her?

She retreated a step, then another, trying to regain her mental balance. Light from the west window behind her slanted across the floor. "How can you just do something like that and walk off? I don't even know what that was!"

He folded his arms across his wide chest. His *bare* chest. "I must really be out of practice."

If he had any more practice, they'd still be out there. Doing more than kissing.

"You can't deny there's something between us, Shelby."

Of course she could! "You know my history. You know I haven't gotten involved since Ronnie. I don't ever want to be in a long-term relationship again."

Chewing on the inside of his cheek, Clay slid his hands into the pockets of his pants, which only drew attention to his flat belly. And the fact that he was aroused. "You've been in one with me since you were born."

"Not like that!" It took some effort for her to drag her gaze to his face. "I know what to do with our friendship. That…what happened out there—" She fluttered a hand. "That—"

"Kiss," he supplied, watching her steadily.

She narrowed her eyes. "Yes, *that*. I don't know what to do with that. I can't get involved with you romantically."

"You don't have to sound like you're talking about the plague."

"I'm not. What happened between us was a slip. It doesn't mean what we think it means. We can still be friends."

"We *are* still friends." His look said he knew this was going to take a while, but instead of his usual patience, she caught a hint of turmoil in his eyes.

The urge to touch him, to kiss him again hit her. She backed up until her thighs hit his huge oak-frame bed. "You know why we're still friends? Because you haven't seen me naked and that's the way it's going to stay!"

He chuckled, though she thought she caught an ache behind it.

"I'm serious."

"I know. It's still funny."

"They don't make men like you, Clay. I don't want to lose what we have." She sounded panicked. She *was* panicked. "Not for great sex. Not for anything. Sex messes up everything."

He scrubbed a hand down his face. "I'm wantin' to get messed up real bad right now, honey."

Oh. My. Gosh. "Clay."

"I don't see any point in denying that I want you."

"How about ignoring it?" She was kidding, sort of.

"I kissed you and I'm not sorry. But if you don't want me to do it again—although that isn't how you acted out there— I'll try not to."

She tilted her head, telling herself she should be relieved but feeling only dissatisfaction. "So you won't kiss me again?"

"I said nothing would happen that you *don't* want."

She started to argue that she didn't want him to kiss her, but the protest died because it wasn't true. "Don't you think we're feeling this way about each other because neither of us have had sex in forever?"

"Who says I haven't?"

"I would've known," she said with a laugh, then she froze. "Wouldn't I?"

He shrugged. "The point is that with you, it's about more than sex for me."

Had he really slept with another woman recently? More than one? Who? When? The possibility hollowed out her gut. "*Have* you been with anyone?"

"Unless you're planning to sign up, I'm not answering."

Her mouth dropped open, snapped shut. She had never heard him say things like this. Never thought she would. Heat flushed her body, urging her to give in to the way he'd made her feel when he'd kissed her. Wanted, sexy. But she couldn't. She struggled to steer the conversation back to something she could handle. "I talked to Erin."

He frowned. "About what?"

"What happened that day you saw me in my under—your bedroom."

"Great. All we need is my sister's feedback."

"She told me that she got involved with Johnny Dollarhide in college and it ruined their friendship."

"Helpful, as usual," he muttered.

"You know how long those two were friends. And now they aren't any more. Look what it did to them."

"We're not them, Shelby."

She eased down on the edge of his bed, then realized where she was and popped up. "We've shared everything else. Maybe it's just…curiosity."

"No," he said simply, his green gaze unwavering.

She chewed on the pad of her thumb. "How can you be so sure? It's not like you've been secretly lusting after me for years, is it?"

He took his time answering, which irritated her. "No."

"So why now?"

"I don't know. Maybe I wasn't ready. Maybe neither of us was."

She paced to the foot of his bed, making a conscious effort not to look at his wide shoulders, that solid chest. "It's got to be the circumstances. I bet if you were with someone else, you'd want them instead."

"Yeah, that's me. Go for whoever's in the room." Annoyance flashed across his features.

"Well," she said tentatively. "You haven't really dated anyone since Megan died so maybe, since we're together so much, that's why—"

"That dog don't hunt, Shelby."

He knew her better than anyone, faults and all. "I can't give you anything, Clay. I can't promise you anything."

"Hey, don't jump the gun," he said softly.

"What am I supposed to do? Just be your friend like I always have?"

"Why not?"

"Because I've never kissed a friend the way you and I just kissed. I've never kissed *anybody* like that!" Her gaze dropped to his mouth and she murmured, "No one has ever kissed *me* like that."

A muscle worked in his jaw. Tension pulsed from him, although his voice remained calm. "It's your choice, blue eyes, and I'll go with whatever you decide. But that doesn't mean I can't hope you change your mind and come to your senses."

"You're not supposed to say that!"

"I'm making this up as I go along." His gaze searched her face, softened. "I have a feeling this is going to happen whether we fight it or not."

"It can't," she whispered. Static crackled in her brain, scrambling her thoughts. Clay was her friend; he couldn't be her lover. Could he? She shook her head, closed her eyes for a second. "I don't know what to do."

"You don't have to do anything."

"Things will change."

"Not unless we want them to."

She wasn't so sure.

"It doesn't have to be a huge deal."

He had melted her into a puddle. It was huge. "Clay—"

"Listen, I don't want you to worry about this. I should've had more control, but I didn't. It won't happen again."

She was uncomfortably aware of the disappointment that pierced her at his words. But he was only doing what she'd asked. "Okay."

"Okay."

After an awkward pause, she asked, "Are you planning to check out that information Vince gave me about Mac Hayward?"

"Yes, as soon as I finish changing," he said pointedly.

She was determined to keep her gaze on his face. Or at least above his belt. "I want to go with you."

He hesitated and she rushed to say, "I'm the person who someone is trying to kill. I should get to be there, especially if the suspect is Hayward. Besides, Vince talked to *me*. I know how he sounded when he told me about Hayward."

"I was going to say you can go."

"Oh. All right." She was relieved, but also a little nervous. Her anxiety had nothing to do with Mac Hayward and everything to do with Clay.

After what had just happened between them, could things really stay the same? It should've been weird even thinking about her and Clay making love. It wasn't. And what really had her head spinning was that she had no trouble calling up a visual of the two of them in his bed. Naked and…busy. A delicious little shiver worked its way up her spine. Oh, my.

She struggled to block the image, forced herself to imagine what life would be like if a romance didn't work out with him, without him as her friend. Long and lonely and dreary. They couldn't cross the line. Keeping things as they were was the right thing to do.

Those sweet lips of hers had torn him up. Clay was turned on and frustrated as hell. He fell back on his cop training, blanking his face and telling her she could come along on this interview with Hayward when what he really wanted and needed was some space from her. He must have managed to hide the lust raging through him because she studied him for a minute, then smiled trustingly. It was a darn good thing she couldn't see inside his head. He'd never been less trustworthy. His expression he could control, but not his body. And his body was straining with the effort not to lay her down on that bed.

As best he could, he focused on what Vince had told Shelby earlier about Mac Hayward, on what he wanted to ask Hayward about the real reason Hayward had stopped going on those out-of-town trips with the science club. And about the hole that had just been blown in the engineer's alibi for the night of M.B.'s murder.

Mac Hayward was on a drilling location in Logan County, which bordered Oklahoma County on the north. As Clay and Shelby drove in that direction on I-35, she turned her head toward him. Like him, she'd changed clothes. She would've changed anyway because her clothes had been spotted with blood from Vince's nose. Instead of the coral top and capri pants she'd worn to lunch with Terra, she had on snug jeans with a hot pink cropped sweater. "Who was that who called you just before we left the house?"

"It was a rig hand who worked with Hayward the night of M.B.'s murder." Clay caught a flash of her taut belly as she lifted a hand to push her hair out of her eyes. "He was out sick the day I spoke to the others and I left my card for him to give me a call when he returned."

A shadow passed across her face at the mention of her friend. She'd held up like a trooper since all this had started.

"The rig hand told me that on the night of M.B.'s murder, he saw Hayward leave the lease about ten o'clock and return several hours later. Since McClain and I estimate the time of M.B.'s death somewhere between 10 p.m. and 2 a.m., it'll be interesting to see what Hayward has to say about that."

"So he lied about that *and* about getting along with M.B. That leaves him on the suspect list for sure."

"Yeah."

She fell silent, laying her head back against the seat and gazing out the window. Clay slid in a Bonnie Raitt CD.

He kept his gaze on the road, but his mind was full of Shelby. Her mouth, her taste, her scent. His nerve endings still hummed. He couldn't make himself regret kissing her, especially since she'd kissed him back. But he shouldn't be thinking about it, either. The bluesy, sultry music flowed around them, echoing the ache in his body for the woman sitting next to him.

It was all he could do not to reach for her, but he didn't because he'd seen the confusion, the anxiety in her eyes a while ago. He didn't want to add to the stress she already had. They talked off and on about nothing, about the visit she planned to have with her mom later. Things weren't awkward, but they were different.

After about forty minutes, Clay exited I-35 and went east toward Cushing, then turned back to the north. They drove through a small town, past a couple of dirt roads and down another into an alfalfa pasture with a gravel road that led to a drilling rig.

Towering over the grassy land, the oil-and-gas derrick was anchored to both sides of a T-shaped substructure. Three separate parts, stacked on top of each other like Lego Blocks, made up the foundation. The top section was a trailer where rig meetings were held, and it was accessed by a ladder on either end of the base.

Clay and Jason had been roughnecks one summer while in college, but Clay hadn't been to a well site since then. He parked about fifteen yards away from the equipment. As he and Shelby got out of the truck, he adjusted the loose open shirt he wore over a plain T-shirt, making sure his shoulder holster and gun weren't visible. He noted the quiet, which was unusual at a well site. He was able to hear the wind ripple through the grass. The rig sat silent. No one was around. He wondered if there was a problem with the equipment, or if operations had even commenced yet.

Midafternoon sunshine glinted off the derrick, this one painted white. A tall, wiry man walked around from the other side of the rig and out of the shadows. He appeared to be in his mid-fifties, and the baseball cap he wore that was emblazoned with a drilling company's name looked to be older than that. He raised a hand in greeting. "Help you folks?"

Clay and Shelby met the man halfway, and Clay showed his badge while introducing himself.

The older man shook Clay's hand, his eyes crinkled in what was probably a permanent squint from years of working outside. "I'm Smitty, the day crew foreman."

Drilling rigs usually ran two crews working twelve-hour shifts. "We're looking for Mac Hayward. His secretary told us he should be out here."

"Yeah, he's in the doghouse." The man hitched a gnarled thumb over his shoulder toward the trailer. "Let me go tell him you're here. A drill bit broke off, second one today. Everybody's piled in there trying to figure out what do to. I don't think anyone else'll fit."

That explained the silence and lack of activity. Clay thanked the man and watched as he nimbly climbed the ladder.

"What's a doghouse?" Shelby shaded her eyes, tilting her head back to look up the one-hundred-foot-plus derrick. "And don't tell me it's that building there. I got that."

He grinned. "It's the base of operations, a meeting place. There are probably also a couple of beds in there."

"I remember that summer you and Jason worked on a rig."

"Yeah. It paid well, but it's a dirty, loud job. If this rig was going, you'd barely be able to hear me."

Just beyond them and to the left of the structure were three circular steel pits sunk into the ground. Reserve pits. One was for drilling mud coming out of the hole, one for water and one for premixing cement or drilling fluids. Wind gusted across the flat pastureland, stirring up pieces of grass and dust. Clay slid on his sunglasses, noticing that Shelby did the same.

His gaze swept the area immediately around the rig, taking in two older-model four-door sedans, three pickup trucks, a rust-spotted blue van and a white SUV. "Recognize any of those vehicles as maybe having been at M.B.'s?" he asked Shelby.

She scrutinized them. "No. I swear! Am I ever going to remember anything?"

"Don't beat yourself up. There's a good chance that the reason you don't know any of those cars is because you've never seen them, not because of the memory loss."

"I guess so." She eyed him thoughtfully. "Thanks."

The slow smile she gave jolted him down to his toes. Heavy footsteps sounded above them, and Clay looked up to see a frowning Hayward moving warily down the side of the trailer and toward the closest ladder.

"I won't get in the way." Shelby edged up beside him, her arm brushing his. "I just want to listen and watch, see if anything makes a blip on my radar."

"No problem." He shifted, just enough to put a little space between them. His attention needed to be on Hayward, not the woman who was tweaking all his senses.

"I keep hoping that a memory will come to me at any time, that a word or a phrase or an image might open up something in my head."

Clay nodded as Hayward reached the ground.

"Detective Jessup, Miss Fox." His hazel gaze shifted from Shelby to Clay. Looking uncertain, the engineer wiped his grease-stained hands on a grimy cloth. "I'd shake, but as you can see I'm filthy. What brings you out this way?"

Clay glanced up and saw Smitty standing in the center of the landing. "Maybe you'd like to step over by my truck, Hayward. For some privacy."

"What's going on?" Alarm streaked across Hayward's blunt features. "Has something happened to my girls?"

"No, it's nothing like that. This is a follow-up to our conversation the other day."

"At the gym?"

"Yeah."

"We can talk here. I don't have anything to hide."

Clay would determine that for himself. "Except for where you really were the night of Ms. Perry's murder."

Hayward gave a nervous laugh. "What are you talking about?"

Clay noticed Shelby was watching the engineer as intently as he was. "I've done some checking on your alibi."

"Yeah, so?"

"There's a hole."

The man frowned. "What kind of hole?"

"Some missing time. Hours."

Hayward shot a look over his shoulder at the foreman, then gestured beyond Clay's vehicle. "Let's talk over there."

"Sure."

The three of them moved to the back end of Clay's truck.

Hayward's voice dropped. "What's going on? Did you contact those people I told you about?"

"All of them." Clay slid his small notebook out of his back jeans pocket. "Including someone who saw you leave the well site at ten o'clock that night and not return until about three in the morning."

The man looked startled for an instant, then recovered. "Oh, yeah, I forgot. I went home to check on my girls."

If that was the truth, it wasn't the whole truth. "Can they verify that?"

"They don't need to be involved in this."

"You were gone long enough to have made another stop before driving back out to that site."

"Another stop? Like where?" His eyes widened and he reared back. "You think I killed M.B.!"

"You had opportunity." Clay scribbled a quick note, his voice tight. "And I've learned that you didn't get along *great* with Ms. Perry, as you claimed. It wasn't your busy schedule that stopped you going on those science club trips. It was her."

An angry flush spread up the man's neck. "No, it wasn't."

"During an out-of-town trip to Dallas, she caught you drunk one night when you were responsible for getting five kids back to the hotel safely."

"Who told you that?" Hayward's voice rose. "One of the kids' parents?"

Clay didn't correct him. "I figure some of them wouldn't mind filing charges."

Mac cursed, clenching his fists at his side. Clay stepped forward a bit to let the man know he shouldn't try anything, and also to put himself between the engineer and Shelby.

"I made a mistake," the man said. "I apologized, but that wasn't enough for M.B.," he stormed. "Yeah, I was pissed, but I wasn't gonna take it out on her. I sure wouldn't have killed her."

"You were angry that she wouldn't let you resume the trips with the science club. Angry enough that you tracked her down after school hours at a restaurant." Clay thought Hayward's getting banned from the trips was a weak motive for murder, but he'd seen weak motives before. And he'd seen murders committed in rage. "Witnesses saw you arguing with her at Little Italy and you were overheard demanding she let you go on the next trip. You were also overheard making threats against her."

"I asked her not to ruin me," he snapped. "I didn't make threats."

"How could she ruin you?" Shelby asked before Clay could.

He started to give her the "let-me-do-it" look, but the intensity on her face stopped him. Maybe this was sparking something in her memory.

Hayward hesitated.

"It's better if I hear it from you, Hayward," he said. "And now. Your lying to me earlier only makes you look bad."

Mac shot an angry look over his shoulder toward the doghouse. Clay followed the engineer's gaze, noting that Smitty was no longer around.

"Okay," the man spat out. "I did go to that restaurant to find M.B. I screwed up that night we were in Dallas with the kids. I admit that, but if M.B. had let that get out, my ex-wife would've used it as ammunition against me."

"How could she use that against you?" Clay looked up from his notebook. The man was showing more emotion about M.B. now than he had during Clay's first interview with him. "In a custody battle?"

"We're not having one of those," he said tersely. "But Dana would use that information to brainwash my daughters, to turn them against me. She works on them every chance she gets."

"Sounds bitter." Clay wondered just how close Hayward was to exploding. The man's face was florid.

"It is."

"And yet you aren't fighting for custody," Clay said skeptically.

"We're not. I don't want it to go that way. Neither does Dana. We're both trying to do what's best for the twins. We let them decide about visitation, and it's worked out just fine. That's the one thing Dana and I have agreed on."

"What's your visitation schedule?"

"Trina and Tessa stay with me on Sunday, Monday, Tuesday and alternating Wednesdays. They're with their mother the other days."

M.B. was murdered on a Sunday night. "So your girls would've been at your house the night of Ms. Perry's murder?"

"Yes."

"And you don't know if they can verify your alibi?"

"They were asleep."

"It's about an hour's drive from that well location to Presley, Mr. Hayward. Coming and going would make it two." Clay fixed the man with a stare. "Did you do something besides check on your girls? Go anywhere else? See anyone else?"

"No."

"Were your girls all right?"

"Yes."

"Then why were you gone five hours?"

Hayward looked away, mumbling, "I might have stopped for a drink."

"Where? What bar?"

"No bar. On the side of the road. In my car." His eyes narrowed. "Are you gonna arrest me for that?"

"How long were you there?"

He shifted uncomfortably. "Until I got back on location."

"That's a lot of liquor. Were you alone?"

"I already said so."

"It would help you a lot if someone could back up your story."

"There isn't anyone." Mac thrust out his chin. "I'm telling the truth."

"Seeing as how your lies are what brought me back to talk to you, I have trouble believing that. If you were at M. B. Perry's that night, I'll find out."

"You can't prove I was there."

"You should be trying to prove to me that you *weren't*."

"I left to check on my girls and stopped on the way back to have a drink. That's what I did. That's *all* I did."

"Then why didn't you tell me this the first time we talked?"

"I can't afford for my ex to find out. She'd never let me see my girls if she knew. You're not going to say anything, are you?"

Clay slid his notebook back into his pocket. "I may have more questions later. Stay available."

He moved up the side of his truck and opened Shelby's door.

Hayward took a step away from the truck. "Are you gonna file charges for me having an open bottle in the car? Or for what happened in Dallas?"

"Somebody might." He could only file charges if he caught the guy with an open container, but he didn't clarify that. He wanted to keep Hayward guessing. "If I were you, right now I'd be more worried about the fact that there's no one who can confirm your alibi."

The engineer glared as Clay climbed into the cab and started the engine. Closing the door, he reversed, turned the vehicle and headed down the road toward the gate. White plumes of gravel dust rose up behind them.

"What about motive?" Shelby glanced in the side mirror, then shifted in the seat to face him, curling one leg under her. Her peachy scent drifted toward him. "Do you think Hayward was angry enough over M.B.'s banning him from those trips that he would kill her?"

"No, but maybe he was determined to make sure she never said anything to anyone about his negligence with those kids. He especially wouldn't want his ex to find out." Clay pulled onto the road leading back toward the highway.

"Custody doesn't seem to be an issue. He gets his kids half the week anyway."

Clay wanted to tug her over next to him, touch her. "If he thought M.B. might do something to mess that up, maybe he'd kill her. Or he could've just been so angry at her and his ex that he did it in a fit of rage. He could also be lying about all of that. Maybe Hayward was M.B.'s lover and saw her with Tyner that night, used the science club trips as an excuse to talk to her."

"Vince did say he didn't hear the whole conversation."

"I can't prove Hayward was or wasn't drunk on the side of the road that night, but I want to find out if his daughters remember him coming home. Maybe they heard him. He had motive to kill M.B. and with five hours of his alibi uncon-firmed, he definitely had opportunity."

"What about Sandoval?"

"He's still on my list, too." Clay had started to tell her about the school custodian when he'd gotten home earlier, but that kiss had blasted everything else out of his mind.

His gaze traced her creamy skin, dropped to her mouth, her breasts. The mystery location of her fox tattoo taunted him incessantly. "Sandoval has no alibi for the night of M.B.'s murder, and the one he gave for the time of the microwave explosion can't be confirmed. The movie he says he saw was playing on the date and time he gave, and the subject matter matched, too, but no one saw him. Not the ticket seller, the ticket taker or the person who worked concessions. Collier and I will definitely keep digging on him."

"What about Vince?"

"He may have had an affair with M.B. And his being at the firehouse just minutes before that microwave exploded makes him look bad. I find it real interesting that Hayward pointed us to Vince and Vince pointed us right back to Hayward."

"What does that mean?"

"I don't know. Maybe nothing. I have no proof of anything as far as Vince is concerned, but I'm not marking him off yet."

Tyner's overzealous attempt to steer the investigation to-ward Hayward guaranteed him a spot on Clay's list. But the reason Clay had asked the jailer to call him when Vince started his paperwork to be released was because Tyner had jumped Shelby. The dirtbag wasn't going to do it again.

Glancing over, Clay noted the knot on her forehead. It re-minded him of everything she was going through. The memory loss, the murder attempts, the harassment by Vince. And, Clay reluctantly conceded, what had happened between him and her.

Sliding her a look, he recalled the way she'd melted into that kiss earlier, and heat charged through him.

For the remainder of the ride, neither one of them said much. The silence wasn't uncomfortable, but it tempted him to sink into the memories of how she tasted, how she felt. He turned on the CD player. Man, she smelled good.

Clay knew she didn't distrust him. He knew her skittishness stemmed from what Ronnie Lyle had done to her. Bad enough that the bastard had been married to another woman in another town and had had a baby with her while he had been married to Shelby, but for Shelby to have found out from the other wife had been utterly humiliating. Since then, she hadn't opened up to another man, vowed she never would again.

Between her memory loss and the close calls she'd had, there were too many uncertainties, but their friendship wasn't one of them. He didn't want her worrying about him or *them* on top of everything else.

He wanted to show her they'd be friends no matter what, but the truth was he didn't know. If she never changed her mind about them, could he stay friends with her? Move on with his life and be with someone else? Watch *her* be with someone else? He didn't think so. He believed they could be friends and lovers, have it all. He was willing to take a chance and find out. Shelby wasn't.

For her sake, he had to keep things platonic. Somehow.

Chapter 8

It was no use telling herself she didn't want Clay to kiss her again because she did. And that wasn't all Shelby wanted him to do. The admission had her squirming. It was a good thing he'd dropped her off at her mom's bead shop and gone to interview Mac Hayward's twins. Surely the time apart would stifle this rushing heat in her blood.

Even though Hayward's answers hadn't sparked any memories for her, she really had wanted to go with Clay to interview the man. But she hadn't considered that being close to Clay would affect her the way it had. Her legs hadn't been steady since that kiss, and spending so much of the afternoon with him hadn't helped.

They hadn't done anything they couldn't move past, Shelby told herself more than once. But she *still* hadn't been able to get that kiss out of her mind. Her brain had tripped over the memory ever since it had happened, even here, now, in the back room of her mom's bead shop.

"Physically I feel fine," she told her captain on the phone.

"Have you remembered anything yet?" Rick Oliver asked.

"Not yet." Before dropping her off, Clay had checked the messages on his home answering machine and there had been one for Shelby to call her captain. The headache that hadn't plagued her in a couple of days flared at the base of her skull. "I'm starting to think I won't."

"How's that concussion?"

"I seem to have recovered from that for the most part, but I still get headaches."

"What does the doctor say?"

"That I have to be patient." Pain moved into her temples, and she pressed her fingers there. "It's been almost two weeks. Seems to me that if I were going to recall anything, I would have already."

"Yeah, you'd think so. Any idea about when you can come back to work?"

"Clay thinks there's still a threat to my safety. He says I have to stay put until he feels there isn't one."

"You've got a good friend there, Fox."

"Yes, sir."

"Keep me posted."

"I will."

"My annual Memorial Day picnic is coming up. I wanted to make sure to invite you."

"Thanks, Captain."

"Think you'll make it? I need to get a count so I'll know how many burgers to make."

"Yes. Put me down for two people." If M.B.'s case wasn't solved by then and Clay couldn't go with her, he'd definitely want one of his sisters to attend.

Oliver gave her the details and hung up. Spending time relaxing and visiting with her station mates would be nice. The bell over the front door jingled, announcing the departure of the female customers who'd been in Paula's bracelet-making class.

Shelby walked out of the room that served as an office as well as a storage area and over to the rectangular work table in the center of the glass-fronted store. As her mom hung up the Closed sign and locked the door, Shelby checked her watch. A couple of minutes past six.

Clear boxes of silver and colored beads, string and clasps, as well as jewelry her mom had made to sell and display, cluttered the table's surface. Shelby picked up a couple of the bead trays that functioned as drawers and slid them into their place in the built-in wall storage.

She thought about Clay. There was the usual warmth she felt when thinking about him, but this time there were also shivers. She wanted him. All of him. It surprised her how much, and it sawed at her resolve to keep things platonic.

"Is Clay coming back to get you or do I need to drive you to his house?"

"He's coming here. He went to interview a couple of people about M.B.'s murder." She thought about what had happened with Erin and Johnny Dollarhide, how their mixing sex with their friendship had ruined things. She was terrified that might happen with Clay. She didn't want that. She couldn't bear it.

Still, she knew things didn't always turn out badly between friends who became lovers. "Mom, tell me about you and Dad."

Paula looked up from the cash register, where she was putting money into the bank bag. "You haven't asked to hear that story in a while."

Shelby smiled, picking up a bowl of colored beads and moving them to their shelf on the back wall.

"When I was working my way through college getting my art degree, your dad was a firefighter and I was the secretary at the fire chief's office. We were already friends because we lived across the street from each other while growing up, but the more time we spent together as adults, the more I liked him." Her mom's voice went soft with memories. "Really liked him."

"And y'all hung out together growing up, didn't you?"

"Yes. He liked me, too, but he was a couple of years older. He thought I was too wild for him, that he might cramp my style."

Shelby chuckled. Her dad had always teased that getting together with her mom had cramped *his* style. Just trying to imagine her quiet, unassuming dad as wild tickled her.

"I tried to convince him that he could keep up with me, but he wasn't too cooperative."

"And he had concerns about y'all working together and dating."

Paula laughed, her blue eyes twinkling. "Do you want to tell the story?"

Shelby smiled. "No, go on."

"It took him a while to admit he wanted to be with me, and to accept that we could be both friends and lovers. I finally had to jump him."

"And you really did."

"I tried everything I knew to get him to ask me out. I dressed in conservative clothes like your aunt Renee. I cut my hair. I stopped smoking, which I needed to do anyway." Paula pushed her long thick hair over her shoulder. "But nothing worked. I finally had to ask him out."

"And you kissed him first."

"Yes, but after that I couldn't beat him off with a stick."

They both laughed.

A comfortable silence fell around them as they finished straightening the store. Had her dad been any more hesitant about getting involved with her mom than Shelby was about getting involved with Clay? Her parents had been each other's great loves as well as best friends, so those kinds of relationships obviously worked out sometimes. The idea to find out if things would work out for her and Clay was tempting.

Maybe she was more like her dad than she realized, Shelby mused. She remembered how often she'd seen her parents express their affection, and not only in lover-like ways. They had always enjoyed each other's company, just as Shelby did Clay's company. And she definitely enjoyed his kisses.

Paula walked out from behind the counter, placing the bank bag on the surface behind her. "What's going on, hon?"

Shelby eased down into a folding chair at the work table. "Clay kissed me."

"Oh?" Her mom didn't even sound surprised as she took a seat across from Shelby. "When?"

"Today. A few hours ago."

"What did you do?"

"I kissed him back, but I shouldn't have. Should I? Oh, I don't know." She propped an elbow on the table, cradling her head in her hand. The headache seemed to be abating. "I'm confused."

"You've both been alone a long time."

"I told him that, too. That it was the reason we were probably feeling this way about each other. He didn't think so."

Paula patted her arm. "That's not what I meant, hon. If it were only hormones, that would've probably happened sometime before now. Megan's been dead for seven years, and you've been divorced for five. If it's meant to be, you shouldn't fight it."

"How do I know if it's meant to be?"

Her mom studied her for a moment. "How did it feel when he kissed you? If you don't want to answer me out loud, don't. But be perfectly honest with yourself."

It felt great. *Right.*

Seeing the look on Shelby's face, her mother continued. "What's holding you back? You're afraid if a romance doesn't work out that you won't be friends anymore? That was one of your dad's concerns."

"Yes. I know Clay would never hurt me the way Ronnie did, but if we got together and it bombed, I don't know if we could remain friends. If *I* could remain friends. If I could get over him. And what if I hurt him? We both know how I've been since my divorce."

"You're the only one who can decide, Shelby. You and Clay have been through a lot together, and I think the two of you would do fine."

"I'm just not sure how I feel."

"I can't tell you that, hon, but I know one thing. If you didn't want to be with him, you'd definitely know *that*."

"I guess so."

Sometimes being friends and lovers did work out, as her parents had proven. Paula and Curtis Fox would still be together if Shelby's dad hadn't died of a heart attack. Clay was the only man still around with whom Shelby had sustained a long-term relationship, and she wanted to protect it. The only way she knew how to do that was to keep things platonic. But after their kiss, she didn't know how much longer she could fight what was between them. Or even if she wanted to anymore.

Vince Tyner had put his hands on Shelby. He wasn't doing it again.

There was plenty of daylight left when Clay parked at the back entrance to the police department and got out of his truck to wait. During his interview with Mac Hayward's twins, the jailer had called to tell Clay that Tyner was finishing his paperwork and would soon be released. Clay completed his interview with the high school girls in plenty of time to meet up with the paramedic. His paying this kind of visit to Shelby's ex was about as far from platonic as Oklahoma was from Okinawa, but he didn't care.

He leaned his backside against the hood of his truck, crossing his legs at the ankle. The sun still glowed hot against the evening sky. The faint scent of newly budded flowers mixed with the tang of car fuel and smells from a nearby fast-food restaurant.

The heavy back door of the jail creaked open and he straightened, but the person who walked out was his sister, not Tyner. Erin wore the garish makeup she'd been sporting for her undercover role as a hooker, but hadn't yet put on the rest of the costume.

She looked surprised to see him. "Hey."

"Hey."

She glanced around. "You alone?"

"Yeah."

She moved across the asphalt and stopped a couple of feet away, studying him with ill-concealed curiosity in her eyes. "How are things going?"

Clay arched a brow. "Don't you mean how are things going with me and Shelby?"

She grimaced. "She told you that we talked about Johnny?"

"That *you* talked to *her* about Johnny," he corrected. "If this is your idea of helping me, Erin, then don't."

"Well, well." His sister's eyes sparkled with mischief as she eased up beside him and propped one hand against his truck.

"Butt out, brat."

"You really want her," she said softly.

When he didn't answer, she nudged his shoulder with hers. "I just don't want either of you to get hurt."

"I know."

She glanced at the building's back door. "Brooke told me

what happened. Are you waiting for Tyner? What are you planning to do?"

"Have a little talk with him."

"Uh-huh. That's why you're wearing that hit-man look and your holster's unsnapped." She flipped back one side of his open shirt to show him she'd seen his sidearm. "Does Shelby know you're here?"

"No, and you're not going to tell her. I don't want her upset, Erin. She's been through enough, plus it's driving her nuts that she can't remember what happened after she went inside the victim's house."

His sister studied him for a minute. "I can't decide if you're being protective or possessive."

He gave her a flat stare.

"I think both," she mused. "Did you kiss her yet?"

His chest caved at the memory, but he kept his expression blank. "Get lost."

Erin peered into his face. "You did!"

Heat raced under his skin, and he hoped the glare of the late afternoon sun kept her from seeing the flush that crawled up his neck.

"Are you falling in love with her?"

"If I were, I think I'd tell her before I told you."

"I won't say anything."

He hooked a thumb over his shoulder toward her car. "Go."

"I don't want you to do something to Tyner that you'll regret."

"Trust me, I won't regret it."

"Clay—"

"Go, sis. I won't do anything stupid."

"You never do. It's just that…" After a moment's hesitation, Erin pushed away from his truck and walked down the sidewalk to her car.

Clay didn't care if it looked as if he were staking a claim

on Shelby. Tyner was going to stay away from her or find him-self in a cell for longer than an afternoon.

Erin returned with a duffel bag that probably held her hooker clothes. "If it helps any, I think she's wavering."

His heart jolted, and it was all he could do to keep a pas-sive face. He wanted to know more, but he wasn't asking. He wasn't in junior high, for crying out loud.

"Sure you don't want me to stay and back you up?"

"Yep."

She hesitated, then started for the back door. "Don't assault him in the parking lot. I don't want to have to clean up any blood."

Clay grinned in spite of the cold determination inside him. He really hoped Tyner would give him a reason to lock him up.

Clay waited patiently for the jerk to exit, knowing he'd be processed out the back door. Thick-trunked oak and maple trees spread their leafy arms, dappling the sidewalk with sun and shadow. The paramedic was still on Clay's suspect list, but learning from Mac Hayward's daughters a while ago that they couldn't confirm their father's alibi put the engineer ahead of Shelby's ex.

The jail's heavy door creaked open and Tyner stepped out, looking angry. He reached the corner of the building before he saw Clay. He stopped cold. "What are you doing here?"

Clay straightened and moved forward, seeing no reason for a soft sell. "Stay away from Shelby."

The other man's shoulders went rigid. "If you're talking about what happened today, I gave her some good information."

"You put your hands on her." Clay's words were low and savage. "Don't do it again."

The paramedic gave a sharp laugh. "She broke my nose!"

Clay gestured to the bruises beginning under Vince's eyes, the white tape across his nose. "I'd say so."

"She'll be lucky if I don't file charges on her."

He laughed. "Yeah, try that." With a lot more calm than he felt, he said, "If you get within a hundred yards of her, you'll find yourself served with a restraining order and I'll enforce it."

"Are you threatening me?" The man bristled and stepped closer, his stance combative.

"Think of it as me trying to help you live a little longer." Clay braced his hands on his hips, making sure Tyner got a glimpse beneath his shirt of the Glock tucked in his shoulder holster.

From the corner of his left eye, Clay saw an ambulance pull up to the curb and stop. Vince glanced over, raising a hand to signal he'd be a moment longer. Since Brooke had impounded Vince's car when she'd arrested him, Clay figured the ambulance driver was Tyner's partner picking him up.

A shrewd light came into Tyner's eye. "You have something going on with her."

I should be so lucky, Clay thought, his hands curling into fists. "This is the only time I'll warn you. If you get near her or contact her, you'll be seeing me and you won't like it."

"You won't get any further with her than I did," Tyner sneered.

"She's told you more than once to back off," Clay warned. "Now I'm telling you."

The muscled jerk balled his hands into fists and stepped toward Clay.

Clay wished the scumbag would swing; then he could throw the guy back in jail.

A vein pulsed in Tyner's neck. After a long minute, he cursed and stalked off toward the ambulance. The vehicle's passenger door slammed, and Clay watched as Tyner and his partner drove away.

Clay didn't know if the paramedic would heed his warning, but Clay would be watching and so would his sisters. If the guy knew what was good for him, he'd back off.

As Clay drove to Paula's store, he tried to calm himself. He didn't want Shelby to pick up on his anger or the fact that he had just laid a claim on her. Tyner had gotten the message that she belonged to Clay, and he had no problem with that. But he didn't know how Shelby would feel.

When he reached To Bead Or Not To Bead, located in a small strip mall, and parked in the front, the Closed sign already hung in the door. At his knock, Paula let him in. As he helped her move a table into the back room, Shelby came out of the small restroom to the side. He met her eyes and she gave him a slow, soft smile. A smile that zinged him hard and hot. He wasn't sure what that was about.

He asked Paula if she wanted to have dinner with him and Shelby, but she declined, saying she was headed to her weekly pottery class.

She thrust a couple of necklaces and bracelets into Clay's hands. "These are for Erin and Brooke. If they don't like the styles, they can exchange them."

"You've given them way too much jewelry already." He tried to catch a slithering silver necklace before it slid out of his hand.

"You know it's no use trying to talk her out of it," Shelby said.

"Yeah, I know hardheadedness runs in your family."

She stuck out her tongue, which made him want to back her into the wall and taste her.

His cell phone rang and he grabbed it in relief. "Jessup here."

"McClain here. Today was the medical examiner's first day back at work. I just got the full report on M.B.'s body. Also the results on the scrapings from her bed and lamp that I sent to the lab, along with the paint shavings from the wall."

"And?"

As Clay listened to the fire investigator, his gaze shot to Shelby's. A sharp jab of adrenaline hit his system. He wanted to see if she reacted the same way he had. He hung up and glanced over to find her studying his mouth.

His heart thudded hard. She was thinking about that kiss. He could read it in the dreamy confusion of her eyes. Maybe it was driving her as crazy as it was driving him.

She pulled her gaze away and grabbed her purse from behind the counter, moving toward him. "We'll get going, Mom. We don't want to make you late for your class."

"All right. I'll lock up behind you and go out the back."

"We'll all go out that way," Clay said. He wanted to make sure Paula got safely to her car.

After securing the store, Clay and Shelby walked out into a back alley with her mom. Shelby hugged her mom and watched her drive away. She fell into step with Clay as they walked around to his truck at the front of the building. "Who was on the phone?"

"Collier."

"Did he find out something?" she asked as they reached Clay's truck.

He nodded, opening her door. As she slid inside, he said, "He got the medical examiner's report. Traces of accelerant were found under M.B.'s fingernails and on her ring."

"And?"

"It was hair spray."

"Hair spray?" Shelby's eyes grew wide. "Remember the night I had that bad dream? I asked you before bed if you smelled hair spray because I'd been smelling it since Erin got ready for work that afternoon. I dreamed I was at M.B.'s. Do you think there's a connection or am I just wishing?"

"I'd say it's real possible. It's too much of a coincidence to be a coincidence."

Fifteen minutes after leaving her mom's store, Shelby stood with Clay on M.B.'s front porch. Late-day sunshine glared off the decorative glass at the top of the door and the large front window to the right. M.B.'s lawn was tidy, her hedges trimmed. The firefighters across the street were taking care of the yard. Dylan Shepherd had told Shelby that during one of his phone calls to check on her.

She had asked Clay to bring her back to the crime scene. Now that she knew about the hair spray, being inside M.B.'s house might jar loose something in Shelby's memory. She wanted to remember, but she was nervous about it, too.

Learning that the accelerant used to start the fire was hair spray had connected a dot for Clay and Shelby. Even though she hadn't consciously recalled that she'd smelled hair spray the night of the murder, the strong odor had to have been what had triggered her nightmare about being at M.B.'s and falling. Could there be another explanation? If so, she didn't know what it would be.

"You ready?" Clay's steady voice reached through the crush of her thoughts.

Her heart pounded in her throat. Sweat slicked her palms. She wanted to grab his hand, and they weren't even in the house yet. "Yes."

He'd been quiet on the drive over, listening and nodding when she repeated her theory about the hair spray three times. They had agreed that she should try to reenact as much as she could. She recalled sprinting from the fire station across the street and up to M.B.'s porch, then going inside.

After a long minute, she took a deep breath and opened the front door. The stench of smoke was strong and immediate. Almost two weeks had passed since the fire and the lingering odor was more stale than bitter, but there was no mistaking it.

She and Clay walked inside, leaving the door open as she'd done that night. The sour smell of mold traced the air. The furnishings were in order, the rugs and floors dried out from the firefighters' hoses as much as possible.

Captain Oliver had told Shelby that once Clay and Collier

had released the crime scene, a dozen firefighters from Station House Three had cleaned up M.B.'s house. Her mom and brothers were still unable to bring themselves to go inside.

Shelby paused at the edge of the living room and a sharp tingle shot to her fingertips. Her gaze moved over the soggy-looking area, the black-streaked brass lamp beside the Queen Anne sofa, the beige-and-green rugs on the dark hardwood floor now warped from water.

"What should I do?" she asked shakily, her voice small in the empty house.

"Just stand here for a minute. Try to let your nerves settle."

"We don't have that much time," she muttered.

Just as it always did, his crooked grin helped calm her a bit. She scanned the room and the kitchen doorway beyond. Her legs trembled.

"We'll stay as long as you want, leave as soon as you want. I'll be here for whatever you need."

There was no way she could do this without him. "Okay."

She walked forward, stopping at the end table that held the brass lamp. "I think the first thing I did was look around this room," she said slowly, catching a faint odor. Dry, sticky.

She turned to Clay. "Do you smell it?"

"What?"

"Hair spray."

He watched her intently. "All I smell is smoke."

"Do you think I'm imagining things? Because of what Collier said, because I think that nightmare might've been triggered by the smell of hair spray?"

"I don't know. We don't *need* to know right now. Just see if anything comes back to you."

She nodded as she turned toward the staircase and looked up at the second floor landing. "I think I went upstairs."

She found herself at the foot of the stairs, staring up the

wrought iron banister. The sharp whiff of hair spray grew stronger. She knew the smell had to be from her memory. A dull ache started at the base of her skull and spread upward.

She closed her eyes trying to picture what had happened, trying to remember. Searching her mind for images, sounds, anything. All she could see was herself, standing there as she was now. Suddenly she felt threatened, and goose bumps rose on her arms. Cold sweat gathered between her breasts, and the trembling in her legs intensified.

Clay had moved to stand at her shoulder and she reached back to link her fingers with his. She didn't understand what was going on inside her. "I must've gone up there. Why can't I remember?"

He squeezed her hand then let go. "It won't all come at once. Just go where your mind takes you. If it becomes too much or you want to stop—"

"I want to know." Her gaze met his. "I *need* to know. For M.B., for me."

He nodded, his beautiful green eyes steady on hers.

She again looked up the stairs. Some undefinable, silent force urged her to climb, but her legs wouldn't work. Her breathing grew shallow. She put her foot on the bottom step.

"I'm here, Shelby."

She didn't know how Clay knew to reassure her, but she was glad he had. Thank goodness he was with her. Her clammy hand curled tightly over the black iron railing and she took a step, then another. The stench of hair spray and smoke mixed. Apprehension pounded like a fist against the wall of her chest. "Are you coming?"

"I'm right behind you."

The ache in her head sharpened, spearing from above her ears to her temples. Her vision blurred slightly as she mounted the stairs.

Moving on wooden legs, she forced herself to walk to the

doorway of M.B.'s bedroom. She stopped. The smell of hair spray overwhelmed her senses. Strong, unmistakable, cloying. Gripping the door frame with a shaking hand, Shelby closed her eyes, trying to visualize what she might've witnessed that night. All she saw were blurs and indistinct shapes, shadows. She was hit with the deep sense that something tangible, something identifiable was just out of reach.

She heard a small sound—a frightened sound—and realized it came from her. Her body went numb; her heart beat erratically and too fast. The headache drilled through her skull.

Still remembering nothing, she opened her eyes. A sudden flash of gray and red hazed her vision. A memory. Smoke and fire. Horror, disbelief, panic boiled in her stomach like acid.

Dizzy now, she backed away, hit the railing and felt the hard iron bar in the small of her back. Terror welled up, cutting off her breath. She'd felt this before. Someone had pushed her. Who?

She clapped a hand over her mouth, sure she was going to be sick. Before she realized what was happening, Clay had pulled her to the top of the staircase and forced her down onto a step. "Sit. Put your head between your knees."

The room spun; tears burned her eyes. She cradled her throbbing head. "What's going on? What's happening in my head?"

"Tell me," he urged.

"I can't see anything in my mind! I just…feel. I smell hair spray and smoke. I know I smelled them that night. I know it," she said fiercely, choking back a sob of anger and fear. "And someone pushed me. But that's all I know. Why can't I remember anything?"

"Shelby, you're as white as a ghost. Take deep breaths. Right now, just concentrate on that."

She swayed.

Clay moved to kneel a couple of steps below her. He steadied her with a hand on her shoulder, ordering quietly, "Look at me, Shelby. Look at me."

She did, focusing on the deep soothing green of his eyes, the steadiness, the strength.

"Breathe."

After several seconds, the nausea subsided, but she still shook as if she had chills from a fever. She had to get away from the bedroom.

She rose jerkily to her feet. Clay stood, wrapping a hand around her upper arm, and she leaned into him as they walked down the stairs.

Even when her feet touched the solid wood floor, her legs wobbled as if they were disjointed. She turned into Clay's chest, burying her face there as her brain locked up. Frustration joined the terror that squeezed her chest. The acrid scent of hair spray still lingered in the air. "Do you smell it now?"

"No," he said quietly.

She wrapped her arms around him, plastering her entire body against his, needing his reassuring warmth, his strength. She thought she felt him stiffen. He turned both of them and gently eased her down into a chair near the sofa.

Something about his actions bothered her, but her foggy mind couldn't grasp what.

"I've got some water in my truck. Let me get it for you."

"No," she said quickly, urgently. "Please don't leave me alone in here." She recognized the desperation in her voice, even though she didn't understand it. She gave a self-conscious laugh. "I know I sound like a big wimp, but I don't want to be in here alone."

"It's all right. I'm not going anywhere."

"I want to remember." Her voice cracked. "I thought I would."

"You did. We know now that you didn't fall from upstairs. Someone pushed you. The rest of what's locked up in your head won't come out by forcing it."

"What if I never recall anything else? I need to know, Clay!" She surged up out of the chair, her foot catching the leg. Faltering, she grabbed a handful of his shirt.

She needed him. Sliding her arms around his waist, she closed her eyes. Some part of her calmed enough to drag in a lungful of air, the first full breath she'd had since walking into the house. She pressed her ear to the steady, regular beat of Clay's heart, her face snuggled into the reassuring warmth of his chest.

Her senses were overloaded and she couldn't sort out why. Too many feelings pounded at her, with no memories to explain them. How could she help Clay find the murderer if she couldn't remember anything?

His hands lifted to her shoulders, but instead of rubbing them as he frequently did or stroking his thumb soothingly across her nape, he gently moved her away from him. Why had he done that? "Ever thought about trying hypnosis?"

She looked up at him, feeling alone. "No, but it's a good idea."

He shrugged, taking a step back. "If it worked, you wouldn't be able to use what you recalled in court, but you'd have some peace of mind and we'd probably be able to get some kind of lead."

"Do you think Dr. Boren will okay it?"

"Yes."

"I'll have to ask Captain Oliver to put in the paperwork so I can see the city shrink and get a referral."

Clay nodded, moving closer to the door. Confused, Shelby followed, aching for him to wrap her up in his arms.

As apprehensive as she'd been about coming back to the crime scene, she'd really hoped to get a tangible memory. She had. Knowing that someone had pushed her from the second floor was scary, but what troubled her just as much was that there was now some kind of distance between her and Clay.

Chapter 9

Shelby had needed a friend last night, and a part of Clay felt as if he'd let her down. He'd let her reach for him when they'd revisited the crime scene, but he'd made sure he kept some distance between them.

Dammit, feeling her touch was agony. And it was getting more difficult to be with her without putting his hands on her. The easiest thing, maybe the best thing for both of them, would be if he let someone else protect her. But he wasn't going to.

As they drove to Leticia Keane's house late the next morning, Clay struggled to force his mind to turn to the questions he wanted to ask the seventeen-year-old, questions that had come up a while ago during his half-hour phone conversation with the male teacher she'd gotten fired last year and who now lived in Tulsa.

"So this Mr. Wyman said Leticia had done this before? To someone besides him?" Shelby sat only inches away in Clay's truck, her soft scent drifting to him. The fitted floral top and red pants she wore brightened her face, but didn't camouflage the circles under her eyes.

He had brought her because there was a possibility she might recognize the girl or that the high schooler might spark something in Shelby's memory. And even if Shelby didn't remember anything, there was the possibility that Leticia might act nervous around her. That would tell Clay something, too.

"Yeah. Wyman said after Leticia started causing all that trouble for him, he did some digging. He knew she'd attended a different high school the year before, one in Oklahoma City. When he checked, he found out she'd done the same thing at that school, too. This is her second go-round as a senior. Because of her grades, she couldn't graduate the first time. When Wyman confronted her and her dad with the information he'd found, they agreed not to go before the school board as long as he kept it to himself."

"So why did he leave? He had proof she had a pattern of this behavior."

"It's still largely a case of he said, she said. The teacher didn't believe there was any way he could stay here after that. Charges like sexual harassment follow a person for a long time. He didn't think he could get a job here, so he moved to Tulsa."

"I can't believe what some people are capable of doing."

"The first time Collier and I interviewed her, I didn't get a sense of this degree of manipulation. But I checked Mr. Wyman's story about the other teacher, and I'm inclined to believe him."

Shelby shook her head. "I guess if she lied about the teacher making advances to her, she's probably lied about other things. Maybe like being involved with Antonio Sandoval. Do you think she is?"

"I don't know. I hope I can get a feel for that when we talk to her."

"If she wanted him and thought he was having an affair with M.B., it's not hard to imagine she might've tried to get rid of M.B. And if I saw Leticia that night…" Shelby shuddered.

Clay turned onto a street in a quiet residential neighborhood with older homes. Thick, full Bradford pear trees along the curb swayed in the breeze. Shelby's theory could be right. Leticia Keane could be involved with Antonio Sandoval. "Sandoval doesn't have an alibi for the night of M.B.'s murder, and his being at the movie the day of the microwave explosion at your station house can't be confirmed."

"What about Leticia?"

"At the time of the microwave explosion, she was in school so she's covered for that, but not for the night of the murder."

"This should be interesting," Shelby murmured.

They pulled up at the curb of a modest home of buff brick with a narrow porch and black columns. The door to the two-car garage was down and there was a red Corvette in the drive.

"I've seen that car! At M.B.'s."

His gaze shot to her. "Are you sure?"

"Yes." She grabbed his hand, looking excited. "That's the one I told you about earlier. I can't remember the exact date I saw it, but I know I did."

"That's good." Startled at the jolt of heat that traveled up his arm at her touch, he pulled away, reaching for his keys.

"I can't believe I finally remembered something. Of course, it isn't about the night of the murder, but at least it's something."

"You never know where it might lead."

They climbed out of the truck. As he came around to follow her up the sidewalk that led to the front door, Clay didn't even try to keep his gaze from sliding down the slender lines of her back to her hips encased in slim red pants. Man, he wanted to get his hands on her.

He shrugged into a lightweight jacket, then checked his badge that was clipped on the waistband of his khaki slacks. He rang the doorbell, more aware of Shelby's soft peachy scent than he liked. He had to keep his mind on Leticia Keane.

A slightly built man with close-trimmed black hair and wire-frame glasses answered the door. Recognition flashed across his pleasant features. "Hello, Detective."

Clay shook Tom Keane's hand, then introduced Shelby. He explained that they needed to reinterview Leticia, and Mr. Keane invited them inside.

Disapproval tightened the man's mouth as he showed them into a small living area with a couch done in a gold-and-cream floral print. Matching tufted armless chairs sat opposite the sofa. "Please make yourselves comfortable while I get Leticia."

As he left the room, Shelby moved next to Clay and said in a low voice, "He didn't look too happy with her."

"I hope that look gets her to cooperate."

Mr. Keane returned with a slender, strikingly pretty black-haired girl. Clay glanced at Shelby, and she gave an almost imperceptible shake of her head. She didn't recognize the dark-eyed teenager. And the girl didn't act as if she'd seen Shelby before.

"Leticia, I'm sure you remember Detective Jessup. This is Ms. Fox." The man pulled his daughter forward, his gaze meeting Clay's. "She's going to answer all your questions."

She smiled coolly. "Is this about the custodian at school? The one you asked me about last time?"

Clay thought he glimpsed apprehension in her eyes. He shook his head, picking up the bitter-ash odor of cigarette smoke beneath her flirty perfume. He hadn't smelled it the first time he'd been here. "I need to double-check some information we got about you and a Mr. Wyman."

Her gaze jerked to her father. Tom Keane's expression hardened. "Why is his name coming up?"

"Like I said, we're double-checking some information." Clay's gaze shifted to the girl. "Leticia, what can you tell me about Mr. Wyman?"

"Does she really have to go through this again?" her father asked.

"Yes, sir." Clay felt Shelby move closer to him and he worked to stay focused. "Leticia can answer my questions here or at the station. Whichever you prefer."

"She'll do it here." The man turned to his daughter, urging, "Just tell them, honey. Get it over with."

A cold look darted in and out of her black eyes so quickly Clay wondered if he'd imagined it. She finger-fluffed her shoulder-length hair and gave a dramatic sigh. "I was supposed to be assigned to him for detention and he creeped me out. I didn't want to go to his class so I made up things about him."

"What kinds of things?"

Leticia slid a look at her dad. "Sex things. I said he tried to get me to do things to him so I could get a higher grade."

"How far did you take it?" Clay pulled his small notebook from his jacket pocket and flipped it open. "Did you tell this to another teacher? The principal?"

"No. I just told Mr. Wyman that I'd tell my dad. That we'd go to the school board if he didn't leave me alone."

Her answers were matter-of-fact, seemingly direct. This was exactly how she'd acted during Clay's initial interview with her, but this time he knew to look beyond that. "Sexual harassment is a serious charge to level against someone. I guess you know he had to leave his job and move to another city?"

"I knew he left the school. I didn't know he left town."

"I spoke with him earlier today."

The girl froze. So did her father.

"He said you were the one who offered to exchange sexual favors for a better grade in his class."

Mr. Keane leveled a stare on his daughter.

Clay went on, "He said that after you threatened him, he did some digging. Found out you claimed the very same thing about another teacher the year before in a different school. Was that charge also a lie?"

She looked ready to stalk off, but she reluctantly admitted, "Yes."

"Why did you threaten the other man, Mr. Lawford? What did you have against him?"

"Nothing really." A cold smile touched her lips. "Kinda twisted, huh?"

She acted perversely pleased with herself. "Sounds like revenge. Why would you want revenge against Mr. Wyman? Or Mr. Lawford?"

"You tell them the truth, young lady," Mr. Keane said tightly. "And remember this is exactly why you're on probation in this house."

She shot him a hateful look and Clay finally began to get a picture of the real Leticia Keane. Wyman had said that the girl had flirted with him, hung around after school hours, shown up in the men's locker room, waited by his car, done everything she knew to get his attention. Clay wanted to hear it from her.

"My dad thinks I did it because I had a thing for Mr. Wyman."

"Did you?"

She shrugged, her gaze sliding over him with such undisguised sexual interest that Clay was taken aback. Shelby made a small sound beside him, and he knew she'd seen it, too. He kept his expression blank. Man, this girl was bad news.

"You had a crush on him and he wasn't interested, right?"

An angry flush crested her cheeks and Clay knew he'd gotten to the heart of the issue. "You didn't like that, so you tried to ruin him."

"He didn't have to be so mean about it!" she burst out. Her dad squeezed her arm, but she jerked away. "Yes, I did it to get back at him."

"And Mr. Lawford?"

"Same thing," she said grudgingly, not meeting Clay's gaze.

"My daughter has problems, Detective," Mr. Keane said quietly. "We're trying to work on them."

"Did the incident with Mr. Wyman have anything to do with your not graduating last year when you should have?"

"Yes. No," she amended when her father looked at her. "I had bad grades. I skipped a lot of school and got suspended."

"And because Mr. Wyman wouldn't get involved with you, you got him fired."

Her father winced, but the girl just stared sullenly at Clay.

"You're at a new school now. How are your grades this year, Leticia?"

She shrugged. "My dad says they could be better."

"Are there any teachers you don't get along with?"

"No."

"I tried to get her in classes with only female teachers this year, Detective," Mr. Keane put in.

Probably a smart move. "What about Ms. Perry?"

Something sharp flared in the girl's eyes. "What about her?"

"Did you get along with her?"

"I was her aide."

"That's not what I asked," Clay pressed.

The girl hesitated. "She was all right."

"What did you do for her?"

"A lot of times she made me work on my own homework. Sometimes I took messages to the office, that kind of stuff."

"I know you weren't in the science club she sponsored. Did you spend any time with her other than the hour a day you worked as her aide?"

"No."

Gotcha. Clay's eyes narrowed on her. "You sure about that?"

"Yes. Ms. Perry stayed late a lot with the students she was teaching to read English, but I didn't stay."

"And you didn't see her away from school?"

"Why would I?" She checked her fingernails, acting as if she were bored.

She wasn't bored; she was hiding something. She was trying too hard to appear tough and unconcerned. "Are you sure you want to stick with your story?"

Clay was acutely aware of Shelby at his side, taking in everything with an intensity he could feel. "I have a witness who saw your car at her house about three weeks ago."

Color drained from the girl's face, her dark eyes burning. "What's going on, Leticia?" her father asked sharply.

"Oh, now I remember. I *was* there," she said too quickly. "I dropped off some papers I'd graded for her."

"So why lie about it?"

"I didn't lie! I just didn't remember."

"Did you go inside?"

"Yes."

"Is that the only time you were there?"

"No, maybe one or two other times."

"Would your fingerprints be on anything?"

Panic streaked across her features. "I don't know. Why?"

"Yes, Detective. Why?" her father repeated.

Clay studied the girl. He thought she was giving him the truth this time, but he bet she wasn't giving him all of it. "Where were you the night of May 9th?"

"I don't know. That was forever ago."

"Think about it, Leticia, and tell him," her father ordered.

"It was a Sunday night, two weeks ago tomorrow," Clay said.

She scowled, and he could almost see her mind racing. "I was at a party."

"On a Sunday night, with school the next day?"

"It was a birthday party, and it was over by eleven. I was home by then. You can ask my dad."

Mr. Keane nodded.

"Whose party was it?"

"My friend, Melanie Adams."

Clay recalled talking to Melanie on his and Collier's initial visit to the high school. "Did you go out again that night?"

"I just told you when I got home!"

"One of my sisters used to sneak out of the house when the rest of us were asleep. Did you do that on May 9th?"

"No!" she declared hostilely.

The weary, disappointed look on Tom Keane's face said he didn't believe his daughter any more than Clay did.

"I didn't sneak out. I came home and I stayed home."

"She did come home by the time she said she did, Detective, but I don't know about the other."

"Daddy!" The girl's eyes filled with tears. "Tell him I was here!"

The man studied his daughter for a moment, sadness settling over his face. "I'm sorry, Leticia, but I don't know that. I'm never sure anymore when you're telling the truth."

Clay couldn't prove the girl *had* slipped out of her house after eleven o'clock the night of M.B.'s murder, but his gut told him she had. And though he wasn't sure what motive she might have for murder, his instincts told him there was more to be learned.

A set of fingerprints had been lifted at the crime scene that hadn't yet been matched. "Would you be willing to let us take your fingerprints, Leticia?"

She looked alarmed. "Why?"

"To eliminate you as a suspect."

"My daughter's a suspect?"

"She's lied, Mr. Keane, which makes me wonder what

else she might be lying about. Since you can't verify that she stayed home all night on May 9th, I need some way to eliminate her as a suspect."

"What possible reason could she have for wanting to kill Ms. Perry? To kill anyone?"

"I've interviewed other students who say Leticia didn't like Ms. Perry, that she felt Ms. Perry demanded too much of her."

"I don't have to give you my fingerprints, do I?" the girl challenged. "Isn't that violating my rights or something?"

"Not if you give them voluntarily."

"Which she will," her father said sternly.

The girl turned hurt eyes on her father. "Do you think I killed Ms. Perry?"

"No," he said softly. "But it's to your benefit if you cooperate. The sooner Detective Jessup eliminates you, the sooner this will be over."

After a long pause, she nodded. Mr. Keane shifted his attention to Clay. "What do we need to do?"

"Come to the station. I'll have the ADA bring forms for you both to sign stating that Leticia is giving her prints voluntarily and that you're giving your permission. The fingerprint tech will print her and she'll be finished."

The other man nodded sharply. Leticia glared, but didn't resist when her dad grabbed his keys from a small table next to the door and herded her out behind Clay and Shelby.

Even if Leticia's prints did match the one found at the scene, it didn't prove she'd done anything wrong, only that she'd been in M.B.'s house.

As they slid into Clay's truck and waited for Mr. Keane to back out of his driveway, Shelby asked, "Do you really think she could be the killer?"

"I don't know if she's strong enough to have snapped M.B.'s neck."

As Clay put the truck into motion, she said, "So maybe Leticia wasn't alone at M.B.'s. Maybe someone who *was* strong enough to kill M.B. was with her. A man."

Clay nodded. "If we match Leticia's print to the one found at the scene, it might spook other information out of her. I might be able to get her to tell me if she was alone that night. After we finish with her at the station, we'll go talk to her friend Melanie."

"To see if she can confirm Leticia's alibi for the night of the murder?"

"Yeah." He glanced at her, his gaze drifting over the curve of her breasts, the gentle flare of her hip. His hands curled tightly around the steering wheel. "Do you want to go with me to interview Leticia's friend?"

"Yes. As long as you think we'll be home in time for me to get ready for Collier's wedding."

"I think we will."

She stared out the window. "I smelled cigarette smoke on her. Did you?"

"Yeah, underneath the perfume."

"If she smokes, she probably carries a lighter. And could've used it to make a can of hair spray into the torch that set M.B. on fire."

"I had that thought, too." He took in her pale face, the way she gnawed on the pad of her thumb. "You okay?"

"Yeah." She shook her head. "Sometimes it just hits me that she's really dead. That I could've been, too."

Something hot charged through Clay's chest. He didn't like being reminded. "You still thinking about getting hypnotized?"

"Yes. I put in a call to Captain Oliver before we left your house. He's supposed to call me back. If I don't hear from him before the wedding and he's there, I can talk to him then."

Clay nodded.

She blew out a breath. "Seems like every time we think we're getting somewhere on M.B.'s murder, we run into a wall."

"We just have to keep digging. Eventually, we'll learn something that will send us in the right direction."

"You have incredible patience. I mean, I've always known you were patient, but to do your job, you have to follow lead after lead, never knowing when you might find the one thing you need. At least when I fight a fire, it's out and it's done. That job is finished. I don't think I could do what you do. I'd feel like I was waiting all the time."

He stared at her until she looked at him. "Some things are worth waiting for."

Her eyes widened a little at that, but she held his gaze. Deep in his gut, he thought Shelby might be wavering, but he had nothing tangible to back that up. Maybe his gut-searing desire for her was clouding his instincts.

He needed to get the idea of *them* out of his head, needed to get his body's reaction to her under control. He just didn't know how.

A little after six that evening, Clay stood at the glass door in his living room looking into the backyard. He glanced at his watch again. What was taking her so long? It never took Shelby this long to get ready to go out.

His sisters had called a few minutes ago, already at the church in north Oklahoma City where Collier McClain's and Kiley Russell's wedding would take place. Erin and Brooke had gone early to watch for Vince Tyner. Shelby's ex probably wouldn't show up—he wasn't invited—but Clay was taking no chances. That had as much to do with his personal feelings as it did his professional ones.

Because Tyner had been in the firehouse just minutes before the microwave explosion, the paramedic was still on

Clay's suspect list. Since his talk a couple of hours ago with
Leticia Keane's friend, Leticia herself was a question mark.
Though Melanie Adams had been cooperative, Clay sensed
she was holding something back and he hadn't been able to
get it out of her. That, as much as seeing a different side to
Leticia Keane today, made him now consider the teenager a
person of interest.

He turned and walked to the couch, snagging his dark suit
coat off the back. Because of the warm temperature, he
wouldn't put it on until they arrived at the church. He'd need
it then anyway to wear over his shoulder holster. He wouldn't
be the only cop packing heat under his suit. Having known
the bride since their days at the police academy, it wouldn't
surprise Clay if Kiley wore her ankle holster under her wedding gown. That ought to give Collier a little jolt later that evening. Clay grinned.

"I'm ready," Shelby said from the doorway.

"All right." He looked up and his breath jammed in his
lungs. *Hell-o. That* was Shelby? Wow. Wow! She looked incredible.

Her short hair was shiny and fluffier than usual, her eyes
a brilliant blue across the room. He registered that even as his
gaze lowered to her breasts, then her hips. The ankle-length
coral gown winking with small gold beads hugged her trim
curves.

The halter neckline bared her shoulders only, but the way
her full breasts pressed against the sleek fabric made it really
easy to imagine the rest of her bare. Her skin glowed satiny
gold.

Uncertainty flickered across her face and she looked down,
flattening a hand against her stomach. "Is this all right? What
do you think?"

Think? There was no thinking, but his body was reacting.
And how.

She grimaced. "Do I look ridiculous?"

"No," he said quickly. "You look good. Great," he said hoarsely, his gaze tracing over her again. "*Really* great."

A blush tinted her skin, and pleasure warmed her eyes. "I'm ready if you are."

I am so *ready*. "Yeah, let's go."

"Your jacket." With a little smile, she pointed at the floor.

He followed her gaze and saw his suit coat. Realizing he must've dropped it when he'd seen her, he felt heat crawl up his neck. "Thanks," he said gruffly, stooping to pick it up.

She turned for the door and when Clay got a look at the back of her dress, he froze in midstep. His hand clenched in the dark fabric of his jacket. The back of her gown was cut out, and from her nape to the small of her back was one sleek bare expanse of skin. The elegant lines of her body were jaw-droppingly sexy. And there was a slit that stopped at the back of her knee, flashing a teasing glimpse of leg as she walked. *Oh, man. Oh, boy. Oh, hell.*

Blood hammered hard in every cell of his body. He wanted some of that woman. *Now.*

She reached the front door and glanced back. "My car, right?"

"Yeah," he said hoarsely, amazed his voice even worked. They'd agreed to drive her little coupe so she wouldn't have to climb into his truck in her gown.

She started out, probably expecting that he'd be right behind her. He should've been, but it took a couple of seconds for his legs to work. Unable to take his eyes off her, he finally reached the door.

There was no way he could go out there with her right now. He was hard and throbbing, and sweat broke across his nape. "Wait for me in here. I'll just be a minute," he called, his free hand sliding into his slacks pocket and curling tight around Shelby's car keys.

She closed the glass door and moved in front of the large kitchen window, giving him a smile over her shoulder that put his muscles into a clench. The evening sunlight filtered through the blinds and brushed her skin with gold. All Clay could think was he *had* to touch her. He had to. She was his. He was going to grab her and— No!

Trying to curb the thoughts, he closed his eyes briefly. She'd said they weren't going there. He started down the hall and went into his bedroom, then crossed to his bathroom and closed the door.

He walked to the sink and turned on the cold water, wetting his face over and over until it tingled.

Other parts of his body were tingling, too. He couldn't let her see him like this and he couldn't take a cold shower. This would have to do. After long seconds, he grabbed a towel and dried his face. He looked in the mirror as the ache in his body throbbed deeper.

All he could think about was Shelby, naked. He wanted to know how she felt against him, how she tasted on her nape, the curve of her spine, between her breasts. And he wanted to know where that tattoo was. There was no sign of it in the sweet line of her back. And having seen her in her bra and panties he knew there was no tattoo on the swell of her breasts, the flat of her stomach or her legs. There were only a couple of places it could be and he wanted to find out where. Right now. It was going to be a long night.

A couple of hours later, Shelby stood beside her captain in the gorgeous hotel ballroom, watching the newlyweds dance.

The faint scent of roses and sweet peas drifted around the room, mingled with the subtle smells of perfume and cologne. Two walls of the large gold-and-white room were windows that looked north over the hotel's manicured grounds and an affluent residential area of Oklahoma City. The strappy beaded heels Shelby wore looked great with this dress, but they killed her feet.

"Sure, I'll be happy to put in the paperwork for you to see a therapist," Rick Oliver said. "Sorry I couldn't return your call this afternoon."

"That's all right. Do I need to come in and type up the request?"

"Nah, you only need to come in to sign it. If you're willing to be hypnotized, it sounds like you're trying whatever you can to get your memory back."

"Yes."

"You really think it will help?"

"I'm hopeful." She glanced at the trim man beside her, barely able to tear her gaze from Clay. Dancing yet another dance with yet another woman. "Clay took me back to the crime scene last night and I remembered a couple of things. If I had a little help, I think I could recall something concrete that might actually help catch M.B.'s killer."

"I've never requested this for one of my people before, Fox, but I don't expect there to be any problems. Might take a week or more for the paperwork to get through."

"All right." Her gaze followed Clay as he swept some woman she didn't know around the floor. The dark suit he wore drew attention to his broad shoulders. The starched white shirt and patterned tie brought out the deep bronze of his skin. He looked delicious. "I didn't see Cindy at the wedding."

"She stayed home with Aubrey. The little darlin' had another asthma attack an hour before it was time to go. I offered to stay and let Cindy come, but she thought I should be the one since I've known Collier for so long."

Clay had danced with every woman here at least once, every woman but Shelby. The realization settled under her skin like an itch. She didn't like it, especially since she was still replaying the look in his eyes when he'd first seen her this evening.

Raw, undisguised desire. As hot and fierce as what had been on his face the day he'd seen her in her underwear. She knew he wanted her, so why wouldn't he dance with her?

She didn't like seeing all those women in his arms, even the ones who were old enough to be his grandmother. And ever since Erin and Brooke had informed her about Clay's conversation with Vince yesterday, Shelby had felt restless. Impatient. As if she were waiting for him to do something. She hadn't been able to stop thinking about it or calm the little flip in her stomach.

She knew Vince would interpret Clay's protectiveness to mean she belonged to him and she didn't mind one bit. But if Clay felt that way, she couldn't tell it. The edginess that had simmered inside her all day grew sharper.

In fact, not only did he act as if he had no claim on her, but he was distancing himself. In small ways, such as not having called her "blue eyes" in two days. And he wouldn't touch her, at least not the way he normally did. That had been what bothered her last night at M.B.'s, although she hadn't been able to put her finger on it then.

She'd kept him in her sights all night since the ceremony, trying to decipher this restlessness churning inside her. They always danced at least twice at events like this and she expected him to ask her. But so far he hadn't. He'd barely looked her way. Frustration burned through her.

Finally, *finally* the current dance ended and Clay returned his partner to some man in the crowd, then moved through a throng of people toward the far wall. She followed the line of his broad shoulders, the sandy hair streaked gold under the chandelier light. He stopped next to Jack Spencer, a longtime cop buddy of his. Tension Shelby hadn't even been aware of eased out of her shoulders.

If Clay wouldn't ask her, then she'd ask him. She excused herself from her captain and angled across the corner of the cream-and-gold bordered rug, then wove her way through the group of people gathered on the edge of the dance floor. A few people stopped her along the way, and she tamped down her impatience.

The band began to play the Patsy Cline version of "Crazy." Shelby was relieved to see that Clay appeared to be staying put. The closer she got, the more flushed she felt. Finally she reached him.

"Hey, Shelby." Jack Spencer peered around Clay to greet her.

"Hi, Jack." She sounded as breathless as if she'd run over here instead of walked. She didn't see Jack's wife or four-month-old daughter. "Did Terra take Elise home?"

"No, just to a room across the hall. Russell provided child care."

"Oh." She smiled, then looked up at Clay.

His gaze was warm as he took a sip of his ginger ale. Since the month-long drunk he'd gone on after Jason's death, he didn't touch liquor any more. The speed with which he'd become dependent on alcohol had scared him. And Shelby.

She touched his arm. "You're not all danced out, are you?"

"I'm not that much older than you," he said dryly. "I'm probably good for one or two more."

She smiled. "Would you dance with me?"

He could turn her down. He should. Dancing with her would not do one thing to help him stop wishing for more between them, but he couldn't have refused even if his job were on the line. "Sure."

He cleared his throat and said goodbye to Jack as he clumsily set his glass on a table behind him. Holding her close, touching her would be sheer torture…and the best feeling he'd had since that kiss on his back porch. He wanted to do this anyway, even though he knew he'd stay awake half the night aching.

Her curvy body in that clingy dress affected him as strongly now as it had when he'd first seen her. He hurt just looking at her. He knew how soft and warm her skin would feel beneath his hand. Knew how her light peachy scent would tease him. He didn't like that all the men she'd danced with earlier tonight knew that now, too. At least in public he'd be able to keep his hands where he should, keep from doing all the things he was afraid he'd do if they were alone.

He folded her left hand in his right and curved his other arm lightly around her waist, his palm gliding across the warm velvet of her back. She closed the distance he'd left between them and her breasts brushed softly against him. His body tightened. There was no way she had on a bra or any semblance of one under this dress. Maybe no panties, either. He struggled for breath.

She smiled up at him, her blue eyes smoky in the soft light. "You clean up real nice, Jessup. Did I already say that?"

He flattened their joined hands against his chest, although what he wanted to do was slide both his palms up her bare back. Did she know how much she was getting to him? "So do you."

If she could've pressed their bodies any closer, she would have. Laying her head on his shoulder, she let her body relax into his. His heart beat strong against her ear; his heat surrounded her. As the band went into Toby Keith's song about two friends falling in love, the slow, dreamy music coaxed the strength out of her legs. The mouthwatering scent of woodsy cologne and clean male had her melting into him.

She curved her free arm over his shoulder, wondering if he was enjoying this as much as she was. Wanting him to *want* this as much as she did. His body was warm and hard against hers, causing a flutter in her stomach. Clay. Clay was causing flutters. The thought made her smile.

She wanted him. The admission came easier now, but she didn't know if she could give in to it. The concerns she'd discussed with her mom were serious. What she had with him held her world together.

He'd told her she could call the shots and he had let her. To the point of frustration. She knew if she wanted things to go any further between them, she'd have to be the one to take the step. She just wasn't sure how many steps she was ready to take.

She was vaguely aware that they were on the edges of the crowd, more in the shadows than out. Soft light from the chandelier fringed this corner of the large room. She smoothed her hand over his shoulder, feeling the slight bump of his shoulder holster.

His chest was solid and hot, his thighs lean muscle against the brush of hers. The whimsical, seductive music honed her awareness of him to a razor edge. His warm musky scent. The tempered lines of his body. She resisted the urge to stroke a finger down his strong jawline. He rested his chin atop her head and the subtle pressure of his big hand against the small of her back felt as right as anything they'd ever done as friends.

"Hey, y'all."

Clay's husky greeting had Shelby lifting her head and turning. The bride and groom danced close, beaming. Shelby hadn't been aware of anyone coming near them.

She smiled at Collier and Kiley. "It was a beautiful wedding."

"And short," Clay put in, earning a soft laugh from the bride.

Collier lowered his voice. "We're going to slip out using that door behind y'all."

Shelby laughed. "Do you think you're going to escape Walker?"

"Right now, my brother's distracted by two women." Collier grinned. "If they fail, I'm depending on the two of you."

"Go for it," she said. The newly married McClains couldn't honeymoon until Collier and Clay had solved M.B.'s murder, but they hadn't wanted to postpone the wedding.

After a quick look around, Collier ducked behind Clay, pulling Kiley behind him, and the pair disappeared. They were obviously crazy about each other and seemed like good friends, too. Shelby knew they had fallen in love when Collier and Kiley were assigned to work together on a serial arsonist-sniper case about five months ago. For years, Shelby hadn't wanted that kind of relationship. Until now, she hadn't been willing to even consider opening herself up to one.

Curling her hand around Clay's nape, she brushed her thumb against the hot supple flesh on the side of his neck. She slid her fingers into his hair, loving the feel of its silky warmth.

His arm tightened around her waist.

"Clay?"

"Hmm?" His breath whispered against her temple.

"Erin and Brooke told me you had a talk with Vince last night."

"I'm going to pound them," he growled. "Sorry if my talking to Tyner bothers you, Shelby, but he's a threat. I want him to know I'm watching him."

"It doesn't bother me," she said softly, looking up. She wanted things out in the open. *Everything.* "What does bother me is that you've been pulling away."

"In case you haven't noticed, almost every inch of my body is touching yours."

"I don't mean right now." She hesitated, her gaze locking on his. "I reached for you at M.B.'s last night and you wouldn't touch me. Every time I reached out, you pulled away. Today, too."

He tensed. "I wasn't trying to hurt you."

"I needed you to hold me, help me know everything was

going to be all right, but you wouldn't." She moved her hand so she could keep her fingers in his hair and lightly trace his earlobe.

He studied her for a moment then pulled her full into him, pressing his erection against her belly. "This is what you do to me. I seem to be walking around like this all the time now. I want you, blue eyes."

She blinked, feeling a flush heat her cheeks as he continued. "I'm not going to pressure you. You've got enough to deal with right now, but I can't just turn my feelings on and off. There might be times I can't hold you the way you need. You get to me, so much that sometimes I don't think I have the self-control to keep from kissing you." His gaze lingered on her lips, slid to her breasts. "Or touching you. You're driving me crazy right now."

Her stomach dipped in delicious anticipation. She loved his touch on her, wanted more. Her gaze drifted over his face, paused on his mouth. "I've been thinking."

"Yeah?" he murmured.

"About us."

He stopped abruptly, his hand going to her waist to keep their balance. "Us? Like friends us?"

"No." In these shoes, she had only to lift up slightly to say into his ear, "Like naked us."

He drew back, heat flashing in his eyes. He swallowed hard and for a minute, he stared at her. "Really?"

"Really." She wanted to nibble at his jaw, kiss her way to his mouth. She'd never put her hands over him so intimately, and it wasn't enough. There was a hollowness inside her and she knew—finally—what would fill it. She lightly brushed her fingertips across his nape. "I didn't like seeing you dance with all those women tonight."

A grin hitched up one corner of his mouth. "I wasn't that wild about all your partners, either."

"My feelings are changing," she said quietly.

His big hand closed on her waist, squeezed. He waited.

"It's frustrating, wanting to remember about the night M.B. was killed and also trying to deal with wanting to kiss you every time I see you."

"I can help with that last part," he murmured, his hot gaze dropping to her lips.

Her pulse skittered. "I know, and I really want that. I really want *you*. I need you."

"What are you saying? As a lover?"

She nodded. "And my best friend."

The longing, the dark want in his eyes made her breath catch. "You have to be sure."

"I am."

He searched her face, saying huskily, "I mean really sure. Don't start this if you're gonna stop."

"I'm not stopping. I'm ready."

He cupped her shoulders, his thumbs circling lightly on her flesh as he held her slightly away from him. "There's no going back, blue eyes. I can wait until you're as sure as I am."

"You told me what you want and now I finally know what I want. You and me, together."

"Positive?"

"Absolutely positive."

"Because right now I can probably stop myself, but later—"

She brushed her lips lightly against his to quiet him. Then she did it again, and this time she stayed. She moved her mouth over his, inviting him in. His long fingers cupped her jaw, held her steady while his tongue swept into her mouth. She could taste a slight hint of ginger ale, a mysterious flavor she remembered as all Clay's from their other kiss.

She felt his restraint, sensed a savage desire just beneath the surface, and her heart raced. She gripped his biceps, pulling away because the feel of him, the taste of him, was too intense for where they were.

She was glad to see his pulse beating as fast as hers. He looked a little dazed and a lot hungry. "Believe me now?"

In answer, he grabbed her hand and headed for the exit behind them.

Chapter 10

The next fifteen minutes were a blur. If Clay had any doubt about Shelby being ready, she put it to rest in the corridor of the hotel. And in his car. Every minute or so, she kissed him, looking as astonished as if she'd recovered something special she'd given up hope of ever finding. As they drove to his house, her mouth skated over his neck, the line of his jaw, teasing, torturing with every soft brush of her lips.

She curled her fingers lightly against the inside of his thigh and his hand covered hers. "I don't want you to stop, but if you don't, I'm not going to last long once we get home."

"I don't think I'm going to last long anyway." She nuzzled his neck, slipping her hand from under his to loosen his tie.

"Shelby."

"I'm just helping you." She bit lightly on a spot just below his ear, trailed her hot tongue along the cord of muscle that ran up his neck. "It'll save time later."

He braced himself against the rush of desire that shot

through him. His blood was already boiling, his body iron-hard at the thought of finally having her.

Grabbing her hand at his belt buckle, he nearly ran the car into the light pole at the end of his street. "Stop that."

Her tongue traced his ear. "How long has it been?"

"I don't know. Long," he growled. His brain had checked out about a minute ago. There was his house, less than a hundred feet away. He hit the remote and the garage door slid open. "Since Megan died. How long for you?"

"A little more than five years. Since before I kicked Ronnie out."

He would ask her about that. Distracted by her body-warmed scent, he decided it would be later.

Pulling the car into the garage and vaulting to the other side to grab her and haul her inside the house barely registered. He jabbed the button to close the garage, slammed the house door shut and made it only through the laundry room into the kitchen before he walked her into the wall, trapping her with his body.

He framed her face in his hands, kissed her long and deep and fierce. Even though he knew how she tasted, her sweet flavor kicked through his system as if it were the first time. She gave a low husky laugh, pulling his tie free and unbuttoning his dress shirt. Silvery moonlight filtered in through the kitchen blinds, enough so that he could see her eyes burn with the same want he felt.

He tried to calm the frantic pounding of his blood. Her light, peachy scent filled his lungs as he streaked his hands over her, wanting to touch everywhere at once. He kissed a path down her velvety neck, across her bare shoulder. "You look unbelievable in this dress."

She brought his mouth back to hers, pushing off his coat, her hands tangling with his as he undid his shoulder holster and slipped it free.

By the time he had the weapon safely set aside, she had

his shirt open and out of his pants. Her fingers mapped his chest, flexed in the hair there, moved to knead his shoulders. Sensation fired his nerve endings. Settling his hands on her waist, he kissed her again, murmuring against her lips, "Are we really doing this?"

"Oh, yeah." Her tongue stroked his as her palm moved down and her fingers closed over him. All his muscles went taut. She dragged her lips from his and kissed her way over his collarbone, burying her face in his chest. "You smell good."

"You smell good, you feel good, you taste good." The cool silk of her hair brushed his chin. Amazed at how soft she was, he coasted his hands down her arms, then covered her breasts.

"Oh!" She arched into him.

He grinned. "I've been wondering all night if you have on any underwear."

She gave him a mischievous smile that dared him to find out. Oh, he was going to. *And* he was going to find that tattoo. Impatiently, he reached behind her to open the catch of her dress. The bodice sagged low on the swell of her breasts, but didn't fall.

He couldn't wait to see her, to feel her. Trying to clamp down on a desperate need that had his hands shaking, Clay eased her bodice down, and when he saw her plump, perfect flesh, something inside him stilled. He cupped her, thumbing her taut nipples. "Look at you," he murmured.

"I want to look at you." She made quick work of his belt, then the zipper. When her hand slipped inside and closed around him, he squeezed his eyes shut, reaching for control. It didn't help that she made a soft sound of discovery, deepening the ache in his body.

His hand went to her right breast as he bent and took the other in his mouth. He tasted her, his tongue curling around her rosy puckered flesh. "I want to take you right here," he rasped.

"Here is good." After pushing off his pants and boxers, she lifted up to give him a hot fevered kiss, trailing her hands down his torso. She scored his belly with her fingernails and his muscles quivered.

He stroked a knuckle along the satiny length of her throat, sipping at her sweet flesh. Sliding a hand into her hair, he tugged her head back and gently bit the curve where her shoulder met her neck. She breathed his name with an urgency that had need shooting straight through him.

He had to have her, all of her. *Now*. Kissing his way down her body, he peeled away the dress inch by inch. Moonlight played across her skin, slipping through the shadow of his silhouette on her. Her hands delved into his hair, fingers curling against his scalp as she toed off her shoes.

This was going too fast. He didn't want it to be over, not yet, but his body was hurtling far ahead of his brain. Going to his knees, he jerked the coral gown past the flat of her stomach, his mouth racing over her smooth skin.

He dipped his tongue into her navel, and she trembled. "Oh, wow," she said raggedly.

He breathed her in, peach and woman and a hint of musk. His body throbbed, muscles coiling against release as he struggled to hold on a little longer.

Hooking his fingers into the fabric at her hips, he tugged down her dress and discovered a sheer ivory thong. He stifled a groan, then almost choked when he saw the tattoo. Just below the jut of her hip bone. His breath hissed out, and he nearly lost it right then.

Stripping the dress and underwear to the floor, he ran his hands up her thighs, over the taut whisper of muscle beneath her skin as she clutched at him. She was breathing hard, shifting restlessly. He gripped her hips, holding her steady as he flattened his tongue over the tiny fox tattoo that matched the one on his shoulder and sucked.

"Clay!" She twisted against his mouth, her voice husky and pleading. Her head went back against the wall, and she held on tight, her short nails digging into his flesh.

More. That one word was all he could think of. She was naked. She was here. She was his. He breathed in her delicate scent, trailed soft love bites low across her belly to the other hip as he entered her with one finger.

She shuddered around him and he felt her go limp. She clutched his shoulder hard, saying something, asking something, but he couldn't hear for the roar of blood in his ears. He caught her to him as she wilted to her knees.

"I can't believe how good this feels," he said huskily as her warm bare flesh met his. "How good *you* feel."

She locked her arms around his neck and found his mouth, eating at him with a greed that matched his. Her hands were trembling, moving from his face to his hair, gliding across his shoulders, pulling him closer.

He laid her back on the cool wood floor, his finger still deep inside her. She moved with each stroke of his hand, and he stared in awe at how beautiful she was in the mix of moonlight and shadow, her eyes bright with need.

"Now," she said brokenly, reaching down, urging him to her. "I need you."

Her firm hot touch had his vision blurring, a flash fire streaking across his skin. It was all he could do to get the words out, "I can't…go slow, Shelby."

"Good. Don't."

His senses swam with the subtle draw of her scent, the honey-dark taste of her, the knowledge that she was here with *him*.

He needed her in ways he never had before, in ways he knew he would need her from now on. Deeper than sex, deeper than friendship. There was no going back. Moving between her legs, he levered himself above her and brushed a kiss against her forehead. "Last chance to change your mind."

She pulled his head down to hers, kissed him wild and deep. The desire, the total surrender in her eyes gathered up his heart and put it in the palm of her hand. "Take me."

He was done. The words went straight to his gut, then lower. He slid inside her tight warmth and went dizzy for a second. He wanted to remember every breath, every sensation—the sleek way her body arched into his, the delicious agony of her breasts teasing his chest, her thighs cradling him—but he was on Fast Forward.

Surrounded by her tight, slick heat, he was dying and it was the best feeling he'd ever had. He couldn't hold back any longer. Sliding his arms under her, tilting her hips into his, he began to move. Something shifted in his chest and opened, as if he'd been suffocating and was finally able to breathe.

She seemed as desperate as he felt. Her strong hands were never still, skimming his shoulders, raking his back, his hips. She nipped at his neck, then his jaw, returning his fevered kisses, bending her knees so he could go deeper.

He heard her breath catch as her body tightened on his. Her arms locked around his neck. The sound of his name spilling raggedly from her shot him to the edge.

She pulsed around him, sleek and wet and hot. Keeping his gaze locked with hers, he held on, pummeled from the inside out by intense sensation as he stored away the memory of her face. Then she let go, and so did he. He could've sworn he saw tears in her eyes.

Hours later in the shower, Shelby couldn't stop smiling. They'd finally gotten to his bedroom and made love slowly, with the lights on. Then fallen asleep.

She'd woken a little bit ago, noting as she slipped out of

bed that it was nearly 5 a.m. Lying beside him, she'd felt so happy that her chest ached. It still did, a little.

As well as she knew Clay, there were things she hadn't known. Like how he would do anything she asked if she touched her tongue to a certain spot in the crease where his thigh met his groin. Like how his eyes darkened to jade when he was deep inside her. The memory caused a little shiver to skip up her spine.

There were things she hadn't known about herself, either, such as how she could melt with just one look from him. That had never happened. Not with Ronnie, not with anyone.

She rinsed the shampoo from her hair and reached for the soap. Her back was to the shower door when she heard it open. She blinked water out of her eyes, slicking back her wet hair.

Before she could turn around, Clay had covered her body from behind with the hard strength of his. He was naked and aroused, the taut sinewy lines of his body holding her in place.

He nuzzled her neck as his arms slid around her waist. "Good morning."

"Morning." She turned her head and met his kiss, tasting the same mint toothpaste she'd used. His mouth was hot and sleek, and need started a slow simmer inside her.

He drew away, his eyes dark with desire. She'd wondered if things would feel odd between them after this, but they didn't. Things felt wonderful. His hands slid up to cup her breasts, rub her nipples.

Her head fell back on his shoulder. "Did I wake you?"

"No," he rumbled lazily. "How long have you been up?"

"Maybe five minutes."

He kissed her shoulder, her neck, lingering on the super-sensitive spot below her ear that he'd discovered last night. "You okay?" he asked quietly.

"Oh, yes," she hummed in pleasure. "I'm good."

"I mean about this. About us."

She shifted slightly so she could look at him. He wanted to know if she was sorry, if she was thinking about running. Why was she surprised?

"No thoughts about backing off?"

"None." The realization that she could hurt him in that way sliced through her like a blade. She hated that her past would make him doubt one thing about them. To mask the sudden tears that sprang up, she narrowed her eyes and gave him a mock glare. "You?"

"No way."

"Good."

He kissed her ear, his thumb brushing against her temple. "You're not gonna cry, are you?"

"Maybe. Maybe not."

He sank his teeth into the curve where her neck met her shoulder, and heat shot straight to her center.

"Most definitely not. No crying."

Keeping one arm around her waist, he trailed his fingers down her torso and reached to link his hand with hers. He lifted her arm, kissing her knuckles, the pulse at her wrist, working his way up with featherlight touches. The sensation of warm water streaming down her body combined with the wet, soft heat of his mouth numbed her mind.

"Sorry I went so fast the first time."

The rasp of his voice in her ear sent a shiver through her. "I'm not."

"Really?"

"Really." Soap-scented steam rose around them, fogged the clear door of the shower. It would be so easy to forget everything except the two of them. She kissed the underside of his jaw. "I'm glad you didn't slow down last night. You were really lighting my fire."

He groaned. "You are so corny."

She laughed and he nipped her earlobe. His hands, deeply tanned next to her paler skin, skimmed the dip of her waist, bracketed her hips. "Every time last night was wonderful."

"I thought so, too." He pressed tight into her, hard and hot and throbbing at the base of her spine. "Especially since I was so out of practice."

"So you really haven't been with anyone since Megan died?"

"Not until you."

Absurdly pleased, she grinned.

He peered into her face. "You like that, huh?"

"Yes, I do." She curled a hand behind his neck and slid her fingers into his wet hair, massaging his scalp. "Why did you wait so long?"

"I wasn't interested at all until about three years after she died, then we lost Jason. That set me back for a while, but when I was ready, I didn't want sex that didn't mean anything." He smoothed a hand over her wet hair. "I'd been out of the dating scene for so long, I didn't really want to get back into it. It was hard enough the first time," he said sheepishly.

Sometimes Shelby forgot how shy he was with people he didn't know.

"What about you? Have you really not been with anyone since Ronnie?" He sounded skeptical. "You've seen a lot of guys since your divorce, blue eyes."

She gave him a look. "I was so angry and felt so gullible after what he pulled that I didn't want anyone touching me like that." She took one of Clay's big hands that had been stroking her hip and folded it over her breast. "I'm definitely past that."

He kissed her, deep and slow, but she felt a readiness in him, a leashed impatience when he lifted his head. "What made you change your mind about us?"

Her voice was husky, barely above a whisper as the water beat against the tile wall. "After you kissed me that first time, I kept imagining things."

"Things like this?"

"Yes, but never this good." She felt him smile against her neck. "But I knew for sure last night when I saw you with those other women. You could've gone home with one of them. I wanted you to go home with me."

She rested her head against his shoulder and watched him slide soapy hands over her breasts, cupping and kneading and holding her. "That feels incredible. I like that."

"I can see." His cheek brushed hers as he grazed an index finger over the swell of her breast and circled her taut nipple. "If this is a dream, don't wake me up."

She smiled at his words, her body tingling at the little sparks of arousal he set off everywhere he touched. "I thought our being together would feel strange, but it doesn't. Things are different, but better."

"Better how?"

She rubbed her cheek against his chin. "Like, I don't know, there's a whole new level to our relationship now."

"Mmm." He kissed her nape, traced a path to her ear with his tongue.

She reached back and ran her hands down his lean flanks. "Are you listening to me?"

"Mmm. I'm looking at you, too. And I like what I see." Holding her firmly to him with one palm flattened on her stomach, he grazed the damp heat between her legs, then cupped her, massaging her lightly.

She made a needy sound deep in her throat that hollowed out his gut. Being with Shelby was better than he'd imagined. Getting better all the time, he thought as she curled a hand around his straining flesh.

"Just think," she said huskily, following his rhythm as she

moved slowly against him. "If someone hadn't tried to kill me, we never would've gotten together."

"I think we would have." It felt as if all the pieces of his life finally fit, as if he understood why things had happened the way they had up until now.

This woman was familiar, but there was so much about her that was new. The hint of an intriguing scent behind her ear, the smooth curve of her breasts, the feel of her warm flesh had his blood churning violently. He couldn't get enough of her, didn't think he ever would.

Resting his chin on her shoulder, he saw the blush of arousal hue her breasts, her cheeks. His fingers slid over her firmly, repeatedly. Feeling her body tighten as she neared climax, he backed off.

He shifted her slightly so that water sluiced between them and rinsed away the soap. His instincts told him they hadn't made a mistake, but something niggled at him. Not Shelby. Not what they'd shared, but something.

He turned her, closing his hands on her waist and lifting her. She couldn't hold back a whimper as she sank down on him and wrapped her legs around his hips. This step they'd taken felt right, but it also felt overwhelming. She belonged to him, and the thought that this was too good to be true passed through her mind.

He braced her with one strong arm beneath her bottom, pulling her tighter into him as his other hand swept down her hip.

Sliding a palm around his nape, she drew him to her for a deep, languid kiss. Long moments later, his breathing as harsh as hers, he lifted his head and the tenderness on his face clutched at her heart. Why had she ever resisted him? Raw, savage need flared hotly in his eyes and restraint tightened his features. Her heart beat wildly with each stroke of his body into hers.

His muscles drew tight and she expected him to move faster. But he pinned her to the wall, moving slowly, drawing out every sensation until she was quivering. Until she could hardly think. Every brush of his mouth on her, every pulse of his body inside hers nudged her closer to the edge. She twined her arms tightly around his neck, giving herself over to the sleek friction of his skin against hers.

Staring into her eyes, he eased out of her, then started again. She couldn't catch her breath. Or tear her gaze from his deep green one. His arms corded from the strain of holding her. His body was rigid with the effort to check himself, to give to her without taking. The pure unselfishness of the moment seared itself on her heart and tears tightened her throat. She kissed him, wanting to feel every bit of him she could as the urgent pulses of her body throbbed heavier, deeper. When she broke apart, he went with her.

"Show-off," she murmured when she could breathe again.

Monday at work, Clay had the attention span of a six-year-old. He could hardly keep his mind on the case. The microwave explosion at Shelby's firehouse had been bugging Collier and the fire investigator wanted to see if Terra or Harris Vaughn, the previous fire investigator, had ever documented such a case.

So what Clay was doing was going over files and trying to pay attention. What he wanted to do was Shelby. He couldn't stop a grin. Couldn't stop thinking about her, tasting her, wanting her, and when Collier's new wife came into the F.I.'s office around one, Clay decided to give them some privacy and grab some lunch. At home.

Since Shelby had begun staying at his house, he'd shown up around noon a few times so his sister probably wouldn't think twice about it. Good thing she didn't know what he and Shelby had done Saturday night. And Sunday night—well, all day.

This morning, she had broached the subject of telling people about the shift in their relationship, and she wanted to tell her mom before they told anyone else. That was fine with Clay. He could wait to tell his family until she'd spoken to Paula.

Coming through the front door, he saw Brooke on the cordless phone in the living room. When she looked up, he asked, "Where's Shelby?"

His sister pointed to the laundry room, and Clay angled left across the kitchen past the large front window to the laundry room door that stood open.

She had her back to him, tossing wet clothes into the dryer. He glanced over his shoulder and saw that Brooke was looking out the patio door, not paying him any attention.

Shelby straightened and turned, her eyes lighting up. "Hey. I thought I heard you come in."

He grinned as he slipped into the tiny room and shut the door.

She arched a brow. "What are you doing?"

"I need some privacy. I'm here to check your temperature."

"What are you talking about?"

He backed her into the door that accessed the garage and braced an arm over her head, closing his hand on a fistful of her loose T-shirt. "This morning when I left, you were hot, hot, hot. Just checking to see if you need any fires put out."

"Oh, good grief." She groaned. "Don't ever call *me* corny again."

"Just thought I'd give you some of that hose dragger talk you like."

She laughed, color flushing her cheeks. Ever since M.B.'s murder, there had been shadows in her eyes; Clay was relieved to see some of the old light finally coming back into them.

He kissed her, tucking her tight against him when her arms

slid around his neck. After a long moment, he lifted his head and she gave a dreamy little sigh that hit his system like a shot of adrenaline.

"What have you been doing this morning?" She slid her hands over his shoulders, kneading and massaging. "I didn't know you were coming home for lunch."

He rubbed his lips over her fresh-smelling hair, nuzzled her temple. "I didn't know, either, until Kiley showed up in Collier's office. There was no doubt I was a third wheel. Newlyweds," he said with a mock growl. "I can tell when I'm not wanted."

"Good thing you came here, then." She hooked two fingers into a belt loop on the front of his jeans and lifted up to kiss him.

He filled himself up with her sweetness, one hand trailing down the satin column of her throat. Her pulse skittered beneath his touch and she moved against him in a way that had impatience firing his blood. He slipped his hand under the hem of her T-shirt.

Dipping just inside the waistband of her shorts, he skimmed his knuckles lightly back and forth across her fine-textured skin. She shifted so that one hip pressed against his growing arousal.

He shouldn't have started this, not when he couldn't finish it, but dang if he cared. Still he had to remember his sister was out there. He drew back to look at Shelby. "This is blowing my mind."

"Mine, too." She nuzzled the hollow of his throat.

"*You* blow my mind." He stroked a hand through her hair. "I've known you your whole life and sometimes when I see you, I can't even speak."

"Clay." She looked up, her eyes wide with surprise.

A flush heated his neck. "Dumb, huh?"

"Yeah." She wrapped her arms around him. "It's so dumb it makes me want to strip you down right now."

He laughed, meeting her kiss. She stiffened, which registered at the same time as his sister's voice.

"Hey, are y'all in here?" The door opened and Brooke peeked around it. "Why is this door closed—get out of here! No way!"

Hell. He lifted his head, Shelby laughing against him.

"Well, well. What are y'all doing?"

"Laundry," Shelby said with a straight face.

Brooke laughed and looked pointedly at Clay's hand inside the waist of Shelby's shorts. "Clay hasn't had his hands on that much laundry in his whole life." Her gaze shot from him to Shelby. "Are y'all together, *together*?"

Realizing all he would be getting now was lunch, Clay reluctantly dropped his hand. "Let Shelby tell her mom before you make some big announcement."

"Does this mean I know before Erin?"

"Before anyone."

"All right!" She looked from one to the other of them. "How long has this been going on?"

"Since Saturday night." As Shelby eased past him toward the other woman, she gave his waist a little squeeze.

He skimmed his hand over her bottom and she swatted at him.

"It's about time," his sister said as she walked toward the kitchen table.

Shelby laughed. "What are you talking about?"

"Yeah, what *are* you talking about?" He shut the laundry room door behind him.

"Dad and I have thought for years that you two should get together."

"No way!" Shelby glanced at Clay. "Did you know that?"

"No."

She looked at Brooke. "Why didn't anyone say anything?"

"Oh, like that would've done any good."

Grinning, he opened the fridge, reaching inside for some leftover pizza while Shelby made sure Brooke was all right with Clay and Shelby being a couple. Brooke was fine with it, just as Clay knew Erin and his dad would be.

He'd finished his second piece of pizza and was reaching for a glass of iced tea when his cell phone rang. It was Melanie Adams's mother, who said that her daughter needed to talk to him about Leticia Keane. Mrs. Adams asked if they could see him at the station. After arranging to meet in half an hour, he disconnected.

"Who was that?" Shelby asked. After Clay told her, she said, "Melanie's the girl who backed up Leticia's alibi for the night of M.B.'s murder?"

"Yes." He'd hoped to get his sister to leave him alone with Shelby for an hour or so, but now duty called. Shoving back his disappointment, he punched in Collier's office number and told the fire investigator to meet him at the PD.

"Do you think she'll have something helpful to say?" she asked when he hung up.

"I hope so."

Shelby followed him to the front door, hooking a hand into the back pocket of his jeans. "Wait."

He glanced back, seeing a flirty smile on her face. She gave his sister a look over her shoulder, and Brooke turned around, dramatically covering her eyes.

Shelby grinned, flattening a hand on his chest. "I'm going to Mom's in an hour or so. Come over for dinner when you're finished, all right?"

He nodded, one hand curving on her waist as he dipped his head. Her mouth opened under his and Clay had to force himself to keep the kiss light. "I'll call you after I talk to the Adams girl and let you know what's going on."

"Okay." Her gaze did a slow hike down his body, and every one of his nerve endings popped.

This morning, his concentration had been poor, to say the least. This afternoon, he'd be lucky if he could remember how to drive.

Chapter 11

An hour later, thanks to information provided by Melanie Adams, Clay and Collier were on their way to find Antonio Sandoval, the custodian at the school where M.B. worked. Clay did his best to keep his mind on what they'd learned and not Shelby. Pulling his thoughts from what had happened between them over the weekend, he focused on the information he and the fire investigator had gotten from Leticia Keane's friend.

According to Melanie, the Keane girl and Antonio Sandoval had been sleeping together for about three months.

Melanie had kept this from Clay when he interviewed her on Saturday because she didn't believe Leticia was guilty of anything, but when she had seen how upset Leticia was over Clay's last visit to her and her father, Melanie became afraid that her friend was hiding something more disturbing than her involvement with an older man. If that were true and Melanie had kept silent, she'd said she wouldn't be able to live with herself.

Clay and Collier reached the high school only to learn today was Sandoval's Monday off. When they couldn't find him at the school, at home or at his complex's laundromat, they decided to stake out his apartment.

After a couple of hours, the man pulled up in front of his complex. Clay radioed dispatch and requested that a black-and-white be sent to this location so they could transport a suspect. A few minutes later, he and Collier were knocking on Sandoval's door.

When he saw them, wariness skipped across the Latino's movie star features. "What do you want?"

"To talk to you about where you were the night of Ms. Perry's murder."

"I told you I was here, alone."

Melanie Adams had confirmed that Leticia had indeed come to her party that night and so had Sandoval. The pair had left together about ten minutes after Leticia's arrival. Clay shot Collier a look as he leaned a shoulder against the doorjamb. "It sure would help you if someone could back that up."

"There is no one," he said stiffly.

"No one?" Clay asked quietly as he and his partner moved into the apartment.

Sandoval's gaze darted between the two men as he grudgingly stepped back to allow them inside. "No one."

"Not even someone like a girlfriend?" Clay suggested.

"I don't have a…girlfriend."

"That's not what we're hearing," Collier said. "Word is, you're involved with Leticia."

"Leticia Keane?" The man's look of surprise was ruined by a flash of panic.

"Yeah," Clay said. "The girl you've been sleeping with for three months." He continued over the man's sputtering protest. "The girl you took back to Melanie's house in time for her to make it home by curfew. The girl you were seen with on the night of the murder."

"I wasn't with anyone! Whoever said I was is lying."

"We have an eyewitness who saw you leave Melanie Adams's birthday party and one who saw you return later. The times you were seen put you with Leticia about the time Ms. Perry was killed. And no one can verify where y'all were."

"That doesn't mean we—I—killed Ms. Perry."

"So you *were* with Leticia?" Clay pressed.

The man's body was rigid, poised for flight as his gaze darted to the door behind Clay. Clay moved to block the exit and Collier put himself to the guy's left so he couldn't run into one of the two bedrooms down the hall.

When Sandoval didn't answer, Clay fingered the handcuffs on his belt loop. "You do realize I can file charges against you for having sex with a minor?"

Which he'd already planned to do. Plus, having her boyfriend in jail might squeeze some information out of Ms. Keane. "If you're trying to protect Leticia, you should know she's already admitted that y'all are involved." Leticia hadn't, but Clay figured that, too, might convince the custodian to talk.

The man's pulse jumped hard in his neck. "She wouldn't do that."

Clay shrugged. "We can do this down at the station if you want."

Unmistakable fear streaked across the man's face. "All right. I was with her. But we were here! We came here from the party and stayed *here*. We didn't kill anyone! That's the truth."

Clay shook his head. "That's the thing, Antonio. You haven't told us the truth in the past so you don't have a good track record with us."

"I'll tell you everything, whatever you want to know." The

more agitated he became, the more pronounced was his Spanish accent.

"Why didn't you tell us this when we asked you the first time?"

"Her father is very strict. If he knew she was seeing me, things would be bad for her."

"Bad how? Would he hit her?" Clay asked sharply.

"No, not that. Just keeping her in the house all the time. Making her see some kind of head doctor."

Clay knew she was already doing that, and from what he'd seen she needed to be. "So tell us what you did the night of the murder."

"Leticia and I met at Melanie's house, then left and came here. We were here the whole time. I took her back there so she could drive home by her curfew."

"What time was her curfew?"

"Eleven o'clock."

"And only the two of you were here?"

"Yes."

"What did y'all do during that time?"

The man looked away, a flush tinging his burnished skin. Clay exchanged a look with Collier, who asked, "Was Leticia jealous of Ms. Perry?"

"Yes." Sandoval hesitated. "She thought there was something going on with me and the teacher."

"Was there?"

"No." He shook his head vehemently. "No."

"Did Leticia believe you?"

"I thought she did."

"But you're not sure?" Clay asked.

Sandoval looked as if he would deny it, then shook his head. "She was very jealous of anyone I saw when I wasn' with her, but she wouldn't hurt them. We went against her father's wishes to be together, but she—we didn't kill anyone."

"Until we know for sure, you'll have to come with us."

The man backed up a step. "I answered your questions!"

"The fact remains that you had sex with a minor. And until I get the full, straight story about you and her for the night of that murder, I don't want you going anywhere."

"Please." The man's voice was labored, and perspiration sheened on his face. "I've told you everything I know. I'll sign something. Just don't arrest me. I can't go to jail. I'll do whatever you want, but I can't go to jail."

Collier's eyes narrowed. "Been there before?"

"No!"

Clay knew that was true or Sandoval would've turned up in the system the first time his name had been run. But the fear in the other man's eyes told Clay the guy was definitely hiding something. What had him so spooked? Had he done something with Leticia besides sleep with her? Something like murder?

"I've done nothing. I shouldn't be taken to jail." His face was pasty beneath his dusky coloring.

Everything Clay had on Leticia was circumstantial. He didn't have enough to book her, and he didn't want to tip his hand. The last thing he needed was to spook the girl and risk having her run off. Arresting her boyfriend might compel them both to cooperate.

Clay cuffed him while reading him his rights and guided him out the door to the waiting patrol car. "Let's go."

After putting Sandoval in the back of the police cruiser and sending him to the station for booking, Clay and Collier climbed into Clay's truck.

Collier stared after the departing black-and-white. "Something's sure got him scared. Do you think it's ratting out the girlfriend? Or that they killed Ms. Perry?"

"I don't know. Their affair being discovered is a good motive for murder. If M.B. found out about them, she could get

Sandoval fired at the very least. If criminal charges were pressed, she could get him deported. And I imagine she could have disciplinary action brought against Leticia, too." He started the truck and wound his way out of the parking lot of the apartment complex. "Seems like Antonio really wanted to protect the girlfriend, but it didn't take much pressure for him to cave."

"Speaking of girlfriends," Collier said casually, "how are things with Shelby?"

Clay's head jerked toward the other man so fast he strained a muscle in his neck. "What?"

"Word's out you guys are together."

There was no way Brooke would've spread that news until he or Shelby had told her it was all right. He cleared his throat. "Who told you that?"

"Some people who saw you at the wedding reception."

"Some people?" He arched a brow. "Like your wife?"

"Well, Kiley noticed something was going on when we left." Laughter underlined Collier's words. "But it was really Terra and Jack Spencer who said you looked like more than friends."

Clay shrugged, unable to stop the grin that spread across his face.

His friend chuckled. "That look's a dead giveaway. Y'all trying to keep it a secret?"

"Not really. We just haven't told our families yet. It happened pretty recently."

"Like forty-eight hours ago?"

"Yeah." Clay laughed.

"I don't know what it is about murder in this town, but a lot of people sure hook up because of it."

Clay knew Collier was referring to himself and Kiley, and probably Jack and Terra Spencer, as well. All of them had worked together on arson-murder cases, then wound up married.

"Speaking of Shelby, I'd better call and bring her up to speed. She'll want to know about Sandoval."

He reached her at her mom's and told her what they'd learned about Antonio and Leticia, then said he'd be there for supper after he and Collier had filed supplemental reports on the interview and arrest.

"I told Mom about us," Shelby said in a husky half whisper that made his body tighten.

"What did she say?"

"She's excited."

He lowered his voice. "So am I."

She laughed. "I don't think she meant the same kind of excited."

"Probably not." Most definitely not, since Clay was thinking about getting Shelby naked and…doing stuff to her. "See ya in a little while."

"Okay."

He hung up, grinning like an idiot. Couldn't stop even when Collier ribbed him about it.

"I thought Clay was going to make it," Shelby's mom said as they cleaned up the supper dishes a couple of hours after he'd called.

They were in Paula's roomy kitchen, done in gray and white with a touch of dark blue and yellow.

"I told him we'd fix a plate and put it aside until he could get here." Shelby had told her mom about Antonio Sandoval and how his involvement with Leticia Keane had come to light. "After he arrested the custodian from the high school, he had something else come up in the investigation. That's why he called again just a bit ago."

"Something more on that man?"

"No, another suspect. Clay said he got a call from the secretary at the school where M.B. taught. Her gym bag was found in the locker room and inside was her day planner. M.B. was supposed to meet with the ex-wife of another of Clay's suspects, but she was killed the night before the meeting was scheduled to take place." Shelby took the last pot from her mom to dry it. "You can't tell anyone this stuff, Mom. If I weren't involved in the investigation, I wouldn't have this information."

"I know. I remember when you told me that before. My lips are sealed, but I do think I should get to know what's happening or if there's progress. You *were* nearly killed, Shelby Marie."

"I know." She squeezed her mom's hand, then dropped the dish towel onto the counter as she bent to return the pot to its place in the cabinet below.

"What about Vince? Has he accepted that things are over between the two of you?"

"Yes. Well, I think so." Shelby had told her mom about the incident at the Fire Investigator's Office. "Clay paid him a visit, and Vince hasn't bothered me again."

"Does Clay consider him a suspect?"

She nodded. "Vince may have been having an affair with M.B., and the fact that he was with me at the firehouse just before the microwave exploded makes Clay want to keep an eye on him. But I don't know if Clay views him as being as strong a suspect as the man he's talking to right now." She explained to her mom about Mac Hayward and what he'd done at a school-sponsored function in Dallas, the abruptness with which he'd stopped going on M.B.'s science club trips.

"So Clay thinks M.B. was going to tell Mrs. Hayward how her ex-husband got drunk and basically lost those high school kids in Dallas?"

"That's what he's trying to find out. Keeping M.B. quiet about that is a strong motive for murder since there's a good chance that kind of information could've caused Hayward to lose joint custody of his daughters. I'm sure Clay will talk to him as well as his twin daughters."

"I can't believe we're having a conversation about people getting murdered, my daughter nearly being one of them."

"I know, Mom, but Clay's taken good care of me. Pretty soon this will be over."

"When do you think that will be?"

"I don't know, but I hope soon. I'm ready to go back to work."

Her mom leaned back against the opposite gray-speckled countertop, studying her. "How are you feeling?"

"Physically, I'm fine. I haven't had the headache in a couple of days, and my wrist only hurts occasionally. The thing that really bugs me is that I haven't remembered anything else about that night besides smelling the hair spray and falling over the railing."

"What if you never do?"

"Clay asked me that, too." She gnawed on the pad of her thumb. "He says we'll deal with it, but he's not the one with a big black hole in his memory."

"Can you live with it if you're never able to recall anything else from that night?"

"I don't know. I guess I'll have to."

"Will your lost memories affect the case in a negative way?"

"He says no. He has to be able to *prove* guilt and that isn't dependent on whether I remember or not. But if I did remember something, it might lead him to the evidence he needs. I spoke to Captain Oliver about seeing a hypnotherapist. If it works and Clay's able to learn something helpful from me, it won't be admissible in court. Still, I'm hoping hypnosis might jog something loose in my head."

"After the case is closed, what will you two do? As a couple?"

"We haven't made any plans. It's still kinda new, Mom."

"I know." Paula's gaze searched hers. "So it feels right being with him?"

"Yes, just like you said it would."

Her mom stepped over to hug her. "I think it's great—"

A series of loud pops sounded outside in front of the house. Shelby and Paula both jumped, then hurried to the front door. Dusk had settled. From here, they could see only the glow of a porch light across the street and the other houses down the block. They moved outside and stepped off the porch.

Across the street and four houses down, fire shot out of one of the large city garbage cans left out by a neighbor for to-day's trash pickup. The flames were high, orange with a dark brown cast, and still contained. There was another crackling explosion, and something popped inside the can.

Several neighbors started toward the heavy plastic container, their excited voices swelling. A masculine voice hollered for someone to call 911.

"It's Faye Quillen's house!" Shelby yelled to her mom as she turned back toward the garage. "I'll get the fire extinguisher. You go check on her!"

The elderly woman had poor vision and could barely get around without assistance. Her granddaughter stayed with her, but sometimes worked late. Which probably explained why the trash can still sat at the curb. Shelby punched in the code on Paula's garage door keypad. As soon as the door lifted enough for her to duck underneath, she sprinted to the back of the garage and yanked the extinguisher from the wall.

She'd automatically grabbed with her right hand, and her injured wrist twinged painfully. As she ran down the driveway, she shifted the canister to her other hand. More neighbors poured into the street, some going to help her mom. Mr. Lancaster, from two doors down, had his fire extinguisher and was racing toward the trash fire, as well. In the distance but growing louder, she could hear the wail of sirens.

Shelby reached the end of her mom's driveway. She didn't see the little boy on the bicycle until he shot into her path from the left. They both cried out, startled.

She jumped. He wrenched the handle bars in an effort to avoid hitting her. The bike veered sharply and crashed, slamming the kid to the concrete. "Ouch!"

Throwing a quick glance toward the fire, Shelby knelt next to the cycle so she could see the child. "Are you okay?"

"Yeah. Just my elbow's scraped. And my bike—aw, man."

"Let me see your elbow real quick."

He angled his arm toward her. In the hazy light, it looked like a good-sized scrape. As she leaned in for a better look, she felt a prickle down the center of her scalp. Like a too strong electrical pulse, or someone trying to yank a couple of hairs from her head. Goose bumps rose on her skin and she jerked around, but saw nothing.

"I'm sorry," the boy mumbled. "I didn't see you until it was too late."

"It's all right. I didn't see you, either." Adrenaline pumping through her, she held the bike so he could get up. "Be sure and wash that with soap and water. Have your mom put on some antibacterial cream and a bandage."

He nodded, standing. She straightened, gripping the extinguisher and glancing down the street. Something exploded in the can and Mr. Lancaster backed away from the fire. The sound of screaming sirens grew louder.

Another boy, maybe two years older than the one on the bike, and a woman with short dark hair rushed toward them. "Derek!" She hugged the injured boy to her. "Are you okay?"

"Yeah."

The woman looked at Shelby. "Are you?"

"Yes, I'm fine." Her heart was still racing.

"I'm so sorry. Derek, did you apologize?"

"He did." Shelby smiled. "It was an accident."

Paula rushed up, panting slightly. "Is everyone all right?"

"I think so." Shelby turned as she heard the push of air brakes, the sharp screech as the emergency vehicles stopped. A ladder truck and rescue truck from Station House One. "Is Mrs. Quillen okay?"

"Mrs. Lancaster got her out of the house and over to theirs. She seems to be fine."

"Looks like the fire is contained," Shelby murmured, her heart rate slowing enough to process the questions crowding in. There was a chance that fire could've started by spontaneous combustion, but most likely someone had started it. Why? Kids pulling a prank?

The young mother touched Shelby's arm, drawing her attention. "Thank you again."

"You're welcome." She smiled at the little boy. "Take care of that arm, Derek."

"Okay."

As the woman and two children walked away, Shelby looked over her shoulder toward her mom's house. What had grazed her head minutes ago? It hadn't been flying debris from the trash can. Even if the fire had shot something into the air, it wouldn't travel this far.

Gripping the extinguisher, Shelby's gaze skimmed her mother's concrete drive, the neatly trimmed grass, the garage. Her gaze caught on the side trim of the garage door. What was sticking out of the wood about two feet above the base?

She retraced her steps until she was close enough to see through the hazy light.

Paula moved with her, staring at the same spot Shelby was. "What is that?"

Shelby shook her head. Even when she identified the object, it didn't register at first. In the wood trim framing her mother's garage door was…an arrow.

Who would have a bow and arrow? And why would they have it in a neighborhood?

"Is that an arrow?" Her mom sounded as incredulous as Shelby felt.

"Yeah."

"How dangerous! That could've killed someone." Paula reached for it.

"No, Mom. Don't touch it." The arrow was what Shelby had felt skim the top of her head. She *knew* it. A chill rippled down her spine as she realized how narrowly she and the little boy had escaped.

One of them really could've been killed. She suddenly realized the implications, and her stomach turned over.

The explosion, the trash can fire had been diversions. Any noise that might've been made by the weapon had been drowned by the sounds of excited residents and rescue vehicles.

Her legs wobbled, and she sagged back against the brick of the house. The voices of milling neighbors and the rescue personnel canvassing the area faded. She didn't think she was being paranoid. She was pretty sure someone had just tried to kill her.

Again.

Clay was leaving Mac Hayward's office when his cell phone rang. Of course, the man denied knowing anything about the appointment his ex-wife had scheduled with the murder victim. An appointment that could've cost Hayward his daughters.

Clay answered his phone. "Jessup."

"It's Jack Spencer." The homicide cop's words were clipped. "Something's happened to Shelby."

Clay didn't remember the drive to Paula's house. His whole body shut down; he felt cold. Fear sheared him straight to the bone. Someone had made another attempt on Shelby's life.

He parked behind the police cruiser blocking off the street where Paula lived and jumped out, flashing his badge as he ducked under the yellow crime scene tape cordoning off the area. He took off at a dead run.

Jack had said she was fine, but Clay had to see her. His chest still ached from the jolt to his heart caused by his friend's call. Neighbors congregated in the street, on the sidewalk and curb. Paula's front yard was empty.

Robin Daly, the detective who'd been called to the scene, was especially good at her job. She would've gotten Shelby inside, out of view, especially since Jack had relayed to Clay that he'd told Robin about the previous murder attempts.

Clay reached Paula's front door and yanked it open, rushing inside. Coming to a stop at the edge of the living room, his gaze skipped over a couple of male firefighters, a patrol officer and a few civilians who were probably neighbors. There were too damn many people in here.

Shelby sat on the couch, her mother on one side and Robin, taking notes, on the other.

She was pale, but calm until she saw him. Then tears started rolling down her face. His gut knotted. He hadn't taken two steps before she was in his arms, holding on tight. He held her to him, squeezing his eyes shut as he backed into the wall for support.

He focused on the rise and fall of her chest against his, the heat of her breath through his shirt. She was okay. He tried to draw in air around a sharp, hard lump in his chest. After a minute, he opened his eyes.

"How did you know?" Shelby pulled back slightly to look up at him, her lashes spiky with tears, her eyes deep blue.

He framed her face with shaking hands and thumbed away her tears. "Robin was with Jack and Terra when she got the call from dispatch. Jack called me."

"Mom called 911," she said in a too calm voice.

Shock, Clay recognized. He pressed her head to his chest, tightening his arms around her.

"I'm okay," she whispered.

"What happened?"

"Mom and I heard some popping noises. We ran outside and saw flames coming out of Mrs. Quillen's trash can. I went into the garage for the fire extinguisher while Mom went to check on her. When I came out, a little boy on a bike and I crashed into each other. I bent down to help him and when I did, something grazed my head."

"An arrow," Robin Daly said quietly over his shoulder.

He half turned, keeping Shelby against him. "That's what Jack said."

The brunette detective nodded. "It's shorter than an arrow for a traditional bow. That makes me think it's a crossbow arrow."

Crossbow? Quiet, powerful, deadly. Clay thought his jaw might snap as he asked, "Any chance it could've been an accident?"

"There's always a chance, but that's not what my gut says," Shelby said quietly.

"Mine, either." He was still frozen inside.

"I'm finished with you, Shelby." The other woman squeezed Shelby's shoulder. "I'm afraid whoever shot that thing is long gone, but I'm going to canvass the area again, then interview the neighbors and after that I'll see if I can find someone who owns a crossbow."

"This is too bizarre." Sliding one hand beneath Shelby's hair, Clay brushed his thumb back and forth on her nape. "I have a few people to check out on my own. Plus, I want to read up on the state regulations. I don't think Oklahoma is-

sues crossbow permits anymore except to someone with a disability that prohibits them from shooting a longbow. Of
course, the shooter might not have a permit at all."

"Keep me posted," Robin said. "I'll do the same."

"I'm going to canvass with you."

Shelby looked a little surprised, but Robin just nodded. A
stillness came over Clay. As he and Robin had talked, the fear
that Shelby could've been killed hadn't subsided, but it had
been overtaken by something hard, something searingly hot
that he couldn't define at first.

As Robin walked away and Shelby pressed tighter into
him, he realized he was furious. At himself. "You shouldn't
have even been here."

"I was safe until I went outside."

"I called Collier after I heard about this." Clay tried to keep
the harshness from his tone. None of this was *her* fault. "I
want him to go through that fire debris. This has to be related
to M.B.'s murder."

Shelby nodded.

His blood was cooling now, his thoughts becoming clearer.
Crystal clear. The call out of nowhere that Shelby had nearly
been killed had jerked him back to reality with the brutal sting
of an ice bath.

He'd been so wrapped up in her, in *them*. Why hadn't he
realized it before now?

"I should've moved you to a safe house a long time ago."
If he'd been thinking like a cop instead of a man who wanted
her, this wouldn't have happened.

She'd nearly been killed, and it had been because of him.

Chapter 12

By the time Clay stepped back inside her mom's house an hour later, Shelby had stopped trembling. But beneath the fatigue that pulled at her, she still felt the pulse of fear. She'd never been so afraid because of something that *hadn't* happened. All she wanted was for Clay to take her home.

"No one saw anyone suspicious, no unfamiliar vehicles." He came to the foot of the couch where she and Paula sat. His voice was quiet, steady with a thread of steel. "There were no footprints, no sign of the weapon. And no one heard anything."

Shelby shifted so she could see his face. "Do crossbows make a noise?"

"Probably a loud cocking sound or something, but it probably would've been drowned out by all the excited neighbors."

"From the angle that arrow came at me, the shooter was probably hidden between two houses." She rose from the couch and took a couple of steps closer to him. Her mom also stood.

Clay's face was hard, and there was a cold fire in his eyes she'd never seen. It made her uneasy. "Yeah, and after the shot, they took off in the opposite direction of the neighborhood. They probably had some means of transportation stashed within a few blocks. Collier's out there now. He found fire crackers and some aerosol cans. From the noise you and the others described, he thinks those were full of some liquid and we both think it was hair spray.

"Rags and paper in the bottom were ignited and once the fire was hot enough to melt the spray tip, the aerosol cans exploded. There was also a melted plastic bottle. He has several tests to run, but judging by the fast spread of the fire, he thinks there may have been gasoline in the bottle. That would speed the fire along and also contribute to the popping noise y'all heard."

"So this *was* related to M.B.'s murder," she murmured, her legs going weak. She'd known it, but she had hoped to be wrong.

"Looks that way. Collier will check everything for fingerprints. I'm taking the arrow to the police lab and see if they come up with anything. Mac Hayward was with me when it happened, so that clears him from being at the scene." Clay dragged a hand down his face, looking haggard and worn. Distant. "And since Sandoval was in jail at the time, we know it wasn't him. But we don't know about Leticia. Or Tyner."

"Did Detective Daly go interview Vince?"

"I'll do it. She's still talking to the neighbors." Clay's sandy hair was disheveled, his voice all business. He was in full cop mode, closed off from her. And still furious on her behalf. "Robin's getting her things together. I'm moving you to a safe house and she'll be the one to take you."

"That's a good idea," Paula said. "Should I go, too?"

"I think you'll be fine here, but if you want to go, you can." Something about this plan niggled at Shelby. She didn't mind her mom going, so what was bugging her? "If you stay with me, Mom, you won't be able to go to the store until this is over."

Paula looked as if she hadn't considered that.

"Clay will be there." Shelby noticed that he stiffened at her words. "I'll be fine."

Her mom nodded, her gaze searching Clay's face. "She'd be okay without me?"

"Yes."

A puzzling heaviness settled over Shelby. He would hardly look at her. When he did, it was as if he were analyzing her. She wanted him to hold her. Instead, he still stood more than a foot away. He hadn't touched her at all. She rubbed at her tired eyes. "I'll need to get some things when we get to your house."

He shook his head. "You can tell Brooke or Erin what you need. You can't go back there."

"All right," she said slowly. This felt wrong. What was going on with him?

He looked away, pinching the bridge of his nose as he jammed one hand into his front slacks pocket. "I won't be coming out there. Whoever is trying to kill you knows you've been with me. I'm not leading them to you."

"You mean you won't be there at all? Not even at night?"

"No. I won't see you until I catch this slimeball."

Panic flared, and Shelby fought to think around it. Something was going on here. Something she didn't understand, something that had her stomach shriveling into a knot.

She realized then that he'd been careful not to get near her since he'd walked in. His eyes were still flat, but twice she had caught a flash of turmoil in the green depths.

Shelby felt Paula's gaze move from Clay to her. She glanced over and her mom pointed into the other room, indicating she was leaving to give them some privacy.

Shelby nodded.

"This never should've happened," he said in a rusty voice. "I'm sorry."

Paula laid a hand on his arm. "If it weren't for you, she could be dead. Thank you."

At the older woman's words, the look on his face changed to one of…guilt? Then disappeared. Unease that had nothing to do with the attempt on her life and everything to do with the man in front of her shimmered across Shelby's nerves. She knew that blank expression. She knew his core-deep sense of responsibility. "This wasn't your fault."

"Yes, it was." The look he gave her was so full of self-loathing that her heart twisted. "What you needed, *who* you needed, was someone who didn't share a history with you."

"What are you talking about? You're turning my case over to someone else?"

"No." His voice was hard, resolute. It hadn't softened at all since he'd walked inside. His demeanor had grown more remote, more tense.

"This is about more than sending me to a safe house." She fought back a surge of dread. "What's going on?"

"I can't get past the fact that I'm the one who put you in danger, and it was because I was thinking with the wrong body part." The scorn in his voice was aimed at himself and started a drum of apprehension inside her.

"The wrong body part?" She stilled. Surely he didn't be-lieve— "Do you mean because we slept together? We both agreed that was right, that we were ready."

"Obviously I wasn't thinking clearly. If I hadn't crossed that line, you wouldn't have nearly been killed tonight."

The relief he felt that she was all right was strong. But the anger that someone had tried again to kill her had turned into steely determination. He was still reeling, so scared that his chest hurt. "No one's going to hurt you ever again."

He hadn't been able to do anything for Jason, but he could, and would, protect Shelby. The way he should have all along.

The exact thing he'd been trying to do was the thing that had nearly gotten her killed. The realization that his feelings for her had compromised his judgment had hit him like a bullet to the chest. "I told myself I was protecting you when what I wanted was to have you with me. If I hadn't been screwing around, literally, none of this would've happened."

She drew in a sharp breath, took a halting step toward him. "What are you saying? That you think it was a mistake for us to sleep together?"

He didn't want to believe it, didn't want to say it.

"You do." The raw pain in her blue eyes, in her voice ripped at him. "You don't mean that!"

But he did. He had to. Feelings had no place in this now. Not anymore. It tore him up inside, but sleeping with her had been the worst thing he could have done. All he could see was her lying dead. Because of him. Cold sweat prickled his nape. "If I'd been thinking like a cop, *doing my job*, this wouldn't have happened." As he spoke, guilt closed around his throat like a choker. "And the reason I wasn't thinking straight is because I crossed a line with you that I shouldn't have crossed."

"Stop talking about me, about *us* as if we're some kind of rule you broke. You weren't the only one there, you know," she said hotly. "We both made the decision. At least, I thought we did. You're blaming yourself, but I don't know why."

Could she really not see? He couldn't let her talk him out of it. Where she was concerned, he had no objectivity and he was rarely able to refuse her. But this time he had to. He carried her brother's death on his conscious like a stone. He was *not* going to let her die, too. "All I care about right now is saving your life, and this is the only way I know how to do that."

Alarms rang in her head. His eyes were so tortured. She hadn't seen such sadness, such loss, since Jason's funeral. "*What's* the only way?"

"For us not to be together."

No, no. no. He didn't mean forever. He couldn't. The *cop* was here now, not the man. Okay, she could deal with that. "I understand that you want to put me somewhere safe and that you probably can't see me or talk to me until you catch the killer, but it sounds like you're saying you don't want to be with me. That you don't want *us*."

He closed his eyes briefly, as if he were steeling himself for a blow. "It's not you. It's me."

Was he breaking things off with her? He was! The air jammed painfully in her lungs. She tried not to panic, tried not to scream at him. "Clay, it's the responsibility you feel for me. That's why you're taking this so hard, but I'm fine."

"Dammit, Shelby, I pushed Jason into going climbing that day, and he wound up dead. I pushed you into bed with me and…" His voice hitched on the image of her lying dead in the street with an arrow through her.

"You didn't push me!" She moved closer, her heart constricting painfully when he stepped away. "You didn't *make* Jason go climbing."

"I don't want to hurt you." Emotion flared in his eyes. "But we have to be honest with each other."

"I know you think that's what you're doing, but—"

"You were nearly killed tonight *again* because of the decisions I made. Decisions that should've been made by my staying clear, objective. Separate."

Pain flooded her. "Do you think our making love was a mistake?"

He hesitated so long that she knew the answer. "I lost focus."

The room closed in on her. It was an effort to keep her voice calm, an effort to force out the words. "You're no more responsible for what happened to me tonight than you were for what happened to Jason."

His jaw set and for a split second, his eyes were savage. "I couldn't do anything to help him, but I *can* protect you and that's what I'm going to do."

"Not like this."

"You're going to the safe house."

No discussion, no argument. "It would be stupid of me not to, but don't push me away. Don't turn away. Don't blame yourself for this, Clay."

"I nearly got you killed tonight!" he yelled.

Shelby froze, her mind racing, her heartbeat thundering. He *never* yelled.

"If you'd been anyone else I was supposed to protect, I would've put you somewhere safe with an officer who wasn't emotionally involved."

"But I didn't want someone else. I wanted you."

"That was a mistake," he said tightly. "It was from the first, but I didn't want to admit it."

"It wasn't!" Apprehension drilled through her.

Stay calm. She was afraid that he truly believed their making love had been a mistake. She would never look at what they'd done as a mistake. They could get through this. "You're afraid for me after what happened tonight. I'm afraid, too. But breaking things off between us isn't the way to deal with it."

"We never should've gotten involved that way."

The words cut deep. She knew how strongly he felt responsibility. Hadn't she told herself when this all began that responsibility was the reason his feelings for her had started to change? She knew her close call tonight was hard on him. Why couldn't he see that none of this was his fault? That it was only because of him that she *wasn't* dead.

A new fear sprang up. Did he think their making love was a

mistake because it had made him lose objectivity on her case? Or because he had regrets about her? About *them*? She could find no answer in his eyes, the stone-cold mask that was his face.

She ached clear to her bones. "How can you just turn your back on what we started?"

"Because if I don't, you'll likely end up dead." There was no inflection in his voice, but his eyes flared hotly. "I can't survive that, Shelby."

"Do you think you can go back to being just friends?" Her voice cracked. "Because I can't."

"Even if it means you stay alive?" he asked harshly.

She choked back a sob at the blame she saw in his eyes. "Even if."

"Maybe you're strong enough to handle something happening to you, but I'm not. Do you know how selfish, how stupid it would be of me to stay involved with you and *hope* you don't get killed? If that happened, I'd eat my gun."

"Clay—"

"I'll do whatever I have to in order to keep you safe."

"Not this!"

"I can't lose another person I love. Not when there's something I can do to prevent it."

"This isn't the answer."

"Why can't you see it's the only one?"

Tears blurred her vision; she wasn't sure if they were from anger or hurt. She only knew that she'd never felt such a hollowness in her chest. And that's when she realized it.

She didn't just love him. She was *in love* with him. "I can't believe this! After how long it took me to see what was right in front of me, after how long it took you, and now you're saying it was a mistake?"

She was hurt. He understood and he hated himself for it. But he couldn't change his mind. He couldn't let himself feel anything right now. As painful as it would be not to have all of her, that was still better than taking the all-too-real chance that she'd be killed, that he'd lose her forever. He had to remember that. "I'm not trying to hurt you, Shelby. This really is best."

"There's no way *that* can be true."

"I think our friendship can survive this."

"Do you?" She bit her lip to keep from sobbing. He broke her heart. "Because I'm not so sure."

His eyes darkened and his mouth tightened, but he said nothing. The doorbell rang, and she jumped.

He glanced over his shoulder. "That'll be Robin. Are you ready?"

Her fists were clenched at her sides. "I've never been so mad at you in my life!"

"I'd rather you be mad than dead," he said quietly.

The pain, the anger nearly choked her. She swiped roughly at the tears on her cheeks. As she watched him walk to the door, she felt as empty as she had the day Jason had died.

The next day just after lunch, Shelby's nerves were still as raw as they had been when she'd said goodbye to Clay last night. And the headache that had plagued her on and off since the night of the murder throbbed at the base of her skull.

She stood inside the kitchen door of the old farmhouse serving as a safe house. On the outskirts of Presley, the decades-old home had been kept in good repair. Sunlight streamed through a window over the sink, making the pale yellow room with white trim feel cozy. She didn't feel cozy. She felt angry. Lost. Hurt.

Since arriving here with Robin Daly, Shelby hadn't been able to get Clay's words out of her head.

I lost focus. Crossed a line. Mistake, mistake, mistake.

How long had she fought sleeping with him? Why hadn't she kept fighting?

"All right, I'll tell her." The female detective was across the room on her cell phone. "Well, I think she's still rattled from that close call last night, but she's holding up fine."

So, Robin was talking to Clay. Shelby wanted to stomp over there, grab the phone and yell at him. She felt like the biggest idiot on Planet Stupid. She *was* the biggest idiot.

Hadn't she told herself that getting romantically involved with him was a bad idea? That it would change everything for the worse? She'd *known* it was a huge mistake to let their relationship shift that way. Now Clay wanted to go back to being just friends. Friends!

She'd fallen in love with him, and she wanted him to be in love with her. But he wasn't. Things could never be the same between them again. They might still be friends, but she would always see him as her lover, always *want* him as her lover, and she would never feel as comfortable around him as she once had.

Just the thought of seeing him every day, having to act as if she didn't want more than friendship from him, sent a sharp searing pain through her chest.

They'd never dealt with anything like this before. Oh, Shelby knew he wasn't turning his back on her, but it felt as if he were. In his mind, he was doing what needed to be done, what he *had* to do. What a *friend* would do. Recognizing that only sharpened the hurt pulsing through her.

Robin hung up her phone, her gray-blue gaze steady.

"I gather that was Clay." Amazed that she could sound so calm with her throat closing up, Shelby leaned against the door frame. She wanted to pound the wall. Or him.

The other woman nodded. "He and McClain just found out something that makes Leticia Keane and her boyfriend prime suspects."

"Am I allowed to know what that is?" Shelby realized her words were sharp and chided herself. None of this was Robin's fault. "Sorry."

The petite detective waved away the apology as she moved over to sit in one of the old wooden chairs at the well-used kitchen table. "After Antonio Sandoval was arrested, the fingerprint tech entered his prints into the system. They don't match the ones already on file."

"Don't match?" Shelby straightened, hope flaring. "He was already in the system? Is he wanted for something?"

"No. At least, not the *real* Antonio Sandoval. His prints were taken when he applied for his work visa into the country. The guy whom Jessup arrested, the guy who worked at the victim's school, is actually named Antonio Perez."

"Perez? How did he get Sandoval's visa and why does Clay think that makes him and Leticia the top suspects?" She took a chair across from the other woman, trying to focus on the information, not the pain caused by the mention of Clay's name.

"Jessup and McClain are checking into how Perez got the visa. Whether it was obtained by foul play or not, he's still here illegally. That's enough to get him deported. If Ms. Perry found out—"

"She could've turned him in to INS and had him sent back to Mexico or wherever he's really from."

"Right." Robin tucked her shoulder-length brown hair behind her ear. "He probably would've served some time in prison, not to mention going on the U.S. national watch list and losing a good-paying, steady job. Leticia Keane would've lost her lover. From what Jessup has told me about this girl, it sounds like she wants to keep whatever or whoever she considers hers. I'd say that's motive to kill your friend."

Shelby tried to envision that night at M.B.'s. Had Leticia and Antonio been the ones she'd seen hurt M.B.? Kill her? Had one of them pushed Shelby over the railing? She tried to call up a memory that placed the high school girl and her lover in M.B.'s bedroom. All she got were fluid shadows, black empty spots, a sense that something tangible was out of reach. "So, are Clay and Collier going to arrest Leticia?"

"They're talking to her now. What they find out will determine if they can arrest her. At this point, they don't have enough."

Shelby recalled Clay saying that Mac Hayward had an alibi for the time of yesterday's attempt on her life, but what about her ex-boyfriend? "Did Clay say anything about Vince Tyner?"

"That he has no alibi for the time of the attempt on you yesterday. But Jessup hasn't been able to find a crossbow permit issued in Tyner's name or any of the other suspects. Oklahoma only issues permits to people with a disability that prohibits them from using a traditional bow. There are less than thirty people in the state with permits, and none of them have a connection to Ms. Perry or you. Or any of the suspects."

"So now what?"

"Whoever's using that crossbow obtained it illegally. It may even be stolen."

"Which means the chances of finding out who has it are slim to none." A chill skittered up Shelby's spine. "I hope it doesn't turn out to be Vince. I dated him. That will freak me out."

"It would freak me out, too."

Shelby was so ready to get out of this house, out of this whole situation. She didn't have a problem with Clay hiding her. Or even staying away from her until M.B.'s murderer was caught. She did have a problem with him breaking up with her. Pushing her away. Going back to being only friends. He'd said they could have it all, and now that was what she wanted. But he didn't.

She couldn't force him to change his mind. And she certainly couldn't tell him that she'd fallen in love with him. He'd blame himself for that, too.

Under other circumstances, she would find this white frame house, shaded by large oak trees, charming and peaceful. But there had been no peace since she'd arrived. The sixteen hours she'd been here felt like a year.

Her cell phone rang and Shelby slipped it out of her jeans pocket, staring at the familiar number for a moment before registering that it was her boss.

She answered, aware of Robin's attention on her. "Hey, Captain."

"Fox, I've been trying to call you all morning."

She frowned. "My phone was on, Cap, but it never rang."

"I heard from three people this morning that you were nearly killed last night. What the hell happened?"

Shelby explained. "I'm okay. Just ready for this to be over."

"So am I," he said gruffly.

Shelby's heart squeezed at the emotion behind his words. Rick Oliver had always been more than a great boss. He'd been her friend and one of the few men who'd given her a fair chance to prove herself when she'd started at his station house.

"The paperwork for you to see that hypnotherapist is ready for you to sign. Where should I bring it?"

"I need to meet you somewhere. I've been put in protective custody, so the detective assigned to my case will have to bring me."

"Is this because of last night?" he asked in surprise.

"Yes."

"Jessup isn't with you anymore?"

"No."

"You still want to see this shrink?"

"Oh, yes. The sooner I can do the hypnosis, the better. Especially after yesterday. If I remember something, Clay can find the murderer and my life can get back to normal." Although after everything that had happened with Clay, Shelby didn't know what *normal* was anymore.

"Right. Well, then, meet me at Keller Plaza in about an hour. It's that new office building off Keller and Fourth. I'm on my days off and I'm doing the final inspection before anyone moves in."

"Let me make sure Detective Daly is okay with this."

"I'll hang on."

Shelby covered the phone and explained to Robin what was going on. The other woman nodded. "Jessup told me you were trying to see the shrink. Tell your boss we can be there."

After arranging to meet Rick, Shelby hung up. She wanted this to be over *now*. Not just because of the threat to her life, but because she also needed some space from Clay. She wished she had never given in to the temptation to sleep with him. She'd screwed up the best friendship she'd ever had.

Maybe when she saw the hypnotherapist, she would ask him how in the hell she was supposed to go back to being friends with someone she'd fallen in love with?

Clay wanted distance. She'd give him distance. But be only friends? She didn't know if she could. It hurt too much.

Clay hadn't had the dream about Jason's death in more than two years, but he'd had it last night. His friend had fallen off the mountainside. Clay had finally gotten to him, tried to find a pulse, lightly slapped his face in an effort to rouse him. Except last night that face hadn't belonged to Jason; it had belonged to Shelby.

Clay dragged a hand across his gritty eyes. He had missed her like hell last night. His whole body ached with it. And when he thought about being without her every night, he realized what he'd done.

The mistake hadn't been their sleeping together. It had

been *when* they'd slept together. The timing was wrong, but *they* weren't.

His brain cells must've started deteriorating that first day his body had responded to hers. He should've waited until the case was over before getting physical. His failure to realize that was only another indication of how he couldn't think clearly around her now that he'd fallen in love with her.

The thought drew him up short. He had fallen in love with Shelby. When had that happened?

Clay and Collier left Leticia Keane's house and drove back to the Fire Investigator's Office. Collier had to be in court in an hour. Until then, they were going to resume their scrutiny of old fire department records in search of the elusive something that was still bothering McClain. They had worked their way back to cases that were dated twelve years ago.

Clay realized his partner was talking to him. He also realized he was grinning like a kid who'd made off with a bag of candy. He might be in love with Shelby, but she didn't know that. And after last night—

Oh, hell. *What* had he done?

"…think about Leticia?"

"I can't believe we couldn't pry anything out of her." Clay hit his blinker and turned onto the street that led to the F.I.'s office. "Not even that she was involved with Sandoval. I mean, Perez. Even after telling her the guy ratted her out."

"Smart girl."

"Frustrating, too. We've got nothing on her."

"Or Vince Tyner, either. Even though he has no alibi for the time Shelby was nearly killed yesterday, we can't prove he was anywhere near Paula's house when it happened."

Clay tried hard to dismiss the image of Shelby that had been flashing in his brain since last night. He could very well have ruined any chance they had. The hurt in her eyes still twisted him up inside. Breaking things off with her had been a knee-jerk reaction to the fear that had sliced through him when he'd learned about her harrowingly close call. The picture of her lying dead with an arrow in her brain had glared bloodred in his mind ever since.

The horrifying realization that it had been his fault that she'd nearly been killed had shocked him into cop mode, and he had handled things with all the finesse of a train wreck. He'd gone on automatic pilot. Protect the witness. Catch the killer. No emotion, no sentiment.

Getting intimate with her had compromised his judgment and he'd taken steps last night to correct that. To keep her alive so they could have a future.

The only place he wanted to be right now was with her, but he had no business being with her. Not until he caught the bastard who wanted to kill her. Clay wanted to call her and explain. Apologize. But right now, he couldn't let emotion influence his decisions any more than he already had.

He knew she was all right physically; she was safe. The sooner he and McClain figured out who'd murdered M.B. Perry, the sooner Clay could get to Shelby. And try like hell to make the woman understand that he'd done what he had to.

Focus, he told himself. "Sandoval was in jail at the time of the attempt. And Mac Hayward was with me, so they're clear."

"We've got little things on several people, but not enough to arrest anyone, except Sandoval-Perez. And that's a separate issue altogether."

They walked into the F.I.'s building, greeting the secretary as they continued to Collier's office. Clay slid off his lightweight jacket and laid it across a chair in the small crowded space.

Collier stepped behind his cluttered desk and picked up a manila folder, passing it over. While Clay opened the file,

Collier pulled a green pressboard file from a pile stacked at least twenty deep.

Clay skimmed the first page. "Didn't find any prints?"

"No. Not on the trash bin, the aerosol cans that exploded or any debris. But I did find traces of hair spray on the cans and places on the melted Dumpster."

"I don't think the debris in that trash bin was the oops-I-didn't-mean-to-put-that-in-there kind. It was intentional."

"I agree. Firecrackers, a sealed two-liter bottle, aerosol cans. All those things are designed to explode, to make noise, to get attention. Like a Molotov cocktail."

"And draw people out. Most assuredly Shelby, a fire-fighter." Clay's jaw felt as if it might snap in two.

McClain's gaze dropped to the file he'd opened, and he thumbed through a few pages. After a moment, he paused. Eyes narrowed, he handed the information to Clay. "This is it. I knew I'd heard about this somewhere."

Clay scanned the report and froze when he saw a name he recognized. Twelve years ago, one of Shelby's fellow fire-fighters had worked a microwave explosion. Had been the one to figure out that the incident hadn't been an accident. Had been the one who'd conducted a demonstration to prove it.

Where had this guy been the afternoon of the explosion at Shelby's station house? The night of M.B.'s murder?

Clay whipped out his small notebook and flipped pages until he found the one he wanted. He passed his notes to McClain. "His alibi for the night of M.B.'s murder was unconfirmed."

"And he was at the station on Shelby's first day back at work when the microwave exploded. He could've been alone in that kitchen, rigging the appliance as easily as Tyner could have."

"We haven't come across his name at all until now. Was he the man having an affair with M.B.?" Clay grabbed his jacket. "I'm going to talk to him, see if I can find a crossbow, find out where he was yesterday."

"I'll walk out with you. I'm due in court." Collier returned Clay's notebook as they moved toward the front of the office building. "Leave me a message on my cell phone and catch me up. I'll be stuck there all afternoon."

"Ten-four. I'll call Robin and give her a heads-up, tell her what I'm going to check out."

Collier nodded as he climbed into his white truck. "Let me know what you find."

Sliding behind the wheel of his own pickup, Clay dialed Daly's cell phone. She answered on the second ring, static crackling across the line.

"Hey, Robin." He reversed his vehicle, then pulled out into the street. "I just found some things I need to check out. Until I get back to you, make sure that Shelby doesn't talk to Rick Oliver. I think he's the one who murdered her friend, the one who tried to kill her."

Despite more noise on the phone, Clay caught the other cop's words clearly. "It's too late."

"What do you mean?" His heartbeat kicked hard against the wall of his chest.

"Hang on. I can barely hear you."

"Daly!"

After a moment, she said, "That's better. I moved to a different spot in the building."

"What building? Where are you?"

"At Keller Plaza. Oliver called to tell Shelby he had her paperwork for the shrink ready to sign. What's going on?"

"It may be nothing." The urgency knotting his gut said differently. He slapped the siren on his dash and flipped it on. "But I don't want her around him until I can find out what I'm dealing with."

"Okay. We'll get out of here. We haven't seen him yet anyway."

"Don't alarm her. Or tip him off." Clay made a U-turn

and started in the direction of the office building. "Just get her—"

A sudden deafening blast sounded on the other end of the phone. Someone screamed. The line went dead.

Chapter 13

The explosion ripped between Robin and Shelby, knocking them both off balance in opposite directions. The policewoman screamed. Wood, metal and sparks shot through the air like shrapnel. Smoke, heavy and thick and black, billowed toward the front door, poured into the area where the two women had started back toward the building's lobby.

"Robin!" Only the width of the hallway separated Shelby from the detective, but the closet that had exploded stood between them. Shelby dropped to the floor and onto her belly, already unable to see through the dense fog of dark gray. Ripping off the short-sleeved cardigan of her sweater set, she pressed it to her nose and mouth.

"Shelby!"

"I'm just across from you." She hoped the other woman could hear her muffled words. She'd smelled smoke in the instant before the explosion. Why hadn't the smoke detectors gone off? "Are you hurt?"

"Yes." Robin sounded dazed. "My head was hit, plus a big chunk of that door went into my leg."

"I'm coming!"

Shelby had to figure out how to get there. They'd come in the front door of the building, looking for Captain Oliver. Before the explosion, Robin had gotten a cell phone call from Clay; when she had moved toward the entrance for a better connection, Shelby had gone, too. They were no more than fifty feet away from the door. Once Shelby got to Robin, they could make it. But going any farther without protective gear would be fatal. Thank goodness the building was finished and there were no workmen.

Before the blast, Shelby had been near the men's restroom. Running a hand along the bottom of the wall, she found a corner and decided she still was. She could make out the opposite wall. Glass and cardboard and metal debris littered the gray-and-green-flecked carpet. The smoke settled everywhere as wisps of flame moved slowly and steadily toward her, across the carpet and the baseboards.

The dark color of the smoke and the red-orange flames told Shelby that petroleum products were involved. She caught a faint, oily whiff beneath the carbon. The fire still burned low enough that she could step or jump over it. Through a sooty haze, she sighted the opposite wall, then leapt over the snaking stream of flame. Once on the other side, she flattened herself on the floor, reached out and touched Robin's arm. Thank goodness.

Her own arms were already baking, as was the exposed skin on her neck, her face, her ears. The heavy smell of burning chemicals registered.

"Stay low, on your belly! Stay with me!" Shelby ordered as she helped the brunette yank off her lightweight jacket. "Put this over your mouth and nose. We're going to crawl out the front!"

Robin nodded to show she'd heard.

The danger here wasn't from burns but from smoke, the silent, relentless killer. They had to go *now*. Flames slithered out of the storage closet behind them. Dark gray smoke spewed and churned and filled every space quicker than she could blink. Why weren't the sprinklers working? Where was Captain Oliver?

Fire crackled and spit as it latched onto the wooden baseboard and chewed at the carpet. Fingers of flame licked at the wallpaper, moving toward the ceiling. The twelve-foot height would serve to dissipate some of the smoke, which would allow limited sight but not lessen the danger.

With Robin moving beside her, Shelby crawled on her belly into the lobby. Having no flashlight, she had to depend strictly on her experience and training as a firefighter and trust she wasn't veering off the path. Even with the covering over her mouth and nose, she wasn't going to last long. And she was worried that Robin, being injured, might not be able to last as long as her.

The heat rose, growing as the fire did. She was going in the right direction. She had to be. Even so, those fifty or so feet from the door felt like a hundred yards in this blistering heat. Already her skin stung as if it had been swarmed by fire ants.

Taking shallow breaths, she kept moving. *Where* was Captain Oliver? He'd been in the back part of the building, and Shelby knew there was an exit there. Surely he'd gotten out.

The thick heat climbed, enveloping them like steamed, scalding wool. Sweat plastered her shirt to her back, ran between her breasts. Her nostrils stung, and nausea rolled through her. Robin had to be feeling the effects, too. They were running out of time.

Charcoal-colored smoke surged around them. The burned-tar smell of petroleum products grew stronger. Shelby's breathing grew labored. A hissing whine intensified, underlined by a deepening throb of sound. Flames slithered along the baseboards, snapping and popping.

The lobby was a cave of smoke except for a wispy wedge of light coming through the glass above the door. They headed for it.

She stayed flat and searched for pockets of air. The smoke sealed off most of the light except for the occasional pale glimmer reflected off the glass. The sweater over her mouth and nose was starting to burn her hand. She was growing light-headed, her throat and lungs coated with carbon.

She bumped into the door. But when she pushed, she met with resistance. It was the wall, not the door! Shifting left, she hit something solid again. The faint glow of light was deceiving her, making her think she was at an opening and not the glass wall. Where was the door?

On her next try, she touched something different. A steel-soled boot. "Captain!"

"Fox!"

Thank goodness! Coughing violently, she managed to say, "Get the door!"

She moved forward, choking on a searing blast of ash at the same time a draft fluttered over her head. The curtain of darkness shifted enough for her to see the captain bend toward her. To help her—No! The smoke distorted her view, as did the protective gear over his nose and mouth, but there was a savage look in his eyes that instantly had alarms ringing in her head.

In a disorienting flash, Shelby's vision hazed. A picture flickered in her mind, too quickly to comprehend, but cold terror gripped her. Moving on instinct and adrenaline, Shelby screamed at Robin and groped along the glass, searching for the door. She felt something swing past her head.

Then there was a whoosh of air. The door had opened! For an instant, the screen of black thinned enough for Shelby to see her boss in the doorway. And another man behind him. Clay?

In the next heartbeat, she also thought she saw the captain's arm slashing downward with…a steel pipe. She lurched to the side. Images popped into her head like camera flashes, out of order, making no sense. Of Oliver rushing at her another time, pushing her. The bottom dropped out of her stomach, just as it had the night when she'd plunged backward over M.B.'s railing.

"It was you! That night at M.B.'s, it was you!"

"Why'd you have to walk in?" Behind his hood, his voice was muffled.

She knew he could see her and Robin. Cramming the sweater against her mouth, Shelby rolled hard into the glass wall. "You tried to kill me! You killed M.B.!"

"I had to protect my family!"

She didn't know what that meant. Too late, she saw the pipe swing down again.

She dodged the weapon, felt a sizzle of pain when it glanced off her shoulder. If Oliver wanted them dead, he had only to wait less than ninety seconds; both she and Robin would succumb to the smoke. Why use a pipe? The answer had her stomach curling. To make *sure* they were dead. To make sure *she* was dead.

Her mind catalogued what happened next, even though it didn't fully register. Oliver swung at her again. A loud pop, different from the noises made by fire, sounded beneath their raised voices.

Suddenly, a long rounded piece of metal hit her leg. The pipe. Wasting no time, she pushed open the door, reaching back to haul Robin out if necessary. Wheezing and coughing, the other woman clawed her way outside. Shelby dragged in fresh air and struggled to keep moving, get some distance between her and the smoke. Clay stumbled out of the building, restraining her captain by angling one of his arms high behind his back. A bloody, wounded arm.

Two large, gloved hands reached down, dragged Shelby a safe distance away onto a grass-covered rise. Only then was she aware of the blare of air horns, the thunder of firefighter boots. She looked up into the face of Jerry French, a veteran smoke eater from Station House One.

"We got you, Fox. Breathe."

Forcing the words past her blistered throat, she croaked, "No one else inside. Solvents in a storage closet, I think."

A look of disgust crossed the man's face. "How many times have we seen this happen at sites waiting on final inspections?"

"Sprinklers and smoke detectors not working."

"Good job. I'll tell the crew."

Three fire engines, a ladder truck, the rescue unit and a battalion chief were in the parking lot. Firefighters teemed toward the building like ants from a hill, rolling out two lines, preconnected to the engine to hook up to one hydrant, running at the smoke that poured out of the building. *Surround and drown.*

Shelby's sluggish thoughts caught on the assumption both she and French had made that the fire was accidental. As Jerry had said, they'd seen plenty of fires that started this way because finishing materials such as paint, thinner and cleaners, along with the cardboard boxes those products had been delivered in, had been stored sloppily. But it also could've been made to *look* like an accident.

Just as the smoke alarms could've been tampered with so as not to detect the smoke at all. That could easily be blamed on improper installation or defective equipment.

But that fire had been set deliberately, for the purpose of killing her. A heavy certainty settled on her. Trembling, she turned her head and saw Robin already wearing an oxygen mask, being loaded onto a gurney by two EMTs. Clay. Where was Clay?

She heard his voice, shifted her gaze and saw him forcing Captain Oliver to his knees, cuffing Oliver's hands behind him. She noted vaguely that blood ran down her boss's arm, streaked Clay's lightweight denim shirt. When her gaze fell on the gun nestled in the small of his back, she understood.

He'd shot Captain Oliver. Saved her life and Robin's, too. Thank goodness he'd been on the phone with the other detective just before the explosion.

Shelby was sick to her stomach, her thoughts fuzzy. Her throat and lungs burned as if she'd sucked down enough fire for a station house barbecue. Another pair of EMTs fitted an oxygen mask on her, then lifted her onto a stretcher, despite her hoarse protests.

Oliver kept his face averted. She wanted to scream at him, hit him, find out *why*. Numb, her insides feeling blistered, she watched the paramedics check Robin's vital signs, then examine her for burns or contusions and attend to her leg. They'd torn her slacks up to her right knee, and Shelby could see a deep gash halfway between the policewoman's ankle and calf. One of the EMTs started Robin on an IV of some clear liquid.

A black-and-white had already blocked off the lot's only entrance. An unmarked police car pulled up, and Jack Spencer stepped out. News crews from three local Oklahoma City television stations descended on the scene like locusts.

Smoke coated her throat and mouth like tar. She watched Clay haul Oliver to his feet and drag him over to a patrolman, who stuffed her captain into the back of the cruiser. Clay slammed the car door and spoke to the officer.

But he studied her, obviously concerned, obviously wanting to talk to her. She was growing drowsy. People stomped and rushed through the lot between the building and the fire trucks. Voices swelled, shouting orders, barking directions. Sooty clouds rolled like a steel-gray tide into the clear blue sky. Reporters pleaded for information from the battalion chief in charge of scene supervision.

Shelby felt hollow inside, completely wasted. Captain Oliver was the one who'd tried to kill her, who'd killed M.B. Was that right? Or was she confused because of all the smoke she'd eaten?

"Miss?" Someone snapped their fingers in front of her face and she pulled her attention from her boss. She felt as if she were waking from a deep sleep.

The female paramedic, a tall, black woman with kind eyes, pointed to Shelby's oxygen mask. "How's your breathing?"

"Easing a little," she rasped, her throat raw.

"Are you nauseous?"

She nodded.

"Light-headed? Confused?"

"Light-headed. Slightly confused." A painful spasm of coughing hit her.

"Shelby?"

Clay. Her gaze shifted to the foot of the stretcher. Soot streaked his right cheek. She saw the concern in his green, bloodshot eyes and felt her own fill with tears. "It was the captain," she said dully.

"I heard him admit to it." He moved up beside her, one big, gentle hand covering hers. "Are you okay?"

She nodded, trying to keep from crying. "Why? Why did he do it?"

"I don't know yet. When I saw him coming after you—" He broke off, squeezing her hand hard.

Her stomach churned; she smelled like the inside of an incinerator. The hair on her arms and neck was singed; her skin burned as if she'd stepped into an oven. But strangely, what hurt the most was looking at Clay.

The EMTs lifted her stretcher into the back of the ambulance.

Clay moved into the open doorway of the vehicle, speaking to the paramedic. "She took a bad fall about two weeks ago and had a concussion. Her doctor is Meredith Boren. She should be told."

"Yes, sir."

"Is she burned?"

"Not that I've found so far."

In her smoke-fogged brain, Shelby realized she'd been a minute, maybe two, away from passing out in there. She also realized she was angry. With Clay. She'd been angry before the explosion.

He looked at the black woman. "I need to talk to her, just for a second."

The EMT hesitated, then nodded. "Real quick."

Shelby knew what he wanted.

"I'm sorry about last night."

Coming so close to being killed this afternoon made her grateful that they still had each other, but it also made her angry. Angry that they both knew how short life was and that Clay wouldn't take a chance on them. Angry that she had fallen in love with him. She wanted to tell him all of that, but her thoughts wouldn't translate into words.

He frowned. "Shelby, did you hear me?"

She turned her head away. He wanted her to say she was fine with his decision that they couldn't be together. But she wasn't fine with it. She might never be.

The EMT leaned forward and gripped the handles to close the door. "Detective, we have to go." She signaled the driver.

"Shelby?"

Keeping her head averted, she closed her eyes and let the tears come as the vehicle rocked into motion.

Clay couldn't believe it. Shelby wouldn't even talk to him. She had been through a horrible ordeal. Two weeks of hiding, nearly being killed three times, learning that her boss was the man responsible for those attempts and for the murder of her friend. She had to be in shock.

But Clay was kidding himself if he thought what he'd said about them last night wasn't part of the reason why she hadn't responded to him. Alarm shot thought him. He was—*they* were—in serious trouble. He wanted to say to hell with everything and go to her right now, but until he gave his statement at the scene, filed his reports and talked to Internal Affairs, he couldn't go anywhere. Frustration sawed at him.

Reining in his impatience, he tried to keep his mind on the case as Jack Spencer took his statement. An hour later at the PD, he stalked out of his interview with Shelby's captain, who had called a lawyer and wouldn't say a word. A crossbow had been found in the trunk of Oliver's car. Citing that, as well as the fact that in the past Oliver had worked on a microwave explosion almost identical to the one that occurred on Shelby's first day back at work, Clay finished his paperwork on the case. He had Antonio Sandoval aka Perez released. INS had been made aware of Perez's false visa and would decide what further action to take.

The next two hours dragged as Clay answered questions from the officers in Internal Affairs. As per standard operating procedure, he turned in his badge and his gun for the routine suspension for officer-related shootings. It chafed, but he didn't dwell on it. All he wanted was to get to Shelby.

Another hour later, after a brief visit with his lieutenant, he finally, *finally* walked out of the PD. He made a quick call to Collier McClain to make certain the fire investigator had heard the news and was on his way to the scene.

McClain had just arrived there and with the information Shelby had provided to the responding firefighters, he had a leg up on determining the cause of the blaze. He expected to find that the fire had started in the storage closet due to spilled finishing and cleaning solvents that had been lit by sparks from either an electrical malfunction or a burst light bulb.

Given that Clay had heard Rick Oliver threaten Shelby's life, Collier also expected to find signs of tampering. Like Shelby, he thought the explosion was likely deliberate, not accidental. Purposely altered wiring could've made a light blow out and drop sparks onto the vapor-producing liquids in that closet.

When Clay hung up from talking to the fire investigator, he focused on Shelby. He had to see her to find out if he'd totally screwed up any chance of having a future with her.

Chapter 14

An hour after leaving the fire scene, Shelby sat on the edge of a hospital bed in Presley Medical Center's emergency room wing. Her mom, who had just arrived, stood to her left. Robin was stable and had regained consciousness, but would be kept overnight for monitoring.

Dr. Boren had just checked Shelby's breathing again. She was being sent home with an oxygen mask in case she needed it. Over the next two days, she was to pay close attention for worsening symptoms of smoke inhalation. Her throat felt as raw as if she'd swallowed glass, and the sleeveless sweater she wore was now black cotton instead of pink.

The doctor pushed her blond curls behind one ear, then made a note in Shelby's chart. "How's your wrist?"

"Still a little tender, but it's fine."

"And your head from the concussion? You've done well since your fall, so I want to be sure that what happened today doesn't cause any problems with that injury."

"I have a headache, but it's from the smoke. It isn't the same pain I felt with the concussion. I had that kind of headache earlier today, just before I was to meet Captain Oliver. Do you think I'll be able to remember anything else from that night at M.B.'s?"

Before the other woman could answer, a masculine voice interrupted, "Hello?"

Shelby glanced over to find Detective Jack Spencer in the doorway. "Hi, Jack," she said hoarsely.

"Just wanted to see if I could interview you after your doctor finishes the exam." The tall, dark-haired man shared a smile with Meredith Boren, who was one of his wife's closest friends.

Meredith closed Shelby's chart. "I'm finished. I'll get out of your way."

"Would you mind staying for a minute?" Jack asked. "I heard Shelby's question about whether she'd be able to remember anything else from the night of the murder. I'd like to hear the answer to that, too."

The blonde looked at Shelby. "Do you mind if we talk in front of him?"

"Not at all."

The woman slid her hands into the pockets of her white lab coat. "I can't say for sure if you'll remember anything else. Your concussion alone wouldn't have resulted in memory loss for this long. I'm convinced that your amnesia is traumatic in nature."

"Meaning it was caused by what she witnessed?" Jack asked. "That her mind doesn't want to relive it?"

"Yes." Dr. Boren studied Shelby. "And you may never remember. Still, the mind is a strange thing and I've been wrong before."

Shelby nodded, her gaze shifting to Jack. "I don't really want to remember. Knowing I saw my captain there, knowing he killed M.B.—" She shuddered. "I'd just as soon not recall seeing or smelling M.B.'s body on fire."

Paula gently patted Shelby's back, careful of her heat-scalded arms.

The detective's blue eyes measured her. "Jessup told me you have an appointment to see a hypnotherapist. Are you still planning to do that?"

"Do you think I should? Would it help the case?"

"With your eyewitness account and Clay overhearing Rick's threats against you, we've got what we need. Clay also uncovered a documented connection between Oliver and a microwave explosion like the one that happened at your station house. And we found a crossbow in the trunk of his car at the fire scene."

"Clay said even if I were hypnotized, it wouldn't be admissible in court."

"That's right." He smiled. "So I'd say, if you don't want to do it, then don't."

"Did you or Clay speak to Captain Oliver? Why did he kill M.B.?"

"Your boss isn't talking. He got a lawyer the second he reached the PD, but from what we've put together and what he said to you, we figure he and Ms. Perry were having an affair. And she threatened to go to his wife about it. That could've cost him his job, maybe his marriage and custody of his little girl."

And other things as well, Shelby realized. "If he lost his job, he'd lose his insurance."

At Jack's quizzical look, she said in a strained voice, "His two-year-old daughter, Aubrey, has severe asthma. With what they spent on her regular medication plus the added expense of sudden attacks, it cost a fortune. I've heard him say more than once—" Shelby had to stop for a breath "—that the only reason his family has survived financially is because of his job insurance. He would do anything for that little girl."

Jack made a note in his notebook. "We think Oliver killed Ms. Perry in a fit of rage. After he did, you have to figure that he realized what he'd done. Then you walked in, and he knew he had to cover his tracks."

She nodded, the horror and anger she felt toward her captain mixed with sadness. How would Rick's wife and child hold up once all this became public?

"Tell me what happened today," the detective said.

In halting half whispers, Shelby relayed the story of Oliver's earlier phone call and their arrangements to meet at Keller Plaza. "He was there when Robin and I arrived, so I imagine he had time to rig things for the explosion. I didn't see him do anything, but you can't tell me that was accidental, especially since he came back in and tried to kill me with that pipe."

Paula stood quietly beside the bed, her blue eyes somber. Pale, she looked alternately worried and relieved.

Dr. Boren tilted her head and eyed Shelby with curiosity. "You've told me a few times since the night of the murder that you've had terrible headaches. Now that you know who killed M.B., can you nail down when you had those? Was Captain Oliver around?"

"You think they could've been related to him?" At the doctor's nod, Shelby's mind flipped through the times during the past two weeks she'd seen or talked to him.

She'd had the headache on her first day back at work, the day of the microwave explosion. Her captain had been there; he'd been the one to run Vince out of the station house. The headache had returned each time she'd spoken to Oliver on the phone. And during her initial hospital stay, when he and Shepherd had paid a visit. "Yes! Every time I was around him or spoke to him on the phone."

"That was your mind trying to tell you something, but you couldn't remember. Probably because it was too painful to accept."

"Do you think the headaches will go away now?"

"I do." The doctor reached into her pocket and withdrew a prescription pad. "But I'll send this script with you for some pain pills. If you need one, take it. I want to see you at the end of the week, Friday or Saturday."

Shelby took the piece of paper. "All right. It'll be nice to be able to get out on my own and do normal things again."

"I imagine," Meredith said with a smile. After making sure Jack had what he needed from her, she said goodbye.

The detective slipped his notebook back into his pocket. "Terra and I are glad you're all right, Fox. I'd hate for something to happen to the firefighter who saved my nephews' drawings during that blaze I was in a couple of years ago."

She smiled, easing herself off the bed. The extra-strength ibuprofen she'd been given after Dr. Boren's initial exam was taking effect and her headache was abating. "Do you have more questions?"

"Not right now. Do y'all need a lift somewhere?"

"I have my car," Paula said. "Thank you, though."

"Sure." Jack's gaze shifted to Shelby. "Jessup was headed to the PD when I left the scene. Because of the shooting, he'll be tied up for a while."

She nodded. Good. She didn't want to see Clay right now.

"Take it easy. I imagine my wife will call later to check on you."

"I'd like that."

He said goodbye, then left the E.R. waiting area. Shelby felt Paula's gaze on her.

"You sure you're okay?" her mom asked quietly.

"Yes." She offered a slight smile as the older woman pulled her close for a careful hug.

"Thank goodness Clay was there today. I don't know what we'd do without him."

Shelby nodded, tears burning her eyes again.

"It's nice to have someone you can count on."

Yes, it was, Shelby thought. And she'd ruined that by sleeping with him.

She picked up the paper bag holding the destroyed cardigan half of her sweater set and walked out with her mom. They were both silent until they reached Paula's sedan.

The older woman brushed a lock of hair away from Shelby's forehead. "I'll take you home. Want me to stop on the way and get anything? Popcorn?"

"No, thanks." The only thing she needed was time. And space. "Mom, would it be all right if I dropped you by the shop and borrowed your car? I need to go somewhere."

"To see Clay?"

"No."

Her hoarse, flat answer had her mother's eyebrows arching in surprise, but Paula didn't say anything else. Neither did Shelby. If she did, she'd break down and cry.

From his truck, Clay called the hospital and learned that Shelby had already been released. He called her cell phone and her house. No answer. There was no answer at his house, either, and neither of his sisters had talked to her.

He knew she was drawing into herself, knew she wouldn't be open to talking to him right now, but he wasn't giving her any more time. He couldn't. He'd missed enough already.

Clay was ready to crawl out of his skin. He might've lost the woman he loved because of the guilt he felt over her brother.

He knew he'd hurt her deeply. He just hoped it wasn't too late for them. It couldn't be too late.

After speaking to Paula, who was at her shop, he learned that Shelby had been there, then gone to shower at her house. He found out what Dr. Boren had said about Shelby's memory and the possibility it might never return. He learned about her conversation with Jack. He knew everything there was to know except where she was. In answer to his question, her mom told him she didn't know and that Shelby had said she wanted to be alone.

That didn't surprise him. He called her home again and about the time he decided she wasn't answering because she knew it was him, he realized where she was.

He drove to Presley Memorial Gardens, guided his truck down the center asphalt drive wide enough for most vehicles, turned at the third lane on the right and got out. There she was, about a hundred yards away, in front of Jason's headstone.

Her head was bowed and she looked almost fragile in her jeans and short-sleeved turquoise top. He knew when she felt him walk up behind her. Her spine went steel-rod stiff.

"I figured you'd be here."

She dashed a hand under her eyes, but didn't turn around. "I don't want to talk to you right now."

"That's fine." He shifted so he could see her profile. She was crying, and his heart clenched. "I should probably do all the talking anyway."

She folded her arms, drawing his attention there. Her light golden skin was redder than any sunburn he'd ever seen and he knew it had to hurt. Her face was washed clean of the soot she'd worn at the fire scene, but the light, fresh scent of soap hadn't completely erased the smell of smoke.

She looked across the rows of neatly laid graves, the sun picking out strands of gold in her brown hair. He wanted to hold her, but he stayed where he was, not crowding, but not leaving, either. Her jaw was set in that stubborn line he knew all too well.

Man, he was in deep trouble here. "About what I said last night—"

"I heard you. I'm fine with it. Today's been tough is all."

Damn. He scrubbed a hand over his face. "I don't want you to be fine with it."

"Clay," she rasped brokenly, her shoulders sagging. "I can't handle this right now."

"I thought you were gonna let me do the talking."

She didn't respond to his gentle teasing. Refusing to give in to the dread pounding through him, he squinted against the setting sun and shoved a hand through his hair. "I know I screwed up, blue eyes."

She wrapped her arms tighter around herself. Her cheek was damp from her earlier tears. He wanted to hold her so badly he ached.

He cleared his throat, pinched the bridge of his nose. "Our being together wasn't a mistake. It *isn't* a mistake."

"Actually, I think you were right."

"No. No, I wasn't." He stilled inside, cautioning himself to lay it out for her, explain why he'd said that, why he'd thought it. "The mistake wasn't us sleeping together. It was when we did it. I shouldn't have pushed you. I should've waited until this case was over. If I had, if I'd kept my feelings out of it and done my job, this might have ended a lot earlier. And you might've been in less danger. When I got to your mom's last night, I just kept seeing you laid out dead with an arrow through you. I felt like I compromised your safety."

"You didn't." She made a soft choking sound. "You protected me."

"That wasn't how it felt."

Long seconds passed. When she didn't respond, he lightly touched her shoulder.

She moved away. *What if there was a next time?* she thought. *Would he react the same way?*

"When I got to your mom's house and realized how close you'd come again to nearly dying, something snapped. All I could see was Jason's grave and yours next to it." The image had him clenching his fists to keep from reaching for her as he said fiercely, "I was not going to put you in the ground the way we did him. First Jason, then you? I couldn't do it."

She took another step away from him, her voice trembling with anger. "You didn't make Jason go climbing, Clay."

"I know I didn't push him off that mountain, but he wouldn't have been there that day if I hadn't pressured him to go. That's on me, Shelby. If I'd put you in a safe house to begin with, Oliver wouldn't have had two more chances to kill you. I know I didn't cause Jason's death, but sometimes that isn't how it feels. And last night, when you were nearly killed *again*, I panicked. I overreacted. The only thing I knew would keep you safe was to get you away from me, so I did."

She didn't answer.

Her silence was killing him, tying his gut in vicious knots. "Honey, say something."

"You freaked out, Clay." She turned, angling her chin at him, tears glittering on her lashes. "I've got a job that puts me in jeopardy every time I go on a call. How do I know you're not going to get scared for me again and pull away?"

His green eyes darkened, and a muscle worked in his jaw. "Because," he said huskily, "for the past twenty-four hours, I've known what it's like to be without you. I thought I couldn't ever hurt more than I did when Jason died, but thinking I'd lost you, knowing it was me who'd put this distance between us, hurt a hundred times worse."

Drawing her bottom lip between her teeth, she turned away. "I needed you last night."

The quiver in her voice broke his heart. "I know, honey. And I'm sorry I wasn't there." He eased a step closer, and this time she didn't retreat. She had to listen. Understand. Forgive him. "I'm trying to explain… Last night, that guilt about Jason was all over me. All I could think was that I pushed him to go climbing. Just like I pushed you into bed with me."

She glared at him over her shoulder. "You left it up to me!

Yes, you told me what you wanted, but it was my decision. Mine!" And she knew she couldn't go back to the way things had been. She couldn't. Looking away from the eyes she loved, the eyes that were so sincere they made her ache, she stared at the green grass, the smooth granite headstone bearing her brother's name. "You were right. It was a mistake. We should've left things alone. If we don't leave things alone right now, I'm afraid we won't be able to salvage any of this."

"Shelby." Damn this distance anyway. He moved closer, sliding his arms carefully around her from behind.

She stiffened. "Don't."

"I want you to listen."

"No. I don't know if I can be your friend anymore, Clay," she choked out, fighting a sob.

"Good. I don't want to be friends."

"Then let me go." She tried to pull away.

"No." Mindful of her raw skin, his arms tightened. "I'm never letting you go. You might as well give in."

"That's what got us into this mess to start with," she muttered.

Was she softening just a bit? At least she was talking to him. "I know the way I handled things was wrong."

"Ya think?"

"I was an idiot."

"Totally."

He brushed a kiss against her temple and lightly pressed his cheek to hers. "I want to make it up to you."

"You hurt me, Clay." A tear rolled down her cheek and caught between them both.

"I know," he said softly. "And I'm sorry. Deeply sorry."

She turned her head away. She was in love with him, and she wanted to tell him. But why? she asked herself ruthlessly. It wouldn't make him feel the same way. And if she told him how she felt, that would be between them forever, too.

She didn't doubt he loved her, like a friend. That was all she'd ever have. But as much as she resented that, could she turn her back on him for the rest of her life?

"I love you," he whispered.

Pain cut deep and she said sadly, "I know you do."

"Not like that. Not only in the way I always have." Carefully, he turned her to face him, then eased his arms back around her waist. "I'm in love with you, Shelby."

Her breath caught as she searched his face.

"You're everything to me," he said, his voice husky with emotion. The same emotion that burned in his eyes. "My best friend, the woman I love. You're my life. I want to wake up with you every day. Have babies with you. Grow old with you."

She couldn't stop the tears now.

He bent and kissed her softly on the lips.

"Clay—"

"I want another chance. I need you to give me one. I promise not to screw it up this time. Please?" he ended hoarsely.

She wanted to, but not if he couldn't get beyond what had happened with her brother. Her voice thickened. "You're the only man who's ever known the real me, all of me. Even though my marriage to Ronnie was good for a while, he never understood me like you do. I've never felt as close to any man, not sexually, not as a friend, as I do to you.

"But I can't be with you if your feelings are tied to Jason. We both know what happened that day. We both know he wouldn't have gone if you hadn't persuaded him, but you didn't *make* him do anything. You tried to save him. Just like you tried to save me. I want us, but it has to be about *us*. No one else."

"I'm working my way through it, blue eyes. I'm coming to see that what I think about Jason's death is more about regret than guilt." His lips feathered across her forehead. "And I don't want to regret you, too. I need you, Shelby."

Her heart melted and she flattened her palms on his chest,

a part of her calming at the feel of his steady strength. "I can't handle it if you change your mind."

"I won't." His gaze held hers.

She knew him. He meant what he said, and she believed him.

"Honey, forgive me. Give us another chance."

She couldn't walk away from this man, and she didn't want to. She pressed into him, savoring the hard length of his body against hers, feeling his heartbeat mirror hers. Pushing the words past her seared throat, she rasped, "I'm in love with you, too."

The pleasure, the desire that flared in his eyes crumbled her last wall. He bent his head and she rose to meet him, her arms going tight around his neck as his mouth covered hers. After a soft, tender kiss, they drew apart.

"So, we're good, right?" he asked.

"We're good." He held her close, and she nuzzled his neck. "I smell like smoke."

"Yeah, I was gonna say something about that."

She pulled back to make a face at him. "Very romantic."

He grinned. "I was gonna say I smell like smoke, too. And maybe we should do something about it."

"Like what?"

A wicked gleam shone in his eyes. "Well, we do that shower-together thing pretty well."

She laughed and kissed him. "My shower or yours?"

"Doesn't matter, as long as we're together."

* * * * *

COMING NEXT MONTH

#1407 A HUSBAND'S WATCH—Karen Templeton
The Men of Mayes County
After a tornado destroys mechanic Darryl Andrew's garage, he realizes that more than a broken arm and livelihood need rebuilding—his marriage is in serious danger of crumbling. While Darryl's secrets continue to plague their relationship, Faith Meyerhauser is torn between her loyalty to her husband and family and following a dream she's buried for nearly twelve years.

#1408 STRAIGHT THROUGH THE HEART—Lyn Stone
Special Ops
NSA agent Dawn Moon is chosen to assist Eric Vinland, the sexy agent whose psychic abilities are crucial in recovering stolen government secrets. But the mission is put in jeopardy when Eric realizes his powers have disappeared, and he doesn't know which is worse…being hunted down by a group of terrorists, or his vulnerability to the only woman he's never been able to read.

#1409 MEMORIES AFTER MIDNIGHT—
Linda Randall Wisdom
When Alexandra Spencer is attacked in a seemingly random mugging, a head injury causes her to forget her divorce from the one man who can save her—police detective Dylan Parker. Dylan senses there is more to the crime and reluctantly takes up the investigation, but finds it hard to concentrate as he is drawn to the kinder, gentler woman who still sparks his desires.

#1410 THE ARSONIST—Mary Burton
Reporter Darcy Sampson is convinced a serial arsonist is still alive, and she seeks out former arson investigator Michael Gannon for answers. When fires erupt in Darcy's hometown, the two must battle to solve the case and the attraction threatening to consume them both.

SIMCNM0206